H. L. CLIFFORD

Doing It the Left Way

First published by Stories Imagined 2020

This novel is entirely a work of fiction. The names, characters and incidents portrayed in it are the work of the author's imagination. Any resemblance to actual persons, living or dead, events or localities is entirely coincidental.

First edition

ISBN: 978-1-7356031-0-0

Cover art by Monika Ostiak-Lobermajer
Editing by Johanna Craven

This book was professionally typeset on Reedsy.
Find out more at reedsy.com

This is dedicated to Tiana and Alexander.
My children, my biggest supporters and the best, most generous humans I know.
Thank you for being patient. Your unconditional love makes it all worthwhile.
I love you forever.

Acknowledgement

There are innumerable people who supported me, and helped me get to this point of sending my first book out into the world.

First and foremost, thank you mom, Eila Trent, for always believing I could do it, and for being my very first editor. I appreciate and love you always.

Thank you, Joe Trent, for always being available with guidance in the technical area. Without it, I would still be trying to figure this all out.

Thank you to my brilliant cover designer in Poland. Monika Ostiak-Lobermajer, you are truly talented and wrapped up this entire journey for me in the most beautiful package.

Thank you to my very kind editor in Australia. Johanna Craven, you are a godsend.

Thank you to all of the amazing baristas in Kona from the (now closed) S.F. Bay Coffee Co. You all are perfect and I miss you so much! I couldn't have done this without you. Your smiling faces and excited support with a side of coffee is exactly what I needed each day.

Thank you to all of my friends at work, here in Kona, Hawai'i. I can't thank you enough for listening to and supporting my passion for these past two and a half years. You're all amazing!

Thank you to the men and women around the world that I have the pleasure of calling my friends. Your support is immeasurable. You have kept me sane.

Thank you to all of my family, for your never wavering support.

Thank you, Yoshua Rosenfeld, for seeing when I needed some peace to finish this, and wrangling my son for me.

Thank you, Shana Ensminger, for putting my 'cuckoo back in the clock' more times than I'll admit. You will always be the best.

Last but not least, thank you Italy, and all of the people there. My friends, acquaintances, random store owners...etc. Each of you has enriched my life in one way or another. Italy, besides my children, you have become my first love.

I

Part One

There comes a time when you're ready for freedom when you have had none, when you realize your thoughts and dreams mean just as much as anyone's and when you know you're truly awake in life.

1

Chapter 1

A loud crack, a heart-racing thump and the airplane drops several hundred feet, then catches again. A few passengers let out a quick scream, and the rest gasp in unison. I'm completely freaked out, but can't seem to move. Frozen to the seat, my hands are clamped onto the arms of the chair. Movement from the corner of my eye makes me turn my head and look out of the window.

A lightning bolt hits the wing of the airplane with another loud crack, we drop again then recover.

"Oh, my god," I whisper in disbelief and utter fear.

I immediately think of my kids, and guilt rushes over me. Why did I do this? If I die, they will be alone. I divorced their father for a reason, and of course my mom will take care of them, but it's not the same as them having me. It's too late in the game for me to do this for myself...

isn't it?

My thoughts and self-scolding are interrupted. Mariano, my plane neighbor, leans in close.

"Are you okay?" His eyes dart to my white fingertips stuck to the edge of the arm rests.

"O-oh yes," I say, forcing a smile while slowly unsticking my fingers. "That was pretty scary."

"It was."

Mariano places his hand on top of mine, which are now nervously folded together in my lap.

"This is Ciro," he says, removing his hand to point to the man next to him.

"Hi Ciro." I smile warily, reach in front of Mariano and shake his hand.

"Ciao," he says and smiles back.

"Ciro heard the flight attendants mention we will all get off the plane in Bari and wait for it to be refueled."

"Oh. Okay."

Off the plane... *where?* A second later the captain's voice comes over the intercom:

"Signore e Signori...questo e il vostro capitano. Ho una spiacevole notizia, l'aeroporto di Napoli sara chiuso per 30 minuti a causa della tempest. Noi devieremo all'aeroporto di Bari dove faremo rifornimento all'aereo. Con la speranza che la tempest passi in fretta, ritornereo immediatamente alla nostra destinazoine programmata."

I can only guess he is now informing the rest of the plane of the information Ciro has

already shared with us. Maybe even something about the freaking airplane getting struck by lightning!

It's almost ten p.m. in Italy and we were scheduled to land in Naples in 30 minutes. I guess I need some excitement even before my feet touch the ground. Suddenly, startled by the loud ding from my phone, I look and see it's from my friend on the ground in Naples. He's waiting for me.

Angelo: Are you landing? You should be landing already.

How am I getting service up here? I ponder this quickly, then respond.

They told us we will fly to Bari, refuel and then fly back to Naples.

Angelo: How much longer? I am waiting here at the airport. It is raining very hard.

Yes – there is a huge thunderstorm up here. They are closing Naples airport.

Angelo: Do you think it will be long for you to land here? Or should I just go home if you will not come back tonight?

For a split second, I think about his question and decide to not have him wait. I hate to make anyone wait or be put out because of me.

You should go back home and get some sleep. I will stay in a hotel room in Naples or Bari if the storm continues. Thank you so much for coming to pick me up! I will take the ferry to Sorrento and see you tomorrow.

Angelo: Okay I will go back home. Message me still when you land so I know you're safe.

I smile at my phone.

Okay, I will.

An hour later, we land. Out of the window I see the storm has not reached Bari and my whole body relaxes into the seat. The flight attendant makes another announcement in Italian, which brings most passengers to their feet, including Mariano. I wait patiently for my turn. When there's an opening, I catch up with him on the stairs to depart the plane. As soon as I'm standing in the doorway, I look up to the sky. It's exceptionally clear, the wind is blowing; but warm. This is all so very interesting.

Big bright lights at this little airport make the runway an oasis in the dark night. With a plane full of passengers littering the concrete, and just the strangeness of this whole excursion, it's very surreal. As my first attempt at travelling alone, it's already so different to what I imagined.

Mariano points to two large city buses waiting a short distance away.

"We will go inside those, all of us, and wait for the plane to be refueled," he says, as it's now our turn to walk down. "No one can be on the plane when they put in fuel."

I nod, my hair blowing strong to one side as we make our way towards the second bus. The warm fresh air feels wonderful.

Two more people jump onto the bus, with Mariano and myself moving closer together to make space. The doors hiss and close, and create an overwhelming excitement in me to see where this bus will take us. Curious as a little kid, I'm facing the huge window and see close to ten airport men, all working on getting the plane ready. Mmm, the airport men. As we slowly drive past, I see a few that are very handsome. Maybe staying in Bari wouldn't be such a bad thing after all. I smile to myself for such naughty thoughts during what should be and has been a stressful time.

"Why do you smile?"

Oops. I didn't realize I was smiling that big and Mariano would notice.

"Oh, I'm just enjoying the adventure we're having," I say and smile back up at him.

Mariano is a nice man and I can see he was probably quite handsome in his twenties and thirties. But as I've come to notice, the majority of men my age let themselves go for the most part. Not all of course, but most. And if I can have men that are in their physical prime... then why shouldn't I?

When Mariano and I were halfway into our connection flight from Frankfurt, Germany, and just before the storm, we struck up a conversation. We are both divorced and both have two children. He told me how much he loves his two daughters and I told him the same of my son and daughter. We talked, and talked even more; about life, love, being a parent and travel. We shared photos and even a sandwich. Yes… he's a very nice man, but I can't help feeling he wants more from me than just a conversation.

We circle the plane and small airport one big time around and the two buses come to a complete stop in the same spot we started.

Inquisitively, I look up at Mariano. "That's it?"

"Yes. We will board the plane again."

We carefully maneuver through the open doors of the bus. Hmm. So, it looks like I'll be staying the night in Naples.

Elated to adjust myself back into the seat on the plane, I take out my phone and message Francesco, my other friend. He just so happens to live in Naples.

Hi! It looks like I will need to spend the night in Naples due to the storm. Is there an inexpensive hotel you know of?

Francesco: Hi. I will find you one now. Wait.

Okay, thank you so much. I am in Bari still, but will be leaving soon.

Francesco: Okay.

The plane taxis down the runway. I'm sad I won't be dinner and dancing with my friend from Sorrento, but now I'm excited to dinner and drink in the big city. I'm also extremely proud of myself for making contacts before I got here. I message Angelo.

We are just now leaving Bari.

Angelo: You are going to Naples?

Yes, we are about to take off. We'll land in half an hour.

Angelo: I will come to get you.

I thought you were home sleeping?

Angelo: I saw my friend first and I'm still on the road. I'm turning around now.

7

Okay, I will see you soon.
Angelo: Message me when you land.
Okay, I will.
I message Francesco.
Hi! I'm so sorry handsome, but I won't need the hotel tonight. My friend from Sorrento is coming back to pick me up like before.
Francesco: Okay amore. Hopefully I will see you soon?
Yes, I will message you. Thank you so much for always helping!
Francesco: It is my pleasure always.

Finally, we've made it to Naples airport. Mariano stands to the left side of the narrow door, like a true gentleman, and lets me enter first. Now I'm a little ashamed that I thought he was only hoping to have sex with me tonight. I really need to stop being so quick to judge men.

I walk past him and smile shyly. "Thank you."

"Of course," Mariano says as he holds his hand with an umbrella, out to usher me forward.

We walk to the baggage claim together to find my carry-on. Since Mariano only has the bag around his shoulder and the umbrella, I know he's just here to help me.

"What will you do tonight?" I ask Mariano as we stop to the side of a group of men from our flight.

"I will have a drink and a massage."

"Oh yes, a massage sounds wonderful after this crazy long day." I imagine someone rubbing my shoulders.

He looks down into my eyes with a small smile. "You know about massage salon?"

"Oh. THAT kind of massage." I'm a bit thrown since I had talked myself out of believing he wanted to only fuck me this whole time.

"Yes. But I was hoping you would be the one massaging me tonight,"

Mariano says in a slow, low tone.

Oh my God, oh my God, I was right the first time! I don't think I've had enough sleep to deal with this right now. I take a deep breath and relax. With it, I remind myself that I am in control of any situation I'm a part of. Politely decline and always be sweet. There are so many goals I have to accomplish on this trip.

My shyness has me nervous and shifting weight from my left foot to my right. I decide to act a little flirty since he's helped me get to this point in my travels. Slowly, I'm regaining confidence since I know my friend will be here to get me. I suppose, in Mariano's defense, it never hurts to ask.

"Ahh well, that's very nice you would spend your evening with me. But unfortunately, I do have my friend coming to get me," I say, slowly blinking up at him.

"Are you very sure he is going to be here?"

He better be at this point; I think almost out loud.

"Yes Mariano, I'm positive he will be here soon. If he's not already outside waiting."

"That's too bad," he says deep into my eyes.

I fight to not visibly squirm. Hold fast, Mila. I calm my ever-growing nerves that are threatening to expose me for the shy, uncertain woman I still truly am. Almost unable to hold his gaze with the confidence and flirty wit I need right now to win this game of cat and mouse, I need to politely decline and be sweet... maybe even a little sassy.

I cut my eyes up at him. "I'm sure I would have had a great time going out for a drink, but as for the massage... I think I need a massage myself, not to be the one giving it."

"Well, we would both reciprocate from a massage together."

I smile faintly. Yes, I'm way too tired to keep up this banter.

"Here," he says as he pulls his phone from his front pants' pocket and finally grants me a reprieve. "Give me your number and if you need anything while you're here or want to go for that drink you can text me."

"Okay, that sounds good. It's 18089375555. Thank you by the way, for all of your help."

"It was all my pleasure. If your friend doesn't call you soon though, you can just come with me." Mariano types my name in his phone and my phone dings. "That's me."

I type in *Mariano* and save his number. It is another goal; to make contacts. Just because he wants to sleep with me doesn't mean he's a bad guy, I remind myself. I may just need his help again. Plus, I'm 42. Ugh... 42. I realized after my divorce that I have no contacts. No one to call to help me with anything in life really. The saying *'it's who you know, not what you know'* became prevalent when I had no one to help me move. Moving furniture with your teenage daughter is not the best idea, pretty much ever.

My phone dings again.

"Oh! There he is," I say a little too loud and startle the men next to us.

"Your friend is here? Where is he?" Mariano cranes his neck to look around and get a glimpse of Angelo.

"He's outside waiting for me by his car. Oh! And there's my bag."

I point to the rather small, mauve carry-on slowly turning the corner of the conveyer belt. Mariano picks it out from between the other bags and sets it up for me to go.

"Thank you again." I smile sincerely up at him. "This part of my trip would probably have been disastrous without you. It would be really helpful if I knew Italian."

"You are very welcome, Mila. You are a gorgeous woman and I wish you a wonderful time here in Italy. But remember, all you need is to call me and we will have that drink."

"Yes. Thank you."

Up on my tippy toes, I kiss his left cheek and then his right. Mariano smiles. At least I know the custom of saying hello and goodbye.

"Okay, now how do I get out of here to where the cars wait?"

Mariano points me towards two large sliding glass doors to the left of where we are standing. "Just outside those doors, take a right and go through another set of doors. That will take you outside. Your friend should be waiting for you there."

"Have a lovely night, Mariano."

"Ciao, bella Mila."

Oh right! "Ciao!"

My smile grows bigger as I walk out of the first set of doors, take a right and leave the building through the last of doors.

2

Chapter 2

How great it feels to be outside of an airport again. The wind is only lightly blowing and still warmer than I expected, especially for being almost two in the morning.

There are cars everywhere. Bumper to bumper, and most are small, like Fiats. Lights are coming from all directions, so it doesn't even seem like night. Horns honking, people and cars maneuvering around one another and I begin to blindly walk across the street, trusting I will see him soon. A couple of irritated drivers are yelling in Italian, what I can only assume is to get out of the way so they can leave. Then, on the other side of the yelling man, hanging half way out of a car window, is... Angelo.

He waves. I close the short distance with my rolling luggage, tired body and huge smile plastered on my face. It feels like we've known each other for a long time; even though we met and have only communicated through text, pictures and video chats. It's amazing how quickly the world has shrunk and how I've learned an astronomical amount of random information in this last year. I think I'm off to a great start with my second life and I'm going to learn how this all works; men, myself, the world, and be the best mom I can be.

"Hi!" I say, finally reaching him.

"Hi!"

I lean in and hug him. His embrace; warm and his neck smells lightly of sweet cologne.

"It's nice to finally feel you," I say and release him.

His smile seems more hesitant than I thought it would be for our first physical hello, but I do feel comfortable with him. I suppose I should, seeing as we've talked almost every day for the past five and a half months.

He sets my carry-on and bag in the trunk of his mid-size car as I slide into the passenger seat, realizing there's still a big stupid grin on my face. I make it not quite as obtuse as Angelo steps into the driver's side. He puts the car in gear and carefully backs out, finding bursts of openings to get us out of the chaos. We hit the tunnels and open road that leads out of the city.

I can't believe I'm really here... in Italy... with the man I've been sharing life secrets and stories with. The sexual secrets I've shared with him suddenly jump through my mind. Everything I want to experience, that I am curious about; he has promised to give me while I'm here. This is the most prevalent aspect of our friendship. Even some things *he* wants me to be interested in.

"I can't believe there was this terrible storm tonight. We have not had rain like that in a long time," Angelo says, looks at me for a second, then back at the road.

I'm almost embarrassed by my wayward thoughts, but realize I did keep them to myself... for now.

"Yes, but I'm not surprised it happened tonight. That's usually my kind of luck." I smile. "I'm not happy that I've missed drinks and dancing though."

He reaches over and rubs the top of my thigh. Tingles shoot through the left side of my body and I relax into his touch.

Suddenly he pulls away.

I fidget with the fluff of material from my ripped jeans and take a deep breath. Maybe he's expecting the things I said I would do on our first car ride together. But I don't usually make the first move. I may *think* naughty things, but *starting* them is a whole other thing.

"It's really nice to finally be in the same space as you after all this time of talking," I say and smile. "Surreal to say the least... but very nice." I look at his handsome face as we drive through another lit tunnel; olive complexion, light brown eyes, perfectly coifed hair... and I want to smell his neck again.

Angelo looks at me and smiles big. "Yes, Mila, it is nice. So, tell me, how are your children? Where are they staying?" he asks and turns back to watch the road.

Well, definitely not a topic of conversation that will segue into the thoughts I was just having, but it's sweet of him to ask about my kids.

"They are doing wonderful, thank you. They're staying at my mom's house and I think I will have a harder time away from them, than they will from me. This is my first time leaving for longer than just a day."

"Do they like their grandma?"

"Yes. They both love her," I say, smiling. "She has helped so much with the kids since my divorce."

"That's great!" He turns and smiles, reaches out and rubs my leg.

And again, my body tingles with his touch.

"Mila, I know I told you I would have off from work the entire time you are here on vacation, but as I mentioned last week, I will have training every day except the weekend. I tried to request it for another time but they denied me."

"Oh. That's okay. I'm sure I can keep myself busy during the days." I try hard to not let my voice drop in disappointment. I know he has tried. At least there's still night, and like he said, the weekends. And, by the way, it's technically Friday morning right now. My spirits lift quick with the prospects of tonight's fun with my friend.

"We're almost there," he says.

It's a blanket of darkness outside as we drive on narrow winding roads. We drive past buildings and occasional tall rock walls on either side. I'm shocked at how old everything looks. I'm in an old country, I remind myself... and it *is* night time.

"We are in Piano di Sorrento now. My house is right before we entered the town." Angelo points to a tall building we're passing on my right. "One of my good friends lives there."

"How far away will I be from you?"

"Sorrento town, where you will be, is thirty minutes away. But faster tonight since there is no traffic. Are you hungry?"

"Oh, yes, I'm starving! I would love something to eat before bed."

He quickly pulls over, stops on the side of the road in front of a tiny store and gets out without a word. The store looks closed except for a couple meandering out of the door. I watch as he walks past them and disappears into the store. The couple hold onto one another, talking and laughing as they walk further up the street and slowly, disappear out of sight. Just as I wonder how long it will take for Angelo to come back, I look up and he's walking towards the car.

"Here," he says, sliding into his seat. He hands me a very hot something wrapped in foil and places a bottle of water and a large beer on the floorboard by my feet. The wrapped treasure in my hand smells so good, I have to peek inside.

"Yumm! This looks amazing... thank you!" I smile from ear to ear and inhale the warm aroma of my meat and cheese sandwich.

"It's a panino," he says, as he pulls the car back onto the road, flips on the headlights and speeds towards the apartment I've rented from his friend.

"A panino," I say, in almost a whisper.

I'm famished and bite into the sticky concoction without even a care of how much it's burning. Sucking air to try and cool what's in my mouth, I'm in ecstasy. Real food and so thoughtful of Angelo to buy it for me. This type of consideration and treatment has been a rare occasion in my life.

He turns us onto an even smaller side road that honestly looks more like an alley to me; I already love how different everything is. We make another corner and slow to a stop under a street lamp.

"We've arrived, but you need to get out here and I will park the car. Wait. Let's get your luggage."

"Oh. Okay," I say, perplexed as to where I'm supposed to go... or wait right here in the road for him? "Where should I wait for you?" I ask and stand beside him at the back of the car.

Angelo places the luggage by my feet and points up another side road, even narrower than the one we're on. I look further up the little road and see it's pitch black in the middle with only one faint street lamp at the far end. This town is exceptionally quiet and we seem to be the only ones awake... besides the grey cat dashing from behind a scooter and into the bushes.

"Just start walking up that way. You see the doors there?"

I squint and do see doors on the side of the tall building. "Yes, I see them."

"Okay good... now just walk up that way and Lorenzo will be here soon."

"Alright." I smile, take my roller carry-on, swing my oversized bag onto my shoulder and begin to trek towards the doors as Angelo drives away.

Seventeen steps on the cobblestone street and a scooter drives up. The driver removes his helmet, looks at me and smiles. He walks over, gives me a quick hug and air kisses on my left cheek, then my right.

"Lorenzo?"

"Hi! Yes! You finally made it! Let's get you into the apartment."

"Yes," I say with a sigh of relief.

Together we walk further up the dimly lit alley. The doors on the building to the right are all different colors and of course, different numbers.

Lorenzo tries his keys on the first door... #42. The green door doesn't budge so we move to the next, further up. Dark blue #45 doesn't open either. On to the next. This door is a very faded red... #53. Still nothing and I'm beginning to think I'm never going to see my apartment.

"Sorry, I don't come to this apartment myself very often and never in the dark," Lorenzo says with a smile. "Let's go to the end. I think it's there."

"Okay," I say with a smile back and pull my roller as quietly as possible up to the end of the bumpy alley.

At this point I don't know what's right, left, up or down. There were two, nine-hour layovers during my total 36-hour flight to get here. Just a little tired. I see Lorenzo at another door. I think we made a turn... maybe? Angelo pops up from the dark all of a sudden. Where did he come from?

A huge distressed brown door that's split down the middle looms in front of the three of us... I hear the lock click and Lorenzo pushes the right side open. Oh my god, yes.

A tiny elevator, two locked doors later and we're finally standing in the apartment. Lorenzo talks me through the Wi-Fi instructions, walks us through each room and quickly says goodbye since it's now 3 in the morning.

"Call me anytime, Mila. If you have questions or need help with... anything."

And with that, Lorenzo closes the door behind him and I'm finally alone in the apartment with my friend.

"Here is your water," Angelo calls out.

I walk into the kitchen where he's placing the bottle of water and beer in the refrigerator. "Perfect. Thank you."

"You're welcome."

He turns and looks slowly at the kitchen, then walks through the little apartment studying each room.

There's one bedroom with a long window that opens up by two glass doors, and those are covered by dark wooden, slated doors. One queen bed sits in the center of the room against the far wall, with two, small white tables on either side. Each holding a small lamp. A large air conditioning unit at the top of the wall next to the window, and a large closet taking up the entire wall across from the foot of the bed, makes up the rest of the room. The floor is covered in large, black and white checkered tile throughout the entire apartment. A small, but cute and functional bathroom, the kitchen with all of the normal amenities, and a little hallway in the middle of these three rooms. The hallway opens up to the living room. Another long window on the far wall, a comfortable looking couch with several decorative pillows, a round table with four chairs, and a tv sitting in the middle of an entire wall cabinet, makes up the last room. Modern art of black and white images with splashes of red, adorn the walls. A full-length mirror and brass hooks hang by the front door. The partly open window's red, sheer curtains gently blow in the breeze.

"Is this okay, this place? Will you be happy here for your stay?"

"Yes, thank you. It's cute."

"Yes, it is, and in a perfect location for you. Right in the middle of town where you can walk to everything."

I flop on the couch; so very happy to finally have my body land on a normal and comfortable piece of furniture. The naughty thoughts I had in the car flood my mind now that we're alone again.

"I'm going to go. I have class in a few hours," Angelo says and takes a few steps in my direction. He bends down and kisses my forehead. "Goodnight, Mila. Go to sleep and I will text you later."

This time, it's harder to keep the disappointment out of my voice. "Oh, okay. You can always sleep here... like you said you would before."

I feel vulnerable, even a little needy seeing as I have major jet lag and I'm in an entirely new country, completely by myself. Angelo is the only person I feel I really know eight thousand and something miles away from home.

"No. I won't sleep here. I need to go home."

I relent. "Okay, I understand. I will talk to you later, when I wake up." With a little smile, I stand and walk him to the door. "Thank you for coming to the airport to get me."

He turns back around and hesitates. "I have to drive to Naples and all of my things are at home. I even told you, right before you got here, I have changed a little. Since my... loss."

Angelo looks sad now and even apologetic. I feel bad for making him feel he needed to explain; that definitely was not my intention. I know he's hurting and it has only been a month since the accident. Angelo shared so much with me during the time we've been talking and this, I believe, is why I feel close to him. We have shared so much more about our real lives than just what type of sex we enjoy.

"Oh... no, I understand. It's okay if you don't stay here tonight, really. I'm sure I will pass out as soon as I hit the pillow." I smile, reach out and rub his arm gently one time.

"Good. Yes. You need to sleep. I will text you in the morning after I get to training; see how you are doing."

"Okay. That sounds great."

A quick hug and I close the door behind him.

"Hmmm... well first things first," I mumble.

I grab my phone from my oversized bag, plop down on my knees, facing backwards on the couch and study the Wi-Fi instruction card from the shelf in the wall. A few minutes later and some of my lucky guessing - because I really couldn't focus when Lorenzo was explaining it - and my phone connects.

"Yes! Now what's next?" I look around. "Clothes."

I pick up my bag and roll my luggage into the bedroom, pull most of the clothes out and hang them in the closet. Now, I feel like I'm finally at my destination.

My body is exhausted as I walk into the bathroom, line up all of my make-up, flat iron, contact stuff and toothbrush. In the kitchen, I open the refrigerator and take a huge swig of water. Then, pretty much like a zombie, I stumble into the bedroom, turn on the air conditioner for noise and fall on the bed; my legs and arms wide open as I pass out.

3

Chapter 3

The sun shines bright in my face from between the long wooden shades. With a moan, I smooth the strands of hair from over my eyes and try to see the time on my phone that's sitting upright against the table lamp.

"Seven-thirty in the morning?!" I rub my face and look again. "That's only four hours of sleep."

I slide off of the bed, walk to the long window and swing the wooden shades all the way open. Next time, I'll have to close these completely if I expect to sleep later than this. With extended arms, I push the long glass windows open... and hear Italy. My mouth stretches slow, into a huge smile as music and faint clanging of dishes drift up from the little café down below. I recognize the song, and can't believe *That's Amore* is really the first thing I hear on my first morning. This is amazing! Yes, I most definitely should be awake and adventure. That, and I'm famished again. I rush, get dressed in tight jeans, a camisole with no bra and my black sandals. Light makeup, my hair in a ponytail and I'm out the door.

Through street restaurants, vendors selling various knick-knacks, meandering tourists and the occasional vehicle making their way past us all, I find my way to the sea.

After a 20-minute stroll and down the side of an extreme cliff, I walk into the first restaurant situated on the first pier I come to. I follow the host and try to ignore all the stares as I walk through the other patrons and servers to a table. I quickly tell the waiter what I would like from the menu and smile up at him. The young waiter looks uncertain of my order and asks me to repeat it as the man at the table in front of me turns around to take a look. The other two servers whisper and nod in my direction.

Really, I need to stop caring if everyone is talking about me and learn to be comfortable eating in a restaurant alone. Why it's such a social stigma when women eat or drink in a restaurant alone, I'm sure I'll never know; but wherever that bullshit came from, I have lived it for my 42 years... and I'm done.

And now all of my plans have changed. I was supposed to be sitting here or somewhere having breakfast with Angelo. But life being as it is, I will find things to do by myself during the day and enjoy my first morning in Italy.

I sit back in my chair and the server brings my order. Well, maybe they had a good reason to stare; I muse at the sight of my coffee *and* wine for breakfast.

I pick up the wine, relax back against my chair and exhale slowly.

With my first sip of wine in Italy, my view is Mt. Vesuvius across the blue sea. The cliffs at the edge of Sorrento beside me and in the far distance, are colored with the pastels of houses and hotels built like they're a part of the rock. The sun slowly illuminates the tips of the shorter piers with more and more sunbathers gathering where the sunbeams touch. I take a few pictures, but nothing will match actually being here. Seeing, hearing and breathing beautiful, magnificent southern Italy.

Now where is that door? I'm almost thinking out loud since I have been lost looking for my apartment for the past half hour. All I can remember from last night are the myriad of doors we kept trying to open. I have tried several today that apparently are not mine. I know this, because the real owners yelled down at me from their windows in such a way that I didn't need to know Italian to understand. Embarrassing. I have given up the hunt though, broken down and called Lorenzo to come and save me. Embarrassed again, because I know the door is close. So now, I'm standing by the little street café I've seen from my bedroom window.

"Hi! Mila!"

Lorenzo is a sight for sore eyes.

"Oh, Lorenzo!" I push my body off of the wall and wrap my arms around him in a big hug. "Thank you so much for coming. So sorry I had to call you for this," I say, as my face cringes in embarrassment.

"It's fine, really. I was on my way past here but I'm glad you called when you did. Otherwise, I would have been in Positano. It would have been quite a wait for you." He smiles and walks us a few feet up the alley and turns right. Only one small store selling yellow and orange liquid in hand-painted bottles to walk past and we are at the big brown wooden doors that split down the middle.

"Oh, my goodness. Now I remember this door," I say. I wonder how I'm going to make it as a grown woman who's never traveled; on her own in a foreign country for nine more days and nights.

Lorenzo chuckles and turns the key. Yep, the door opens. I think he sees the dread on my face.

"It's okay. You know where to find it now." He smiles sweetly. "Come, I will make sure you get all the way into the apartment. I know you have had a long trip to get here."

23

Sprawled out on the bed, on my back, I'm exhausted. The way back up the steep walkway on the side of the cliff from the sea was merciless; gorgeous, but merciless. I strip down to my bra and panties without sitting up or getting off of the bed, so happy I left the a/c on. I hear my phone ding. Shit. Where is it? I stretch up to the pillow as far as my body will allow. My hand feels for and finds my phone. It's Angelo!

Angelo: How is your morning?

Hi! It's good thanks. I ate breakfast by the sea and then got lost. Lorenzo came to show me where the apartment is again.

Angelo: Okay, good you ate. How did you get lost? Anyways, I will come to get you tonight.

I was just jet lagged and didn't look around before I walked away. What are we doing tonight?

Angelo: My friend is the owner of a bar close to where you are. He has happy hour for a few people every night, then we are going to a club after.

Okay, that sounds nice.

Angelo: Good. I will pick you up around 6.

I'll be ready.

Six oh three and my phone dings.

Angelo: I'm downstairs

I don't waste time answering his text and quickly descend the stairs to the big door that leads to outside Italy. Angelo is the first thing I see in the small street and he looks exceptionally debonair in his jacket and scarf. Tight faded jeans, fabric dress shoes and the umbrella he's carrying just adds to the ensemble.

"Good evening. You look nice," he says, giving me the once over and a quick kiss on the cheek.

"Thank you. You look very nice as well."

Angelo's smile seems a little uncomfortable again. I wonder if there's something else going on with him or if he's just shy in person.

"Look there," he says. "Down at the end of your street."

"What am I looking for?"

"The big clock at the end. Your street is the only one that has this. You shouldn't get lost again. This is a very small town... I can't believe you couldn't find your apartment."

Oh. Well I guess he's not shy. I try to laugh it off.

"Oh my god I can't believe I didn't notice that either. Other than the fact I have an amazing amount of jet lag." I look at him and smile.

"Yes, that's true," he says in a much less condescending tone. "So now you know and can find your door always."

"Yes, thank you. I didn't enjoy being lost today."

This evening is a little cooler out, but still feels wonderful as we walk up the cobblestones. Aromas from the street restaurants wafting in the air are unbelievably delicious and unforgettable. I'm so excited to be out tonight and elated to have a friend here to show me Sorrento; to show me Italy. I notice I have a huge, stupid grin again and quickly fix my face. I don't want Angelo to get any wrong impressions.

Here in Italy, I knew there were cobblestone streets. What I didn't realize, is it's the majority of the roads. They are endearing, but walking in skinny heels is definitely a challenge. Then again, I *am* here to challenge myself, and I'm starting to see I just might like it.

We turn the corner and halfway down another alley, we end up in front of a glass door. His friend's bar is in the middle of a long white cement building that I personally, would have just walked by without noticing. Apparently, I need another goal; of paying closer attention to everything around me.

The doors slide open.

"Ciao!" a man Angelo's age greets us emphatically from behind the bar.

"Ciao!" we both say in unison as Angelo motions for me to walk in first.

I step over the threshold, look up and notice there are two other couples sitting at the bar watching us. Ugh. I suppose it's time to practice the new me and get comfortable talking to strangers. Angelo's friend walks out from behind the bar, smartly dressed in a long sleeve blue button-down dress shirt and black slacks. He's definitely not bad to look at.

"Mario, this is Mila. Mila, please meet my good friend Mario. He is the owner of this dump."

I giggle. "It's very nice to meet you, Mario."

He leans in and kisses my left cheek then my right. "Very nice to meet you as well."

Mario leans in to hug Angelo. Suddenly, he slaps his cheek instead, shocking us all. "A dump huh? You obviously don't want wine tonight."

The room erupts with laughter.

"You're lucky you're my good friend, Mario." Angelo grabs him by the back of the neck and plants a quick kiss on his cheek.

We walk to the bar and sit with the others. Mario introduces everyone and we find out the two couples are both from the United States; one set from Colorado, the other from New York and both are here on their honeymoons. Perhaps I shouldn't have worn the dress that ever so slightly, shows my nipples through stretchy material with tiny holes.

Wine is poured, snacks are brought out, my friend and his are going back and forth from speaking English to Italian and I'm holding my own, I think; carrying on conversations with everyone. Of course, as it seems to happen... the couples are curious about why I am traveling so far from home all by myself.

"Oh... well it's my celebratory divorce trip," I say quickly. I pause with a thought and a gulp of wine. "Oh, I'm sorry, that may be a little too honest to tell people on their honeymoon. But I'm sure you both will be great!" Ugh. I don't know what to say.

The woman I'm sitting next to, who looks to be close to my age, picks up her wine with a smile. "I'm not worried. You see, we have decided that neither of us want to have children. So, I think our marriage will last since all of the attention will be just on the two of us."

"That *is* good. It's very challenging to juggle the time for kids and time for each other."

The woman sitting across the bar from me, who looks like she's in her early thirties' chimes in. "So, you're here for your divorce trip? You look amazing... would you mind if I ask your age?"

Oh god. Here we go with the age thing. You know, I wouldn't feel too bad about it if age was just never brought up. But now that I'm *seeing* men younger than myself, it seems to enter a conversation sooner than later. It's to the point where I feel I should wear my age on my chest like a scarlet letter.

A quick sip of wine again and I catch myself turning to look at Angelo. For his approval? Nervous what he's thinking about this conversation? He knows my age, but I wonder if it makes him uncomfortable in front of anyone else.

Angelo doesn't look. I wonder if he's ignoring it or unaware since he seems to be in deep conversation with Mario on the other side of the bar. I turn back towards the four faces waiting ever so patiently for my reply.

"I'm 42."

"Wow," they say in unison.

I force a smile.

"You're making us look bad," the lady next to me says.

She seems to be the most... well... confident in herself. I sip more wine.

"Why would you say that?" I ask, now interested. "How old are you two?" If they have no qualms asking me my age, then I should have the same luxury.

"I'm 28," the overly confident one next to me says, tossing her dark brown shoulder length hair.

"I'm 25," says the blonde across the L-shaped bar.

I like her the best.

"Well I'll take that as a compliment then." I'm shocked at how far off I was with their ages.

"Oh yes… it is a compliment," the blonde says.

I sip more of my wine and change the subject back to them. I ask what they've seen in Italy so far and how long they will be visiting. Any other time I would be ridiculously uncomfortable, especially after that age discussion. But wine being the amazing elixir it is… I am accomplishing some of the goals I set for myself and start to feel good about tonight.

The conversations vary from where the couples have been in Italy to the diverse wine bottles Mario has on display. I look towards Angelo and smile. He makes eye contact with me and looks away.

"Mario. Take down the bottle I gave you. Let them look at it," Angelo says.

The mood with him seems to have changed to a different vibe. Did it happen with the age talk earlier? But then again, he has been acting somewhat distant since we sat down. Well, I sat down and he has been standing at the end of the bar just a little to my right. He walks around from time to time, joins the conversations with the couples or with Mario… but very little interaction with me. He did say something to me about a friend's birthday today; but was vague about any details. I get it. I do. I feel he doesn't want anyone getting the wrong idea about us. But again, if that was the case, why did he bring me here?

I shrug off this growing, shitty feeling so I can enjoy the rest of our hour here. Back to feeling sexy in my outfit; I've decided I deserve to – and the women's men are their problem.

A couple glasses of wine later and we say our goodbyes to everyone. I wound up having fun after all. How interesting it is to fill my life with many diverse people. I have missed out on so much... until now. From now on, I'm going to change my world; make it stretch far and wide with the people I meet on my new journey. I'm beginning to see; life is so much richer when you go out of your comfort zone and relax in your own skin. I'm happy I came all this way.

During our social hour, it rained but now has stopped. The cobblestones are slippery as I take my first step out and feel the slight slide.

"She's very nice looking," Angelo says out of the blue.

"Who? The brunette?" I say, knowing full well that's who. But I'm distracted by trying to step in the right places so I don't fall.

"Yes. She has a nice body."

"I suppose so. It seems they were impressed with me as well."

What the hell is he playing at? Why would he tell me something like that? Is this a test, maybe? He wants to see if I would be jealous?

"Yes, they were. Just look at you... and that dress." His eyes move down to my ever-so-slightly-exposed nipples.

My right heel suddenly slips on the wet stones, I let out a little scream and grab onto Angelo's arm. "Sorry, I'm just going to hold on. That would have been embarrassing," I laugh nervously.

We make it to the end of the alley. I lean my back against the corner of the building and Angelo stands in front. The air between us has again changed.

"I'm going to my friend's birthday party at a pizza place now." Angelo takes a step back and looks down the road.

"What? You're going now?" I'm so confused.

"Yes. I told you in there. I have a friend who I haven't seen in a while and it's his birthday."

"Oh. Okay. I just thought we were going out?"

"You know..." Angelo says with a new tone of voice. "I don't hold hands in the street. I don't kiss out in public either. I'm still wanting a wife and kids." His words are sharp and sting.

What the... I'm utterly shocked and pretty sure it's written all over my face. My mouth has fallen open and my eyes feel like they're popping out of my head. I try to understand what the fuck just happened.

"Tonight, at my friend's bar, you act like you're my girlfriend."

Oh. I see.

"Angelo... I don't know what you're talking about. I know I'm not your girlfriend, but I did think I was your friend. You realize, right? I could have been in Naples instead of here? I had five other men that wanted to show me around but I chose you. You promised me everything and I believed you. You even told me to screenshot the text that..."

"Stop. Things have changed." Angelo's eyes narrow and he steps back a couple more times. "I don't know if I even want to see you anymore."

Mario suddenly appears on a scooter, smiling. Angelo digs a helmet out of the back compartment of the bike and straddles behind him.

Wow. Is this even really happening? I can only stand here, dumbfounded.

"I'll call you as soon as I'm done," Angelo spits out.

The two men speed off past my apartment door and turn at the end of the road; out of sight.

Well.

I look down at my shoes, the damp stones beneath them, and feel lost. What the hell just happened? I should want to go find a nice glass of wine in a restaurant and something to eat, but I just can't. I'm tired and now, emotionally drained. I suppose I'll go back to the apartment; get out of the middle of the street. This is dumb and awkward, all dressed up and abandoned on the rain-soaked corner.

I look around and there are people everywhere. Seven-thirty in the evening and it seems everyone is happily walking to dinner with friends or their lovers. Just being out here with them all... I'm even more sad. A sad, abandoned, damp dog in the middle of an Italian cobblestone street. Yep, I'm going inside.

I open the distressed wooden door and enter the dark, quiet foyer of my apartment building. My phone dings several times. Oh yes... I forgot the Wi-Fi in Lorenzo's apartment connects as soon as I'm through this door. I look at my phone. Messages from Angelo. I read the first one as I climb the stairs to the next door.

Angelo: You're making me feel worse than I already feel.

Angelo: I have done so much for you.

Angelo: You don't appreciate anything.

I feel myself getting angry, can't wait, and text him back.

What? Why?

Angelo: I invited you here. I want you to enjoy. But I am busy sometimes and since the accident, I am strange I know. And you put me down. You talk about the other men from Napoli.

I only told you that so you could understand it's you I wanted to spend my time with.

Angelo: I don't like the feeling of having someone pushing. I like to have fun with you baby but when I see it's forced... I don't like it anymore.

Ok then just do what you need. Don't worry about me anymore – really. I want to have fun with you but only because you want me.

Angelo: You only want to fuck. You traveled all the way to the most beautiful county in the world and all you are concerned about is sex. Go out and see the town. Have a glass of wine and meet new people.

31

I'm sorry if you don't understand. All we ever talked about is what we would do once we were together. You knew why I came here and the things I want to experience far from home.

Angelo: You are crazy. No one travels just to have sex. Go do that when you are home.

Angelo: Now I don't even feel like seeing my friend. I just want to stay here at home. You make me feel bad and I already told you I am sad all the time.

I throw my phone on the couch. Big drops finally breach the edge of my eyes and stream down my face as I pour myself another glass of wine.

He said he would spoil me. Said he would show me everything and do everything with me.

I have been drinking since the second I got inside my apartment. Why not? Angelo said he doesn't want to see me anymore. Obviously, my night has gone to shit. And here I am... 8000 miles from home and chose poorly. Why do I always do this?! My ex-husband was the wrong choice. All of my boyfriends before that were the wrong choice. Now this. I had a plethora of men to choose from and this is where I am; my entire vacation planned around a man who has decided he doesn't want me.

I stand in front of the full-length mirror halfway between the front door and the living room. I stare at myself drinking wine and self-pity takes over as I examine the woman staring back at me.

"Why?!"

It's shocking and strangely comforting to hear my own voice. I look at myself, from my heels to my hair, and take another drink.

"Why are you so lame?!" I angrily ask my reflection.

"What are you even doing here?! Why did you think you could do this?!"

Another gulp of wine.

"You're old. Get that through your head. No man really wants to spend time with a 42-year-old woman when they can have someone in their 20s or 30s."

I break down. Crying uncontrollably, I watch in the mirror as I squat down and feel sorry for myself. What am I doing here? I thought I knew. I thought this would be an amazing adventure that would let me find who I really am. Not a man's wife, a mother's daughter, a brother's sister or even a child's mother... I want to know me.

My face is red and blotchy now. I look pitiful. All dressed up in a sexy, strapless, navy-blue dress, nude suede heels with straps around my ankles and the sides of my hair pulled up; the rest of my dark brown locks cascading down my back.

"Sad."

My phone dings just as I stand up to refill my glass. I roll my eyes. "What now?"

Mario: Hello. What are you doing? Are you getting ready?

The bar owner? Now I'm even more confused.

Getting ready for what?

Mario: To go to the club in Positano.

Angelo said he doesn't want to see me anymore.

Mario: He did? Well I'll take you tonight. Get ready.

I'm already drinking. Kind of drunk.

Mario: Take a picture and send to me.

What? He wants a picture? Okay – I take a picture of just my face with the wine glass to my mouth and send it.

Mario: Are you crying? Why are you crying?

Shit. Well I'm drunk enough. I might as well tell him.

I'm sorry. I'm just sad my friend doesn't want to see me anymore.

Mario: I don't believe that. He's just at his friend's birthday and he'll be here to go with us to the club.

No. He told me I make him feel bad. Also, I think it's because of my age.

Mario: Why would it have anything to do with your age?

I'm drunk as hell now. I've stripped my dress off and I'm walking around the apartment in just panties and heels.

Because I'm old Mario

Mario: You are not old. Why would you say that?

It doesn't matter. He doesn't want to see me.

Mario: Well I want to see you. You shouldn't be drinking alone. I'm getting in the shower now. Go lie down, take a little nap and I'll text you when I'm done.

Mario: I'll see you soon

Okay.

I roll over, look around the room and wonder what time it is. I look down and see I'm naked. Oh. I cringe; I remember now, Mario told me to lie down until he called. My phone. Where's my phone? I sit up and find it on the pillow next to me. It's dead. Shit. I brought the wrong adapter from home, so I borrow the plug from the wireless Wi-Fi after a bit of scrambling around. I plug in my phone and in a few minutes, it's back on – 4:03 a.m.

"What?! Oh noooo I slept all night."

I run and plug the Wi-Fi back in and open my phone quick. So many texts chime one after the other. There're texts from Mario.

8:30pm - *Mario: Okay I'm done.*

8:43pm - *Mario: Text me back I'll walk over to get you.*

9:00pm - *Mario: I hope you're not sleeping. Text me.*

9:08pm – *Mario: I will be at the bar until 9:30.*

And very curious; there's also texts from Angelo.

9:24pm – *Angelo: Hi baby I'm leaving soon.*

10:pm – *Angelo: babyyyyy*

12:32am – *Angelo: You are making me feel worry like never before.*

3:00am – *Angelo: Baby I hope you're ok pls message me as soon as you* can.

Baby? And why would he be worried? What the hell? I thought he didn't want to see me again.

"Ugh. I can't believe I missed the whole night."

I text Angelo.

Hi. I just woke up.

I fell asleep and my phone died.

Hope you had a good time with your friend from Brazil.

Mad at my choices, I toss the phone back down on the pillow and walk to the long windows. I open the shutters and look out to the dark empty street. It's quiet now. No Italian music playing from the little café down below, no one briskly walking through the alleyway to rendezvous with a lover or even a tourist meandering through the streets in search of the perfect memory to take home. It's just quiet, dark and the air is cool.

My first real night in Italy and I get drunk, feel sorry for myself and pass out. Well I guess it can only get better from here; and I got the cry I was needing... I guess.

I close the shutters and fall back into bed, under the covers this time; close my eyes and fall back to sleep.

4

Chapter 4

It is 9:43 a.m. and I wake up to the ding of my phone.

I roll over, moan and rub my eyes... gently; I definitely don't need anything that speeds up aging my face. I check my phone.

Angelo: He is from here.

Who is? Oh... his friend from last night, the birthday boy.

Angelo: Anyway, I'm really sorry I fell asleep. I missed u.

Angelo: What are you doing?

I message him back while going pee. I need to get ready fast to get out of this apartment and go see Italy.

I woke up at 4, then went back to sleep. I'm up now. Drank a whole bottle of wine after I got home last night and woke up with a headache.

Angelo: Yes I know. That's silly. We were supposed to drink together.

I know... I was wanting to.

Angelo: Well I missed you. What will you do today?

I stare at his words *I missed you.* I know I didn't imagine him telling me all of those hurtful things last night.

I'm getting ready now to go explore and find something to eat.

Angelo: Yesterday I told you to go shopping. Just walk around. There are 1000 shops and all of them sell food.

Okay I'll do that. Thanks
Angelo: Let me know what you're doing later okay?
Okay yes, I will.
I'm not going to overthink this – him. I switch my phone to play music; Coldplay's "Hymn for the Weekend".

The alleys and streets are all abuzz. Tourists slowly making their way through the various shops lining every building, selling everything from magnets and postcards, to music boxes and the colorful liquid I pass near my apartment every day, it's called limoncello. I love the energy of tourists adventuring, mixed with locals on a mission. Or even the store owners; lazily enjoying talking to each other, standing outside of their shops as they, like myself, watch the array of people walking by.

Only a few steps outside of the door and my phone rings.

"Hello?"

"Ciao, Mila. This is Mario. Are you okay?"

"Hi. Yes, thank you, I'm fine. A bit embarrassed from last night though," I say as my body automatically withdraws into itself. I cringe at what he must think of me.

"Yes, I was worried about you. What are you doing now? Would you like to have a coffee with me?"

"Umm sure… that would be nice."

"Okay good. Come to the bar. I am here now."

"I'm on my way."

"Great! See you soon."

I hang up, put my phone back in my purse and head around the corner to Mario's bar. How interesting. Well now I can try to redeem myself and explain in person my issues last night. I hate trying to convey feelings and emotions on text; it just doesn't translate well.

I walk through the sliding glass doors and Mario is behind the bar at the far end of the room. I didn't notice last night how bright and cheery it is in here.

"Ciao! Come in. Sit down."

"Ciao. Okay thank you."

I sit on the tall stool right on the corner of the bar. The same one the *nice-looking* woman from last night was on and I roll my eyes at the memory of it all. Mario smiles and asks what kind of coffee I want; a big cup of coffee or an espresso? I haven't tried espresso yet and I'm feeling somewhat vulnerable now in front of him, so I go with what I know.

"A big cup please."

"Okay."

He turns around, adjusts his machine and quickly makes me a cup of coffee.

"So…" Mario says, placing a steaming coffee in front of me with a little napkin, a tiny silver spoon and three long, skinny packets of sugar. "Tell me what happened last night."

Oh god here it is.

"Well, I took your advice and lay down for a quick nap. Unfortunately, I didn't wake up until a little after four." I look down to my coffee and stir in two sugars.

"Because you were drinking alone."

"Yes. Because I was drinking alone," I say glancing up at him. "I also had extreme jet lag… which I'm sure exacerbated the whole situation for me."

"Yes, that's true." Mario sips his espresso quick and it's gone. "I need to check on my other bar. Hurry and finish your coffee."

"Oh. Okay."

I down my coffee and get up to leave. I guess I'll go back to checking out the town. Mario places my empty cup and spoon into the sink and throws away the paper things.

"Thank you for the coffee," I say and grab my purse.

"We will only be a few minutes at the other bar, then we'll come back here."

Oh. I guess we're not done. Okay... again, interesting.

Mario is tall and walking like a bat out of hell. I have a hard time keeping pace and wonder if it will be noticeable if I just jog a bit. Yeah... he'll notice. Just longer strides, Mila.

Across to almost the other side of town and we climb what seems like a thousand steps, walk through a narrow doorway that opens up to a large room and we're in a bar. It's dimly lit and cozy. Wooden tables, benches and chairs are set up strategically throughout the room with a long, robust bar along the left wall.

"This way," Mario says as he walks through a door to the right.

We've entered his bright office and he sits down at the cherry wood desk in front of a window. It's littered with stacks of papers, all in neat piles, with a small plant and *Mario Bellini* on a name plate in the front center. He starts rummaging through his top drawer while I spin around and sit in the chair facing him.

Mario pauses and looks at me with a curious face. "Why were you crying last night?"

I feel my cheeks grow warm with him staring into my soul. I was wrong... this was a lot easier to talk about while drunk texting. I take a breath.

"There were several reasons."

Mario looks at me for a moment more then goes back to looking through the drawer.

"Go ahead..."

"I had terrible jet lag, I'm having issues with my age and..." I hesitate, to get a grip on myself. "And I was very sad at what Angelo had said."

Really quick, I wipe away the stupid tear that is escaping my eye. Oh god, just in time; Mario looks up again, with the paper he apparently was hunting for in hand.

"What about your age?"

I uncross then cross my legs the opposite way.

"I'm 42, Mario."

"So?"

I try not to roll my eyes.

"So... I'm feeling kind of old right now. Seems like it's always a topic of conversation. I don't remember talking about my age this much when I was in my 20s or even 30s."

"You are not old. And you don't even look your age. So, I don't understand the problem." He scribbles on the paper, places it on top of a pile and grabs another.

"I honestly don't know how to explain it to you and I'm sure it's just me. But it *is* how I've been feeling lately. I'll get over it eventually."

"And Angelo? You will get over him as well?" He scribbles again and compares it to another paper.

"I don't want to get over Angelo. I consider him a good friend and that's why what he said hurt me last night." I take a breath and steady my emotions. Goddamn emotions. I exhale slow, then take a deep breath in. "I'm not sure if you know this, but Angelo and I have been talking for five months prior to me coming here. He and I talked about everything; from general day-to-day life, to what we would do when I got here to Italy. I was even there through his sister's accident. We talked almost every day."

Mario looks up but doesn't say anything.

"I know he's hurting. I know he's sad. I just don't understand why he won't tell me he can't do what we planned. Instead, he makes plans and then blames me for acting like I'm his girlfriend when he breaks them. I want to be here for him but I don't think I can keep taking his mood swings. This morning he texted me saying how much he missed me last night."

"See… he is still your friend." Mario stands up and I follow him out of the office. "I will give you some advice on Angelo. He has been my very good friend for a long time." Mario opens the door to the street and motions for me to go out ahead. "Do not argue with him. I lost my father over a year ago and it's taken me this long to feel okay again. It will take Angelo just as long. Just don't argue with him. Nothing good will come from it."

I scoot slowly back onto the tall stool. I like this first bar. I'm used to it now. I sit and watch Mario grab various things, but I'm thinking about Angelo. What should I do? He tells me one minute that we will have amazing sex like I have never experienced before, then almost in the next breath, he's condemning me when I want to do just that.

"What's on your mind, Mila?"

I jump out of my thoughts and back to where Mario is looking at me with something in his hand.

"Would you like a small tiramisu?"

"Yes, I would love one!"

And with that one question, my mood is changed to happy. Who can be upset while eating tiramisu?

He sets up a small glass jar, napkin and spoon in front of me. It looks delicious. I take a bite and it is heaven; perfectly moist and so much flavor.

"My mother made these," he says, opening a small refrigerator with about twelve identical jars in it.

"Well it's amazing! The best I've ever tasted. Please tell your mom thank you."

"So, tell me," Mario says, washing my spoon from earlier. "You keep saying Angelo promised you things. What things would that be?"

Oh... this took a while to come up. I almost thought he really only wanted to be a friend. I gently place another spoonful of tiramisu in my mouth and think deep on whether I should answer this honestly or not... I know where it will lead. Should I care what Angelo thinks or says anymore? But then again, why else would he have introduced his friend to me? I do know more about his friends than they are probably aware of. Angelo told me a lot about them all over the last five months.

One last bite of delicious tiramisu and Mario disposes of it for me. He walks around the bar and I slowly spin in the chair to face him. He is standing so close I can smell his cologne. He smells nice; intoxicating.

"So, tell me, Mila, why would Angelo promise so much?"

"I'm not quite sure why exactly." I try not to gulp. "Maybe he was just being nice, or because he enjoyed our conversations."

"Yes... perhaps. Would there be any other reasons?" Mario places one hand on the bar and leans a little closer into me.

I laugh. "Yes Mario, I suppose there were a few other reasons he would promise me so much."

"I'm listening..."

I take a deep breath and decide to open Pandora's box.

"It just might be the naughty factor."

Mario's eyebrows arch up and a small smile crosses his face.

"The naughty factor? Please... explain."

"Talking sex. About things I have done or not done. And pictures."

"Ciao!" A woman walks up behind Mario and he spins around, startled.

"Ciao, Teresa."

Mario and this new woman start a conversation in Italian. I spin my seat back towards the bar after a smile and a wave. Only a couple of minutes and I hear "Ciao" ... "Ciao."

"That's Teresa," Mario says with his attention back on me. "She's here to take inventory, and after that, to set the bar up for tonight."

"Oh okay. She seems nice."

"So, show me the pictures that had Angelo promising you so much."

I turn and smile but my mind is racing. Should I? Shouldn't I? Once I do, it will be just the beginning... I know.

Fuck it. I shouldn't care what Angelo thinks. He's not taking care of me or my needs.

"Hold on."

I pull my phone out of my purse and find what will turn this friendly chat into a naughty day. I turn the screen to Mario and he smiles.

"That's very nice. Do you have another?"

I pick another picture, one that shows more of me and turn it to him again.

"Yes, I like that very much... any more?"

I show him three more. Each photo naughtier than the last.

"Okay now you've made me horny and I want you," he says and reaches out. He takes my hand and holds it against the front of his pants. "See? You've woken him up."

We stare into each other's eyes as I move my hand to feel the hard bulge beneath it. Oh. Now I'm turned on. "Well Mario, now you've made me wet."

Not breaking eye contact; he pulls my body a little further off of the chair, caresses my knees with his warm hands and spreads my legs open. Slow but steady, he slides one hand between them; up through my skirt.

A sharp inhale from me as I feel his fingers lightly tickle the upper part of the inside of my thighs, pull my panties to the side and lightly touch my wet clit. I gasp when I feel him slide in further; penetrating my lips.

Oh... this... feels so good.

With my left hand holding onto my chair, I unbutton his pants and pull the zipper down with my right hand. I work my hand between his underwear and tight stomach, down to his hot, hard cock. I wrap my fingers around him and stroke slowly, as much as the constricting pants will allow. Mario exhales. He slides his two fingers in and out. I can hear how wet I am.

"Mila, you are so horny," he breathes and moves close to my ear. "I love how you feel," he whispers in a deeper voice.

He is so close to me I feel his breath. The warmth and the light touch of his lips send shivers down the right side of my body and makes me want more. I moan as quietly as I can and close my eyes. I feel him push his fingers further inside.

"Shhh. We don't want Teresa to hear."

I look back into his eyes and nod with an almost desperate look.

"Come. Let's go to your apartment."

He read my thoughts. Mario slowly slides his fingers out of me and I pull my hand from his pants. He buttons up while I straighten my panties and skirt.

I smile to myself. Hmmm, that was fun right here in the open.

Mario swings open the door to my apartment and I'm going crazy with needing to continue. He closes the door behind us, picks me up with my legs wrapped around his waist and sits me on the couch. My feet are on the edge and he kneels down on the floor between my legs. He pulls my panties off and slides his fingers inside of me again. Faster and harder. Deeper and more urgent he shoves them in my needy pussy, making me squirm and moan. He yanks down the neck of my shirt; my breasts exposed.

"I noticed you weren't wearing a bra... I've been wanting to do this all day."

He grabs, squeezes and sucks on them both, still with his fingers penetrating deep inside while I writhe in ecstasy. I am not quiet at all. Suddenly my stomach clenches, I grab tighter onto the cover of the couch… and squirt.

The look on Mario's face is one of happy surprise. He rubs my clit fast, side to side and makes it keep coming… makes me keep cumming.

"Oh, you didn't tell me you can squirt."

"Oh… right… maybe that's… another reason… I was promised so much," I say between breaths and moans.

"You are very bad and I'm going to fuck you hard."

"Oh god, yes. I need you to."

He slides his hand from my clit, I hear him pull down his pants and I'm wet with anticipation.

"Do you have a condom?" I whisper, my head still back.

"No. Do you?"

What? I sit up a little and look at him. "I don't. I'm sorry but you cannot without a condom."

"Are you sure?"

"Mmmm… as much as I don't want to be… yes, I'm sure. I'm adventurous, but not that much."

My head falls backwards again. My hands reclaim the couch in a tight grip and I'm louder than before. Mario's fingers are back inside me, fast and deep. I begin squirting again, all over the floor. He pulls his fingers out and stands in front of my face. I sit up quick with my mouth open and engulf his hard cock.

Oh my god this feels so good… and even more naughty. A moan escapes his mouth as he holds the back of my head, his fingers entangled in my long hair. I'm so wet and I want to feel him inside me, but I can't be that reckless.

Mario stops me, slides out of my mouth, pulls me up by my shoulders and leads me into the small kitchen. My ass, pressed against the sink with him in front of me, his hard chest rising and falling with each heavy breath. My head falls back as he pulls a fistful of my hair... my mouth is filled with his tongue. He spreads my legs wide apart with his other hand, his tongue still dancing with mine. I feel him lightly running his fingertips up my inner left thigh, up to my wet clitoris and through the lips. Slowly, I feel his fingers penetrate deeper until his fist is against me.

I let out my breath in ecstasy.

Mario suddenly swings my body around, his fingers still deep inside me, and lays me on top of the kitchen table. On my back, feet on the table with my knees bent and legs spread. He grabs my breasts as he fucks me hard, deep and fast with his fingers.

Two, three then four fingers inside my wet pussy. Oh my god, it's so good. I feel my body build again.

"Squirt! Squirt now!" Mario calls out.

He quickly pulls his fingers out of me and I gush all over the table. "Yes!"

Mario's fingers are quickly on my clit, rubbing back and forth, making me continue. I clench my left hand around his forearm. This is so amazing and so bad.

Lying on top of this table, my legs spread wide open, I see how he loves watching and making me continuously squirt for him. It's almost as good as an orgasm.

The second I finish, Mario pulls me off of the table and down to my knees on the floor. He slides into my open mouth. I can tell he's close. I suck and stroke him deep and fast. I pull my mouth from Mario's pulsing cock and he shoots his cum all over my breasts. I look up at his face, his mouth slightly open as he watches it drip down my skin, over my nipples. I rub the rest of his cum from the tip onto my breast.

"Hmm thank you, Mario." I say slowly, and with a little smile.

"You're welcome. You were very horny," he says and pulls me up to stand.

"Yes. That's what I've been trying to tell your friend."

I slide my panties back on, wet a towel and clean my breasts. I adjust my shirt into place then wipe him clean too.

"Do you feel better now?" he says with a sly smile, zipping up his pants.

"Why yes I do... that was a nice little release. I needed it very much."

"I have to run now. I need to get back to the bar and ready it for tonight."

"Okay yes, I understand."

He leans in and kisses my cheek before I close the door behind him. I throw my arms up above my head, sway my hips from side to side and happy dance myself into the bathroom to turn on the shower. With a huge grin on my face, I step into the falling hot water and think of how naughty I just was. Oh, how perfectly good and naughty.

5

Chapter 5

O h, yes – I'm in ecstasy once again. The sun is bright and warm under the red shade of the Blue Water restaurant as I savor each bite of this amazing caprese salad. I have seen it in magazines but it's my first time tasting these delicious flavors. The tomato is cool and crisp with the very best mozzarella. I never knew arugula had such a wonderful unique flavor, and with the olive oil and a few basil leaves... this is the perfect, pure pleasure lunch. After my late morning session with Mario, this is especially delicious. I smile to myself and realize I probably look crazy smiling to no one. This is a good day.

My phone dins as I sip the last of my rosé wine. It's Angelo. It has been several hours since Mario left my apartment.

Angelo: Hi. I hope you're having a nice day. You should wear something sexy.

Yes thanks! I just finished eating a late lunch. I might have a friend from Naples come visit me tonight.

Angelo: oh ok

You are busy yes...?

Angelo: It's ok.

Okay then I will.

Angelo: Enjoy.

Thanks.

Angelo: Do you trust this guy?

Yes, I do. I've talked to him for a few months. I trust him as I trusted you.

I pay for my meal and the waiter's smile adds to my good day. The waiters at this restaurant are all men and very friendly. It's kind of funny everyone at this restaurant sees me leave my apartment each time since they're directly across from the big wooden door. I wonder if they know who I know?

I look back at my phone.

Angelo: Okay good 4 u.

I need a release. I need no stress.

I take a few steps away from the restaurant, turn my key in the distressed door and walk into the foyer of my apartment building again.

Angelo: You could have fucked Mario.

He didn't have a condom.

Angelo: Why call someone from Napoli? I just said to wear something sexy. I'm coming for you.

What? I scroll back up in our conversation. Yep there it is. But he only said to dress sexy... I didn't know he meant he was coming to see me. I shake my head. Is it just me or is he vague about most things? I open the next two doors and enter my apartment, set my purse on the table in the living room and walk into the bedroom.

If you are really coming ... I would rather spend time with you. And I'm already wearing a sexy dress.

Angelo: Show me.

I walk to the long window for light and snap a picture of what I have on.

Angelo: I like that.

49

Thank you.

Angelo: But show me another. Something sexier. One you said you were bringing with you.

I know exactly what outfits he's talking about and dive into my suitcase. I find the one I want to wear for this particular occasion and quickly slide it on. I take a picture when my body is all in place and hit send.

Angelo: Yes that one. Very sexy.

Heels or no heels?

Angelo: Heels. Oh I should bring my whip.

Hmm, a whip. That's new.

Yesss I have never had that.

Angelo: Okay. I will whip you.

Yes please.

Angelo: Good. I will try to come see you quickly. Then I have to be home. I'm having dinner with my parents.

Okay yes.

Angelo: If you want.

Yes of course I want.

Angelo: Good. I need to whip you. For being bad. Why did you blow Mario?

Ahahahaha!

Yep. I knew Mario had told him. I laugh out loud at him calling me out on it. It makes sense now why he's so adamant about coming over.

Angelo: Horny girl. Hungry for cock.

Yes, so hungry. Bring condoms please.

Angelo: Okay. How hungry are you?

Why...? I can go all night if that's what you're asking.

Angelo: Good we will.

With this new turn of events, I message Francesco in Naples, explain that I have plans for the night and will let him know when I'll be free for us to meet. I toss my phone onto the couch, run around quick to grab the few clothes and shoes I have scattered and throw them into the closet in the bedroom. I rush to the kitchen and pour myself a glass of the wine I'm so happy I bought today. Okay, maybe another... and yeah, one more just in case.

My phone dings.

Angelo: I'm driving

Okay.

My mind is racing... what's the most important? Makeup. I rush into the bathroom, touch up my makeup, fluff my hair and adjust my boobs. Okay. That should do it.

It's been fifteen minutes now and I'm starting to feel the effects of the wine. This is perfect because I'm a little nervous. I don't like to disappoint and my god, we talked so much about this moment... and now it's here.

My phone dings.

Angelo: I parked.

And now *he's* here.

Angelo: Can we come?

Wait a minute... I look back at that last text. 'Can *we* come?' What the hell?! Is it Mario? It has to be. Why didn't Angelo say anything about it being two of them?! Well shit. I'm glad I had the wine.

Angelo: We are here.

I'm coming down.

Angelo: We are already up at the second door.

Oh shit. My nerves are jumping. I hope they like what I'm wearing. I hope I can handle this.

I swing my long, light sweater jacket around my body and walk out of the apartment to the middle door. This door is at the end of a half wall and I can see them right there, on the other side, with big grins.

"This is a surprise," I say removing my jacket as they follow me into the apartment.

I'm still in shock this is happening, even though I know how Angelo is about sex. This is one of the fantasies we had talked about; in great detail actually. This is an experience I have had only once before... with two brothers from Naples. Oh, the brothers. The very reasons why I chose Italy for my first international trip.

Angelo is right behind me and Mario closes the door. Neither of them responds to my statement. Instead, Mario walks through the living room - taking in the atmosphere.

"Ohh it's very different in here from this morning."

"Yes, I suppose it is."

I walk slowly into the living room behind him. I had time to prepare and set the mood this time; music is playing and the wooden shades on the window are mostly closed, making the lighting inside, perfectly dimmed.

All of a sudden, I'm looking at the ceiling.

Angelo has walked up beside me, wrapped his hand around my long hair and pulled it straight down. My arms relax by my side as he kisses me. My mouth... filled with his as his tongue slides in, deep and slow. He starts to pull his tongue back and I suck it on the way out of my mouth. The wine has kicked in and I'm ready. I know what they're expecting and I think I can do it. This is what I wanted. This is what I need to experience.

Angelo turns me around to see Mario sitting on the couch completely naked. He's hard and slowly stroking. I smile a little devilishly as I kneel down in front of him, between his legs...

Wait.

I stand back up, grab a throw pillow from the other end of the couch, place it on the floor between his feet, then kneel down again on top of it. Much better.

"You'll appreciate the pillow," I say with a raise of my left eyebrow.

I take over stroking for Mario. I feel his dick grow a little more, and again, a naughty smile crosses my face. I slowly bend over and slide him into my mouth, my eyes locked on his. I'm so turned on. Exhilarated. I'm aware of every part of my body and I can feel Angelo watching, which is making me even more wet.

My skin tingles on my behind, up my back and on my shoulder as Angelo runs his hand over my body; my mouth and hands are full of Mario.

"Yes... yes... suck his dick. Yes, Mila, just like that."

I feel Angelo's hand on my head, coaxing me to go down more. I silently obey and swallow Mario. A low moan slides out from between his lips. My head is gently pulled up by my hair and my mouth is free again. I follow where I'm directed, with no one saying a word. The air is full of lust and need.

I straddle Mario as he slides inside me. I stretch around his throbbing cock and start to move my hips. Oh fuck, I'm loving Angelo watching me on his friend and I can't be quiet about it. My body moves back and forth on top of Mario deep inside of me... so deep. Both of their hands; roaming everywhere. My back, my heaving breasts, my face, my ass and through my hair.

I moan loud, and after the third time, Mario sticks his four fingers in my mouth. Angelo has moved my outfit to the sides of my breasts. Mario sucks and slaps one, then pulls his fingers from my mouth just to lead it to Angelo's hard cock. I'm greedy and take it all.

I am in the moment. No appointments, no responsibilities, nowhere to be but right here, letting them please my body and me pleasing theirs. Every part of me is tingling. My senses are heightened and my nerves are on fire. I follow their lead and love not having to think about what to do next or what they will enjoy; they are doing it all... I just have to relax, perform and love it.

6

Chapter 6

ngelo: You are really a sex machine.

After about two hours of playing with Angelo and Mario, they needed to go and see their families. I have just gotten out of the shower and see Angelo's message. I wrap a towel around my damp body and message back.

Why thank you. I'm happy to hear that. I was concerned you didn't like it.

Angelo: No baby I told you before, sometimes I'm having a hard time with breathing.

Oh right I'm sorry, I forgot. You felt amazing. I just wanted to hear you tell me.

Angelo: Yes. That's why I'm scared to fuck. It is just recent. I will see a doctor about it soon.

I'm sorry love, you felt so good. But you didn't use the whip.

I see another message come through.

Mario: Ciao bella Mila. I and some friends are going to a pub in a couple of hours. You should come.

Angelo: Yes, I know. I will bring the whip another time when it's just you and I. I think Mario and a couple other friends of ours are going to watch a football match in some pub.

I giggle. Are they sitting next to each other messaging me?

Yes, he just told me

Angelo: Perfect. Maybe you can change and join.

Hmm. If Mario is anything like me, he's insatiable. Do I want to? Should I want to? I know Angelo told them all about me. My divorce, my age, kids... everything. And I'm still in need. I can't seem to not want more. But how will they view me, knowing I've already had sex twice today?

Oh, to hell with it. I'm going. I'm only here for eight more nights and I'm supposed to not care what people think.

Okay yes, I'll go. What should I wear?

Angelo: Whatever you like babe.

The air is perfect, the mood sexy. It's night time and outside, the streets are bustling with sharply dressed people once again. The clang of dishes and chefs cooking in the side restaurants, the low roar of so many people enjoying conversations over dinner, the hum of distant cars maneuvering through the little roads, and me; briskly walking the cobblestones to meet Mario... somewhere. The blue line on my phone is slowly becoming shorter and shorter as I follow it to him and his friends.

It's day two and I'm still trying to not worry about what other people think as they stare at me wandering around looking lost. I am in desperate need of accomplishing the goal of not giving a fuck.

I come to the end of the blue line, look up and see debonair Mario standing five feet in front of me smiling... well, looking amused is more like it.

"Ciao, Mila!"

55

"Ciao!"

I turn off my phone and close the small distance between us, lean up and give him the customary cheek kisses. I'm feeling good about tonight. Seems like it's going to be an interesting adventure as I follow Mario to a brand new, little four-door silver and blue car.

"Here," he says, opening the back driver-side door.

I peek as I step in and I'm shocked to see a very well put together man looking back at me. He has a young professional look but with longer, crazy styled hair on top. Professional with an edge.

I smile. "Ciao."

"Ciao," he replies and slowly pushes the middle of his glasses up higher on the bridge of his nose.

I scoot in, Mario closes my door, jumps in the driver's seat and looks in the rear-view mirror. "Mila, this is Federico."

The man sitting in the passenger seat next to Mario turns around with a big grin and puts his hand up. "Ciao!"

"Ciao!" I say in just as an excited tone.

"And that's Marco." Mario nods towards the sexy sexy sitting next to me.

"Hi," he says again, with a small, very reserved smile.

With moments like this, it's easy for me to forget all about the number of my age. Sitting in the back of a car filled with sexy younger men, I see myself on the outside exactly how I feel on the inside. I grin, say hi back and try very hard not to revert to my shy self.

Off we go as Mario pulls out and barely misses two lovers walking hand in hand in the narrow alley. I love how fast and crazy we're driving through narrow winding roads. So much so, that I giggle around a blind corner that has me almost in sexy Marco's lap. He just slightly smiles again and I'm so glad it's dark in here. Pretty sure my cheeks are a nice shade of red.

"We know the owner of the small restaurant we're taking you to,"

Mario yells over the music and honking horn of an oncoming car we barely miss. "He has the football match on and amazing food."

"Okay, that sounds good," I say with a big smile.

"It's located up the hill a bit and can get chilly at night, so I'm glad to see you wore a jacket."

I did. I have on a strapless cream-colored summer dress with my short Converse and a cream colored, long but thin sweater jacket. I look pretty cute tonight if I do say so myself. Plus, I chose this outfit tonight for another reason as well.

We've arrived and park across from the restaurant. I step out of the car on the side of a dark road; the air is crisp, just as Mario had said. We walk a short distance to a small, old looking building made entirely of dark wood. Marco opens the door and it squeaks as we enter the warm, quaint restaurant. Inside, it looks and feels like what I thought a pub would be; exactly what they said... but I don't get out much, I muse.

I follow behind Mario as we pass several people on both sides of the large room and sit down at one of the eight wooden booths situated against the walls. I scoot in next to Mario, Marco and Federico scoot in across from us.

Nervous but exhilarated, it's amazing being here... out with three handsome Italian men at a local restaurant. *This* is what I was wanting, what I imagined I would be doing in Italy. Well, this and the fun I had earlier today; I smile at the thought.

After wine is brought to our table by a very young man that popped up out of nowhere and startled me, I relax a little and look around while the three decide on what to order. The soccer game, err... I mean football match is playing on a huge flat screen TV behind us in another area, a little smaller than this one; I assume it's where the kitchen is too. A low rumble of conversation is coming from the other tables filled with men around their twenties and thirties. Oh, and one woman at the table right across from us. She looks to be about my age. Interesting. I try not to stare, but find myself glancing back at her, wondering what it's like to be a middle-aged woman living in Italy. She's wearing all black; what we women do when feeling the need to hide a few extra inches, but she is showing off her assets perfectly with the front of her outfit a plunging neckline. I look at the men sitting across from her and notice that her carefully planned outfit is working. Each man cannot help but to glance down at her ample breasts as she laughs and ever so slightly arches her back. I giggle to myself at how easily she has them.

Eventually, I return to filling my eyes and memories with this lovely place, where the walls are covered with America memorabilia. Everything from Marilynn Monroe pictures to license plates with *California, Arizona* and *Colorado* scrawled on them. None in pristine condition.

I nudge Mario and look back to the walls. "I almost feel like I'm back home."

"Haha yes! Fabio is a big dreamer of America. He travels there at least two times a year."

Mario looks beyond me.

"Guarda le tette di quella donna all'altro tavolo."

Marco and Federico both look towards the table across from us.

"Ahaha! Yes, I noticed that as well," I say with a raise of my eyebrows. Mario looks at me a little puzzled.

"Oh, come on. I don't have to speak Italian to know what you're looking at."

We all laugh and I glance up to see sexy Marco studying me... almost as much as I've been studying these walls.

The food comes shortly after Federico orders for everyone, my wine glass is continuously filled and I'm relaxing more with my fun company.

"Federico knows how to order food," Mario states between stabs of what looks like pork and beans from home. "We always have him order because he orders the best on the menu. Even the chefs didn't know it could be so good."

Federico smiles shyly and looks down but doesn't say anything. He's cute and shy. Quite a contrast to Mario and I haven't figured Marco out yet.

"Federico doesn't speak much English, but we are teaching him. And Marco knows some."

"Ah okay. That makes sense," I say with a smile. "I thought you just didn't like me." I look at Federico and everyone laughs after Mario translates for me.

They go back to eating and switching conversations from Italian to English and back again. I'm not hungry since I ate a delicious filling lunch, so I'm just observing, enjoying the company and drinking wine. Mario continues to give me the *I know how you really are* look throughout dinner and it's making me giggle. I'm positive the boys on the other side of the table have an idea of what's going on. It's good. I'm enjoying being coy tonight.

Federico reaches for the wine bottle and I watch as the liquid splashes into the bottom of my glass, filling it up half way. I think it's cute how each one of them has made sure my wine glass is never completely empty and also how Mario has been little touches here and little whispers there in front of his friends.

I'm getting to know this game.

"So, Mila…" Mario leans closer. "You'll have to let us know what you like."

My cheeks instantly feel warm. Apparently, we're done with the pleasantries and just getting right to it. Hmmm, good thing I already had a feeling this wasn't just a normal *one of the boys* get together. So, as quickly as I blush, I put my wine glass down and flow with confidence

59

instead.

"Well… how can I say this?" I look directly at sexy Marco. "I follow, I don't really lead." I'm shocked. I think I actually see his eyes glimmer. Instantly, I'm shy again.

"You will have to let us know what you want us to do," Mario reiterates. "Direct us."

"Seriously, I don't do that," I say, grateful for the distraction from Marco's gaze.

"You want us to do whatever we like?" Mario again squeezes my thigh under the table and smiles.

"Yesss," I draw out the *s* and cut my eyes up at Mario and then Marco. "I don't want to think about… anything."

I see Marco's eyes glimmer again.

"But for tonight…" I look back to my wine glass that has one more sip left, slowly pick it up and look at each man. "I will go home to rest for tomorrow."

"You don't want us?" Mario says, sounding disappointed as he reaches over and rubs the softest part of my inner thigh.

I set my empty wine glass back down. Oh god, they are all waiting, studying my hesitation now. Do I want to go down this rabbit hole? I'm really not sure if I *do* want to go home, I just didn't think saying yes right away would have been a very good look.

I take a breath and make my decision. With Mario's hand still caressing my thigh and their collective faces waiting for my next few words…

"Is everyone finished?" I jump as the young waiter appears beside me. Holy…! He keeps sneaking up on me. Mario squeezes my leg before letting go and euros are dug out of wallets and thrown together in a colorful pile in the middle of the table. Mario collects it all and says something in Italian to the boy.

Damn. I felt like I had a handle on this conversation.

"Yes," I squeak out as soon as the sneaky waiter turns to leave.

"Yes?" Mario responds with his eyes wide and bright.

"Yes... okay... why not," I say with a little more confidence. I've always been a competitive person, although I think this is a bit extreme. But then again, I'm here. It is an experience I've wondered about in secret. Wondered how it would feel with three men, if I could do it, if I would like it and now... it's placed in front of me. All I have to do is... say yes.

I look towards the other men and can see Marco's mind already churning. I'm not quite sure if this is good or bad, but the way he looks at me now is making me *pleasantly* uncomfortable.

"Okay. Let's go," Mario says with a huge smile across his face.

I stop Mario and motion for him to come close as the other two are scooting from the table. "Did you call Angelo? Does he know about this?"

"Yes, I did just a few minutes ago." He looks deep into my eyes. "Here, I will tell him again now."

"Yes, thank you."

Mario messages Angelo of their plans with me, I gather my jacket and purse and look one last time at the Italian woman. She seems to be enjoying herself immensely. One more man has joined and she's now surrounded by four, younger, alluring men. Maybe this is how it's done here.

We walk past the other tables and no one pays us much mind as we leave the warm, cozy restaurant through the squeaky door and head back out into the brisk, dark air. I wrap my jacket around myself, Mario again opens the car door for me and I slide in. Marco gracefully enters from the other side. The sexual tension between us is evident and I can't help but watch him as he fits carefully into the seat.

His jeans; rolled at the ankles above white Converse. Long legs bent high to fit in the back seat of Mario's small car but he doesn't look uncomfortable. The crisp, white, button-down dress shirt shows his thin but muscular frame and I want to rip it off of him right... now.

Marco hasn't looked away from me since he opened the door to get in and I'm trying my best to hold his gaze.

"You said you follow, yes? You do what I say?" he says in a very low tone, loud enough for only me to hear.

"Yes," I say breathlessly.

The streetlight is shining into the car and again, I see the glimmer in his eyes. The thoughts he must be having behind those glasses.

I hear Mario say something in Italian and soon I'm scooting in the middle, close to Marco as Federico slides in the back with us.

"Federico will sit in back with you too," Mario calls through the door before closing us all in.

"Okay. Hi," I say awkwardly to Federico.

"Ciao." He reaches under my very short dress and caresses my thigh.

My body automatically tenses. Relax, Mila, relax. I'm trying to get into the *wing it* moment, but what will they all think of me after this night is over? What will I think of myself?

I shake the thoughts and questions out of my mind. This is something I can't overanalyze if I'm going to do it.

I feel Marco's body warmth and hear his breathing since I'm so close to him now. Sitting sideways in the middle of this small car, my left knee is over my right and both of my hands are on the seat to the right holding myself up. I look to Marco's face as I feel Federico's hand slide from my thigh to my bottom.

"You do as I say, yes?" Marco asks again.

I nod my head. "Yes." Comes out as a whisper.

"Good. Suck me."

Oh god.

Mario is driving the car just as crazy as before, weaving around scooters and barely slowing for corners. I'm having a difficult time not just face planting in Marco's lap as he undoes the button on his pants and pulls the zipper down.

The streetlights, intermittent and flashing a dim yellow glow into the car like an old-time movie. I can see my reflection for a millisecond, in Marco's glasses, each time I look up to his face.

His face. Attractive, mysterious, controlled. He's a Dom.

I can now feel the wet between my legs and my insides clench as Federico's fingertips lightly pass over my clit. His hands are roaming everywhere on the bottom half of my body as I look down and see Marco's nice sized cock spring free of his pants.

"Suck."

I obey. I turn my body more and pull my knees under me, wrap my hand around his warm throbbing shaft, steady myself with my left hand on the seat between his knees and slowly slide my mouth down. He fills my mouth and moans with pleasure as I take him deeper. It's satisfyingly naughty with Federico penetrating me with his fingers and making me gasp. Marco in my mouth and Federico in my...

A few more corners and the car slows to a stop. I continue to slide my mouth up and down on Marco and Federico has not stopped pleasuring me.

"You are bitch," I hear from the front seat.

I stop and look up to see Mario watching in the rearview mirror, smiling. He winks at me and steps out of the car. My panties and dress are put back into place by Federico as Marco fixes his pants and slides out of the car, his hand extended in for me. I reach out, my hand sliding into his and I notice his grip is tight and warm. He takes command; with his elbow bent, he keeps my hand in his and my arm between his side and his forearm... like a precious package he's carrying. Marco says nothing as he sets us off, across the barely lit street towards large, old cement stairs as we leave Mario and Federico behind.

With his long legs and longer strides, he's on a mission and I am walking so fast that every five steps, I have to do a quick little run for three paces just to keep up. Five quick steps... three little jogs.

Marco doesn't slow much as he takes me quickly up the very large and wide staircase built into the hill. Trees, bushes and out of control flowers infringe on the sides, with weeds trying to grow in between the cracks. I realize there's a church on the right, behind the tall iron fence that looms up the hill. It adds, I think, to the naughtiness of this adventure. The church, I can tell even in the moonlit night, is very old; but every building here is very old.

Hmm... a little more guilty doing what I'm about to do in front of a church that's been here for probably hundreds of years? I'm not sure if that's a turn on or kind of freaking me out. But being led with determination *is* turning me on. My hand is warm and held tight; but with care and want, so I make myself forget my guilt and go with the moment.

We make a left turn up the cracked, wide steps.

"Here."

Marco stops and quickly scans the area around us one more time. My eyes have adjusted to the night and the vague glow of street lights from down below. I turn toward the stairs we just climbed and see there's a large bush of vines on the right and behind us. It has small dark blue flowers and is perfect for hiding us from wandering eyes below. To the left, the stairs seem to go on indefinitely up the hill into an abyss.

Suddenly, Marco's hands are on my arms just below my shoulders. He turns my body around to face him, grasps my arms again and he kisses my lips.

I exhale and melt... finally, his touch.

His tongue slides soft and deep into my mouth, his hands tighten on my arms indenting my skin and he pulls me into him. With the cool air around us and his body warmth radiating against the front of mine, I'm instantly in the moment forgetting whatever worry I had.

The brush of his hand slides between our bodies and I hear his zipper pull down.

"Suck."

I obey, bend at the waist and take him into my mouth again. Tight yet soft, I slide my hand back and forth at the base with my mouth taking half of him. Slow, steady and meaningful.

I feel my long jacket slide up over my bottom and with it, my dress. Marco pulls my black lace thong panties to the side. I gasp as his fingers slide into me and can hear how wet I am. I take him deeper in my mouth.

"Yes. Like that," Marco growls.

Oh my god... I feel more hands pull down the top of my dress. And even more hands on my ass. I knew this was the perfect dress for tonight.

Marco's cock in my mouth, his fingers inside me with Mario and Federico's warm hands grabbing and caressing my bottom and breasts. My nipples are hard and my insides clench with the thought of how I must look right now. I can't believe how turned on I am. Three men with all of their attention on me and my body. I'm almost overwhelmed, my mind spinning with anticipation of what's next.

Marco pulls out of my mouth and with his hands holding on to either side of my face, directs me to Mario. Mario is out and ready for me. Opening my mouth, I take him, my right hand wrapping around his shaft. Marco behind me as his hands caress my ass; squeezing my cooled cheeks, spreading and tilting them upward, I feel him against my wet lips. Parting them with the tip of his cock and skillful as he slides deep into me... oh my god. Down my throat, I engulf Mario out of pure bliss.

My head is spinning again, my skin heightened with sensitivity, cooled from the air. My body yearning for their touch. It's amazing feeling their hands; so warm, they're almost hot. Two pairs of hands caressing my neck, down my shoulders and under, to my breasts; all while I feel Marco sliding in and out of me. Another extreme sensation for my mind to try to process and yet, another to enjoy. I'm still trying to grasp that I'm even here.

Mario slowly pulls out of my mouth, leads my face away from him and directs me to another. Federico; the other set of warm hands I feel. He is not as skilled as Mario and Marco but he is gorgeous. His black t-shirt is tucked under his chin and I can't help myself; I reach up and run my fingers over his chiseled chest and stomach. Mmmm... I lean in closer and take him deep, filling my mouth. Marco is now by my side as he caresses my breasts and Mario is behind me, rubbing and squeezing. Mario slides his hard cock up and down between my slightly swollen lips and slowly starts to push. My pussy stretches around him as he pushes inside of me. I quicken and begin to not care about anything at all. Not how badly society would think of me for taking three men, not that I'm a mother of two, not that I'm a clichéd foreigner; and right at this moment I definitely don't feel bad for liking how amazing they are making my body feel.

"Oh, my... Go...d." The building inside of me; my legs quiver and my nipples harden to stones. My breathing is short and deep... my body finally releases. Marco muffles my moans as he and Federico exchange positions and Mario buries himself deep inside of me.

"Mila, you are so sensual," Mario whispers in my ear as he slowly slides out.

Both Marco and Federico have already adjusted their clothing back into place and are now helping put my clothes back to where they belong. Mario smooths out his shirt after the last button is in place and picks up the condom wrappers.

I look up at all three men as I adjust my dress over my breasts and tug my jacket back over my shoulder; I smile a shy smile. There is an air of knowing, of mutual understanding and it comes through, as each one smiles back at me.

Marco takes my hand and leads the way as we all walk down the now too familiar large steps back to the car. Random people are meandering below, but no one seems privy to what just transpired halfway up the staircase. I giggle, and Marco squeezes my hand one quick time to let me know he gets it.

"So." Mario starts the car looking in the rear-view mirror. "Back to your place?"

I smile. "Yes, sure."

I should probably ask more questions. Like: *Back to my place to drop me off?* Or: *Back to my place to keep fucking?* But I can't. I can't make my thoughts vocal and if I'm not playing naïve, I know it's the latter of the two. Good. I want to do it all again.

7

Chapter 7

The sound of my phone, again is what wakes me. I feel around by my head and the other pillow, then open my eyes. I know it's seven in the morning. It's bright in the apartment and my body is still on Hawai'i time. Plus, I've learned to appreciate the sun even more since it makes me get up early to enjoy Italy.

"There you are," I say as I see my phone on the nightstand. I open the app and see the message that woke me is from Angelo.

Angelo: Good morning. How was your night?

It was good, thank you. Your friends were very nice.

Angelo: Yes, I heard. Why didn't you wait for me?

What do you mean? Mario said he told you but you couldn't come.

Angelo: You played with three of my friends. Why do you think I would not want to be there?

Holy shit. I drop my phone on the bed and rub my face hard with both of my hands. I need to understand just what the hell is going on with this guy. One minute he's telling me to go and have fun, then the next he's asking why I did.

I pick up my phone and text back.

You told me to go with your friends. You know how they are, so I assumed you knew what they had in mind. I even asked Mario to message you. To see if you could come. Please don't do this.

Angelo: Yes, he did tell me, but not that you were all going back to your place. You didn't have to fuck them. You could have just had dinner.

I read the last part over, then over again. And here I thought I was feeling empowered over my own body, my own choices. Nothing like being condemned early in the morning for decisions I made as a consenting adult.

I have to go.

I exit out of the app, turn on "Hymn for the Weekend," plug my phone into my portable speaker and turn it up. Yes, much better.

A light sundress, sandals and a bigger purse that I can carry across my body, are all spread out on the bed and I'm almost set to go on an Italian adventure. In the bathroom, I put on makeup and fix my hair.

Who does he think he is?! Angelo has some nerve.

I pull out the mascara and tug my eyelashes upwards.

I need to just forget him. What the hell is his issue?

His sister passed away, I scold myself.

But can I continue to ride his rollercoaster of emotions?

He's my friend.

Yeah, for the last five months. But is that enough to take this type of abuse for the next seven days? This is my vacation, my holiday I spent over four thousand dollars to be on.

Does money override a friendship?

Wait... am I the only one that believes this is a friendship?

My hair is done and my makeup flawless. I dress and throw everything I need into the bigger purse. I also throw out all thoughts of Angelo. Now I'm ready for Italy.

I lean against a skinny tree surrounded by the sidewalk as I wait for the next bus. More and more young people gather around to wait as well.

"Excuse. Is this the bus to Positano?" I ask as a small bus slows and stops in front of us.

A tall thin man in his thirties looks at me in what could be taken as irritation. "No."

The doors close and the bus pulls out into the street.

Another bus arrives in roughly ten minutes.

"Excuse, does this bus go to Positano?" I ask the older bus driver.

"No," he says and closes the door behind the last people obviously knowing where they're going.

I'm loving the tree right about now; lean back against it, take a look at my surroundings and wait for the next bus.

Across the little street, I'm pleasantly surprised. Wow, I didn't notice the beautiful church sitting in the middle of town. A maize yellow with white trimming. It stands out and blends in at the same time and I have to take a picture. I take several pictures. One of the beautiful church and one of the gated restaurant directly across the street from me. It has dark green vines with purple flowers growing up and around the entrance. I also have to take one more picture of all the traffic filing through the roundabout. Little cars, small tour buses, children on the back of their moms' scooters, people on bikes and the bus I hope I've been waiting for, are all carefully dancing around the tall statue in the middle of the square.

A considerable number of Italian teenagers have gathered around me again and are filling the new bus.

"Excuse, is this the bus to Positano?" I ask a rather cute man watching the door from the inside.

"No," is all he answers. Just like the others.

And again, I am the only one left on the sidewalk by the little tree. I take out my phone and video the vehicles around the turnabout, follow them in front of me and past, on the road out of town. A man that looks like he's in his mid-thirties with a perfectly shaved head, waves at me as I video down the road and sidewalk. Oh shit... here he comes. I quickly smile, put my phone away and sort of try to hide behind the little tree with my shy self, but I'm not *that* tiny.

"Ciao! Come stai?" he says with a huge smile, stopping in front of me.

"Ciao. I'm sorry, I don't speak Italian," I say sheepishly. I feel really bad not knowing the language of the country I'm visiting.

"Oh. I thought you are Italian. How are you? Where are you from?"

"That's nice." I smile and enjoy the compliment. "I'm very good thank you and I'm from Hawai'i, here on holiday."

"Oh Hawai'i! That's very nice. I dream of going to Hawai'i," he says with an even bigger grin.

"Yes, it's very nice, just like here is beautiful. You should visit, but it's a very long trip."

"I saw you with your phone doing video. I thought you wanted a picture of me." He smiles wickedly.

"Ahaha! I was taking video of the traffic. Everything here is different and amazing to me."

"Hahah! Yes, I suppose it is. So, what are you doing waiting here?"

"I'm trying to get to Positano. Do you know when the bus will be here?"

"Oh." His face drops to almost dread. "The bus to Positano is not here at this place. It's..." He looks down the street from the direction he walked. "It's down this way."

"Oh no! I'm not even at the right bus stop?"

"No. No this is not the right one. But... come. Don't worry, I will

71

show you the place." Smiling, he stretches his hand out for me to walk with him.

We maneuver around all of the people on their own journeys and try to stay close so we can talk as we walk together up the road. He is very polite, always having me pass in front when there's only room enough for one.

"How old are you?" he asks with an inquisitive look.

Here's my favorite question again, but with this man I'm fine. I'm getting used to it, I think.

"I'm 42," I say nonchalantly and walk around a bicycle.

"No."

I walk a few more steps and turn to smile. He's stopped right in his tracks in the middle of the sidewalk behind me.

"Ahaha! What are you doing?"

"You cannot be 42. It is impossible." He walks again and is soon right in front of me. "I wasn't sure if I should come to talk to you. I saw you and you are very pretty. But I thought you were a teenager, like 18. There were all of the teenagers around you. I thought, I cannot talk to someone so young, but I decided to find out for sure. You are really 42?"

I feel my cheeks warm. One of the many good things about having tanned skin; no one can really tell when I'm blushing.

"Yes." I smile big. "I really am 42. And thank you, that's very nice of you to so ferociously say I'm not."

His eyes, still in disbelief, are making me feel great.

We continue our fast-paced walk. The sun is climbing higher in the sky and the weather is perfect. A small warm breeze and no clouds. I can't wait to get to Positano and sit on an Italian beach.

"And what's your name?" I ask and turn to look as he steps to the side for an older woman carrying more bags than she probably should.

"My name is Pietro." He bends a little at the waist with his left hand to his chest then looks up. "And may I have the pleasure of your name?"

"Ah… Buongiorno Pietro! It's very nice to meet you. And yes, I'm Mila."

"Oh, you *do* speak Italian! Buongiorno, Mila from Hawai'i."

"No, no," I giggle. "Only *hello* and *good morning*. And two of those can use the same word."

"Okay, that's okay. You should learn. I can teach if you want."

"Thank you, that's very sweet," I answer, still smiling, and at the last second, missing a business man in a suit walking fast, paying too much attention to his phone.

I am pretty much under the impression that no man does anything for a woman unless there's an ulterior motive. Now I should ask the important questions.

There is a break in the traffic of bodies on the sidewalk and we've come back together side by side.

"So, Pietro, how old are you?"

He looks at me with hazel eyes through thin glasses. "I am 39."

"Oh, not too far from me." I'm happy I'm not the only one.

"No, not far at all." He smiles in my eyes.

"And are you married? Have a girlfriend?" I jump over a hole in the side road as we cross it.

Pietro looks up the street. "I am married."

I'm a little shocked. "Do you normally help lost women on the side of the road?"

"No! You are the first woman. You were so beautiful standing there; I couldn't help myself. I had to come say hello."

I have a hard time believing that, but smile and thank him anyways.

"How long have you been married?"

"For twelve years now, but my marriage has not been going so well lately. We are thinking of having another baby… so maybe it will bring us closer again."

He moves around a mother holding her small son's hand.

"You have other children?"

"Yes." His smile stretches across his face. "We have a daughter. She's 10."

"Cute. Yes, a new baby always seems to bring everyone closer. I wish you luck." I smile and nudge his shoulder a little with mine.

He relaxes and smiles bigger. "And you? Are you married? Do you have children?"

"I was and I do." I turn, curious to see his reaction. It's such a relief to say I *was* married. Such liberating little words. I never would have guessed they would bring me so much joy.

I see the question on his face.

"I was married for fifteen years. This… here, now in Italy, is my celebratory divorce trip," I boast, really quite proud of myself.

"Wow, that's a long time you were married. Good for you! And you are traveling alone?"

"I am."

"You are an amazing woman."

"Well I don't know about that, but I do feel in control of my life now." I blush once again at the generous compliment.

"And you have children?"

"Yes. A girl and a boy. My girl is 14 and my boy is 11. They are with my mom right now."

"This way." Pietro ushers me to the right and up another small road, past a little corner café. "We're almost to our destination."

Single file now, as there are more cars driving down this road and the pedestrians are crowding the small sidewalk. We reach the end.

"Ohhh. Now I see, I was definitely at the wrong bus stop!" My eyes are wide, taking in the obvious differences.

At the very top, is the end of the road where a long building sits. Many doors line the front with people filing in and out. Its distressed wood was painted dark green at one point and the patrons, walking away from the building, are all trying to find their way down the two staircases built into the small grassy hill that sits across the road and parallel to the building.

"A train station," I murmur.

"Wait one moment." Pietro touches my arm and walks to a man sitting to the left of us, under a red umbrella anchored by a red podium.

They speak in Italian and Pietro walks back.

"This is the line for the bus to Positano," he says and points with an outstretched arm to a long line of people waiting against the side of another hill by the umbrella man. "It is very long I think."

"It's okay. Do you know if the bus is coming soon? I can wait, it's fine."

"I'm unsure. He said the bus will be here in the next fifteen minutes but there are so many people already waiting. You may not get on this one."

"It's okay, Pietro." I smile at his concerned face. "It was my fault for not being at the right bus stop. I can always catch the next one or even come back tomorrow instead."

"Are you sure you will be okay?"

"Yes, I'm positive. Thank you so much for helping me and I'm sure you had other things to do." Smiling, I lean into him and air kiss both sides of his face.

He hesitates. "I can drive you," he suddenly blurts out.

"What?"

"Yes. I can get my car and drive you to Positano," he says with more determination.

"No Pietro, you don't have to do that."

"It's no problem, but can you wait here for me? I have to get my car from Piano di Sorrento. About thirty minutes."

"Is your wife at home? Would she be mad if she knew you did this?"

75

I know, of course she'd be pissed. And here... is the ulterior motive.

"Yes. But I have never done this before and you are very nice."

I would love to have a private car and someone to show me the real Positano. I'm dying to have some company. But... I can't do that to his unknowing wife. I also can't put myself in the situation to have to fend off unwanted advances. Usually, I make the bad choices. But not today.

I reach out and hold gently onto his left arm. "Pietro, I'm sorry, but in good conscience I cannot take you up on your generous offer. It just wouldn't feel right. You are an amazing person helping me as much as you already have."

"Okay yes, I understand. Well then, take care, Mila and know you are a stunning woman. I hope you have a wonderful time here on your holiday."

"Thank you, Pietro." I pause and think. "Grazie!" I give him my biggest grin.

"Yes! Prego Mila, wonderful! You are learning." He smiles and begins to walk away. He turns back again. "You are sure?"

I smile back. "I am. Thank you so much."

With a wave and bit of a disappointed smile, he turns, walks around the corner and out of sight. I spin to face the ever-growing line behind me and take my place with the rest of the people waiting for the bus to Positano.

The sun is at its highest in the cloudless blue sky. This is a burning situation, waiting here, and I'm starting to question my morals. Like: *Why do I have them?* Ugh, I could have had a private and free chauffeur to Positano and not be dying in this unforgiving sun right now.

No, Mila. I scold the wanting selfish part of me. This is the right thing.

The huge bus arrives and the line moves fast but I expect the doors to close at any moment. I reach the front and they're still open with the driver waving me to step up; I do and hand him my ticket. Every seat is taken and from the back of the bus to the front, the aisle is filled, with standing room left for only two more... myself and the lucky woman that was standing in line behind me. The doors close, the bus lurches forward and we're off. The woman and I both grab onto the metal bars attached to the seats beside us as the bus turns the sharp corner and out into traffic.

Traffic. Is a bitch. Now I understand why it takes Angelo so long to reach the middle of Sorrento town from his home. We are moving an inch a minute and I wonder if I will even get to Positano today. An adventure, I'm on an adventure. And with that thought and reminder, I relax and start enjoying watching the Italian life surrounding me.

On the bus is an equal mix of teenagers and adults of varying ages. In the seat to my right is an older woman holding her oversized purse on her lap with a teenage boy sitting next to the window beside her. Turning to my left, I notice right next to me is a nun. She's wearing her black robe with the head piece. I wonder what that's called and I wonder if she's going to a church in Positano. I look out of the huge windows past the woman in front of me and see we've stopped for a pedestrian.

Finally, we are out of town traffic and the line of cars turn off to their own destinations in other directions. The bus down shifts and picks up speed. I can see a town in a valley and the mountains are fantastic. The blazing sun makes every color vivid and brilliant. Italy is... amazing.

Not much longer and we reach the top of the road to Positano. I had no idea just driving down to the bottom is an adventure in itself. Out of the windows to my right, I see we're hundreds of feet above the sea on a very sharp and unforgiving cliff. I suppose this is my chance to overcome my fear of heights and try not to gasp too loud. My grip tightens on the metal bar. I can do this. I'm fine. I'm sure no one would be on this bus if they drove off of the cliff very often... Right?

The front of the bus has a massive window I'm lucky enough to look out of as we head straight for the tiny guardrail on the first scary corner of the road. The guardrail; it disappears from sight under the front of the bus as we make the turn.

Holy shit.

I look around and no one seems to be fazed. My hand fumbles around, inside of my purse, until I pull out my phone and switch to video. This will give me something to do and also posterity for if I survive this trip. Or, like the little black box in an airplane, it will explain what happed in my demise.

It really is an unbelievable view. The azure sea with its white foam as the small waves crash against the bottom of the cliff. The glimpses of Positano town far in the distance, only visible around each terrifying corner. I am scared out of my mind but at the same time, in awe of this crazy gorgeous country.

My attention drifts to the man I'm entrusting my life to today. He's middle aged, with a bit of a pot belly and what's left of his hair is very short. I realize now he's been chain smoking the whole time. I'm divided in my feelings; either very safe because I'm sure he's been doing this forever and can probably drive this road blindfolded, or still scared out of my mind because he could have a heart attack any moment now.

I shake my head to get the last thought out of my mind. Focus, Mila. There's no getting off of the bus now. I look to my left; there's the nun. This has to be a good sign.

8

Chapter 8

F inally, the bus nears the bottom of Positano; I made it, but not without a few more mini heart attacks of my own. The doors open and I step out onto the road; never thought I'd be this happy to see cobblestone.

I walk past four women taking pictures for each other with a stunning view of the sea down below, behind them. I want to ask if they'll take my picture too, but I just smile and walk past. I guess it's easier for me to talk to men than to women. This is the first time I wish I had a girlfriend with me on this self-changing adventure and I definitely need to work more on my communication skills.

I have no idea where I'm going, so I just follow the small crowd of tourists up the tiny road and take pictures of buildings and houses with vines climbing up the outside walls. Crossing the street, I look over the rail. Oh my... magnificent.

The sea, now not too far below, is alive and sparkling in the bright sunlight. I look out and to the right. There are the iconic pastel squares and rectangles of houses big and small covering the side of the mountain. It looks as if someone took their liberties with a palette of watercolors. Underneath the dancing colors of the mountainside is a beach, which I believe is Spiaggia Grande. I'm super excited now and take a quick selfie with the sea, the beach and the chromatic mountain as my background. Perfect, that's where I want to be.

Picking up the pace, I make my way to a very wide and long stone staircase I assume is the way to the beach. The stairs are cluttered with people; tourists with and without children, elderly couples, best girlfriends on holiday together and the occasional Italian lovers, never without a part of their bodies touching. Both sides of the staircase are lined with little shops, and if there is a break in the shops, there are artisans selling their wares. From marvelous hand painted sceneries of Positano to hand sewn wallets and handmade jewelry. I'll have to stop and buy a souvenir on my way back, but now, I visit the next shop on my left and purchase a beach towel.

Finally, I reach the mouth at the bottom of the staircase. Positano beach. I smell and hear the salty sea and watch people gather in the scattered restaurants to the right of me as I walk parallel to the water, looking for a bathroom. I found out earlier today in Sorrento while waiting for the wrong bus, the public bathrooms charge to use them. I figured I can just pay the 50 euro cents here and change into my swimsuit.

My body is tingling from the sunbeams warming my exposed skin. I have found a small patch of beach, light brown sand mixed with little pebbles, to call my own. I exhale until all of the air is out of my lungs. With a long breath in, I close my eyes, relax and stay half in and half out of reality.

Not sure how long I've been out, I wake from the sun not shining as strong as it was. Some clouds must have formed. I slowly open one eye and see a figure standing over me. Both of my eyes pop open.

"Ciao. Scusami, ti dispiace se metto il mio asciugamano qui?" I hear a man's voice say.

Elevating the top half of my body onto my elbows, I squint at the open piece of beach he's pointing to near me. He's still a silhouette and I think, asking if he can sit there... but I'm not quite sure.

"Ciao," I say, half smiling, and shade my eyes with my left hand. "I'm sorry, I don't speak Italian."

"Oh, no problem. Do you mind if I lay my towel here?"

Honestly, I was so relaxed, I wish he hadn't woken me up just to ask this.

"Sure, of course," I say and lie back down.

Five minutes later and I just can't get comfortable again. Not like I was. I turn my head to the right and notice the man facing me, lying on his side.

"Ciao!" he says in a cheery tone. "You are awake. I hope I didn't disturb you very much."

I lean back up on my elbows, reach over my body with my right hand and find my sunglasses. Ah, now I can see. I turn back to the slight intruder and... holy shit. My mouth wants to drop open, but I fight the urge... hard.

A golden tan from head to toe and shiny dark black hair cut into a definite European style. He has straight, blindingly white teeth behind sexy pillow lips turned up into a seductive smile. His biceps, chest, abs, legs... all cut and built to make any woman, or man, want to just reach out and touch. Tattoos decorate his chiseled body in an array of colors.

Hmm, I wonder if there are any hiding under that very small speedo he's wearing. Oh god, how long have I been staring at him?

I smile nervously. "Oh, umm no... I didn't mean to pass out the first time."

"You are here alone?"

I think I don't like that question. I'm beginning to hear it as a *poor thing* statement rather than just normal small talk.

"Yes I am." I manage to keep smiling. "It's my celebratory divorce trip."

I might as well just get this information out there. Also, I have an uncanny knack for sabotaging possible connections when I feel someone might be out of my league.

"Oh, that's very good," he says showing his pearly whites. "And you are staying here in Positano?"

"No, I'm staying in Sorrento. I have seven days left after today. This is my third day in Italy and I was given free bus tickets here... to Positano."

"I'm on holiday as well. I have been working for three months straight with no time off. I needed to sit in the sun." He leans his head back so his face gets the full effect of the sunrays.

"Yes, the sun is perfect today. So, what do you do for work?" I ask, trying to refrain from taking this opportunity to get the full effect of his perfect body.

He whips back around to look at me. "I'm a physical therapist and part-time personal trainer."

I suppose I could have guessed that. Makes perfect sense and it's a good thing I wasn't staring.

"Everyone wants to have their beach body back after the winter, so I am always busy until around this time."

"Well I'm very happy to meet you. My name is Mila by the way," I say, smiling, and extend my hand.

"Sebastiano. The pleasure is all mine, bella Mila." He reaches over his glistening body, takes my hand, brings it to his lips and kisses the top.

So damn nervous, I don't know what to do with this. I want to pull my hand away and I want his eyes to get out of mine.

"Um... thank you," I try not to stammer and slowly, he gives me my hand back.

We sit and talk about his life and mine, where I'm staying in Sorrento and his upcoming travel to northern Italy. Soon, all of my nervousness is gone and I tell him about my children, my divorce and my dreams. He shares how he learned English so well; which was through an ex American girlfriend, tells me about some of his clients at work and that he lives close enough to Sorrento in another town. Sebastiano has his own opinions on marriage and asks more about my children.

"Why are you here and your children are at home?"

Why are you sounding so judgy?, I think almost too loud. "Because. I have been a good mother and wife for a very long time. I have never left my children even for one day in 14 years. Finally, I decided just because I'm a mom, it doesn't mean I should stop being myself or stop being a woman."

"Okay, yes. I understand... you are right," he says with an almost apologetic look and slowly stands.

I shade my eyes from the sun and he becomes a silhouette again.

"Come. Let's go to the sea."

His hand is outstretched and I want to touch him. I've been wanting to touch him this entire time. He's gorgeous... and I'm still wondering, *why is he here with me?* My self-consciousness rears its ugly head. Oh hell, I don't look nearly as good as I should, to be next to this Adonis. My stomach... the things a C-section can do to the human body is not nice. I suppose I could have bought a tummy tuck instead of an Italian holiday and a sexy one-piece swimsuit to hide it.

I reach up and take his hand.

"Good," he says and doesn't let go until we reach the water.

Cool and crisp is the sea. It thrills every inch of my skin and makes goosebumps until I dive under. I come up and feel amazing! Refreshed and energized, I open my eyes and see Sebastiano watching me; a smile instantly pops onto my face.

"You have an amazing smile, bella Mila," he says walking slowly towards me.

Is this really happening? He's so sexy and it's making me nervous as hell.

Sebastiano presses his tight body slowly against the front of mine. My breasts push into his muscular pecs and my nipples harden. His hands gently run up my arms; from my wrists, to my shoulders, to my back as he leans into me. His tongue is soft and warm, salty and sweet. My skin is cold from the water and slight breeze but my insides are melting. I forget about the rest of the world around us and easily forget all about time. We kiss for what seems like an eternity, neither one of us wanting to stop.

Coming back to the reality of just meeting this random man, I giggle. I think Sebastiano knows why I'm laughing and starts laughing too. I love times in life where nothing is said but the mutual understanding is loud and clear.

He kisses my lips with a quick peck, backs up and splashes me.

Oh, it's on!

We spend a long time splashing and playing in the blue sea. He dives under and pulls me down with him, I grab onto his back as he swims. He lifts me out of the water on his shoulders then throws me off, I swim under and try to pull him in… it never works. I do enjoy a strong man.

Some time has passed and now I hang onto his back while he floats us around. He slips me around to hold me in front of him; we kiss again for another eternity.

The sun has started its decline. We walk together out of the sea and back to our towels, but we can't stop smiling at each other. He reaches across and pats my face dry with his extra towel since I only have the one I'm sitting on. I get lost in his intense hazel eyes as he moves a strand of hair that has fallen in front of my face. How is this man really here with me? He must have a girlfriend... or wife. I won't ask. I don't want to know anymore today; everything is too perfect.

"I have to go now, Mila," he says as I watch him drag the towel over his biceps and those perfect pecs.

"Okay, I should go too. The last bus shouldn't be long after I make it back up that way." I check the time on my phone.

"Would you like a ride back to Sorrento? I have my car just up the hill."

"Really? That would be very nice." I'm shocked at the offer.

"Yes of course. We are going in the same direction," he says gathering his shirt and sunglasses, then looks up into my eyes. "And I would not be unhappy to spend a little more time with you."

Oh my. I feel the same way and my cheeks blush. I quickly look down into my bag and fish out a skirt to wear over my swimsuit. "This was a very nice meeting," I say softly. "I would not be unhappy to spend more time with you too." I cut my eyes up while I slip on the little skirt.

Sebastiano's look is intense and erotic. "Good. Then let's go."

He stands up and... god, he has such a nice butt. I avert my eyes before he catches me admiring him again and I take his outstretched hand. He pulls me up and keeps his hand around my waist, gently resting it on my right hip as we make our way to the long stairs.

"Oh! I need to stop here."

I pull him gently to one side of the large stairs and pause at a table with long paintings of Positano. We look at the various scenes on thick white strips of paper.

"These are very nice," he says standing in front of more paintings on the tall wall behind.

I join him and see exactly what I want. "This one," I whisper to myself. "Scusi," I say to the woman selling them. "May I have this painting please?"

"Si. This?" the woman, about my age, asks and touches the corner of the painting.

"Yes, thank you."

She takes it down and rolls it into a scroll. "Twenty-five euro."

We exchange money for the painting, say grazie and Sebastiano wraps his arm back around me as we continue up the stairs and then up a small hill.

"Here we are."

A cute little car beeps, headlights blink and he opens the passenger door for me. We smile at each other as I pass very close to his body and slide into the seat. He leans in and kisses my lips once more before closing the door. Holy shit, holy shit. I can't believe I'm here, still with him, in his car. I straighten my flowy skirt out of nervousness. Keep it together, Mila. I watch his sexy body walk around the front and open the driver's side door, effortlessly ease into the seat and smile at me again. "Ready?"

The drive back up the Positano road is much better than the trip down. By a landslide. Maybe *landslide* is a bad metaphor. As I think of a new word to use, since I will be telling my best friend in the world all about this sexy adventure, I see Sebastiano look at me with a small smile.

"Do you live close to Sorrento?" I ask, turning towards him.

"Kind of. I live in Salerno but I have some business in Pompeii, which is pretty close."

We come to a complete stop on this very busy road with a lot of buses; both city and tourist. There are cars of all shapes and sizes with scooters and motorbikes filling in any possible open spaces. I like to look at the people and wonder how their lives must be. At least on this day. What brought them here at this time? Is that their wife or their lover on the back of the scooter? Hmm, maybe the man and woman in the back of that expensive looking car are married... or maybe he bought her and the driver. I giggle at my wayward thoughts.

"What is funny?" Sebastiano looks in the direction of my gaze.

"Oh, not much. I was just watching the people and wondering how their lives must be."

"Like who? Which ones were you laughing about?"

I get a little shy but decide to tell him. "The man and woman there." I point low, past his chest. Mmmm his chest. Ugh! Such a distraction.

"In the expensive car? With the driver?" He nods towards the correct car, then turns back to me. "What about them?"

I bite my bottom lip. "I started out thinking she must be his wife, but then thought... what if she is his affair or even a paid-for woman, along with him paying for the driver?"

"Ha! I wouldn't doubt it. I have several friends that do this. They don't have time for a relationship but they do have money for company."

The traffic starts moving and we pass the car in question. We see the man run his hand up the inside of the woman's leg; she leans over and they kiss passionately.

"Paid-for woman!" we both exclaim in unison and laugh.

The rest of the ride up the hill is slow but steady. Just right for me to take a few pictures and enjoy the view outside. The clash of light blue sky with dark green mountains, the curves of the asphalt road as it swerves around each one. The sun is starting to set, creating a brilliant, pinkish-orange glow on everything it can reach.

"So beautiful," I whisper in awe.

"Yes... you are," Sebastiano says, turns to look at me then back at the road; but not before he finally sees my face flush.

We reach the top of the road and pass through Piano di Sorrento.

I recognize where we are and enjoy that I'm getting used to Italy. Sebastiano hits the brakes as the bus in front of us slams on theirs. A little old lady gives the bus driver her index finger; backwards and straight up... aggressively, before she crosses in front. Oh my. It's a different finger than I'm used to seeing, but the message is definitely the same.

We both laugh, Sebastiano reaches over and rubs my bare leg. The mood instantly changes. My insides clench with want as he slowly runs his hand further up my leg and under the little skirt I'm wearing. His fingertips brush lightly over my clit; back and forth, but never harder. A perfect tease, it makes me want more.

I gaze at the side of his handsome face as he watches the road. All the while, his fingers are dancing between my legs, over my swimsuit and making my body want to go crazy. I have to feel him. I reach over and rub the palm of my hand over the top of his lap. Underneath, he twitches and grows.

We make it through Piano di Sorrento and follow the traffic to the right as the cars split, branching off again towards separate destinations. I slide my hand down the front of his shorts. He's warm, smooth and hard; getting harder.

Sebastiano turns to me, a devilish smile on his face. "Mila, you're a very sensual woman. I like your hand there."

The corners of my mouth turn up and I can feel my eyes grow with intensity at his words. "I like my hand there too... as much as I like what you're doing between my legs."

With my words as a catalyst, his hand twists slightly and two fingers slide under my swimsuit. "Oh my god," I quietly gasp.

"Do you like that, baby?" he asks as his fingers find their way inside of me.

"Oh... yes... I do," I breathe softly, slightly tightening my grip around his now very hard cock.

"Good. I like you touching me. You are making me so hard I only want to pull over and do more."

For a few quiet minutes we pleasure each other as much as we can in this restricted situation. His fingers gently and slowly sliding deep in and out of me, as I stroke him back and forth underneath his shorts. I feel a few drops of pre-cum from the tip and run the pad of my thumb across it. He twitches in my hand and becomes even harder. I am so very wet, as we look at each other with want and need.

We drive into Sorrento and both of us finally pull our hands back. Short car, small roads and lots of people on the sidewalks. We smile at each other. Me, a little bashful and Sebastiano with a naughty look as he shocks me; raising his hand to his mouth, he licks and sucks each finger that was inside of me.

A sharp inhale and I giggle. "You are a very naughty man."

"Yes I am." His smile wraps around the finger still in his mouth.

Holy hell. I haven't been licked in 15 years, that so wasn't fair; watching him tease me. I want him to do that between my legs, to feel his breath there. His tongue. But I can't bring myself to tell him this.

"We're here," he says, abruptly bringing my wanting thoughts back to reality. "You said you live near Saint Antonino square, yes?"

Sebastiano has pulled up behind the cars parked in the square close to my apartment. I only need to walk down a small alleyway and past a few shops to be standing in front of the distressed wooden doors.

"Yes. I didn't know the name, but you remembered from our Positano talk. Very impressive."

"I remember everything you told me." He winks. "Will I see you again soon?"

"I would like that very much."

"Okay good. Me too. I will contact you and we can organize another meeting. Maybe go out for dinner." He smiles.

My phone vibrates and I have a feeling I know who it is. I gather my bag and check that I'm not leaving anything behind. I look back up into his gorgeous face. "Yes, please do. I would love to go to dinner with you."

"Good."

And with that, I lean over; he kisses me deep and slow, our lips lingering at the end.

9

Chapter 9

The sound of my purse is loud as it lands on the dining table. I plop my body on the couch and with my phone in hand, I open the message app and yep, the messages are from who I thought.

Angelo: Hi. How is your day? Did you use the tickets to Positano?

Hello. Yes, I did. Thank you, I had a wonderful time. It's nothing I've ever seen.

Angelo: Yes, it's too bad we didn't go to the club there. It is where I was going to take you on your first night.

I'm still sad about that.

Angelo: Don't worry, we have another weekend you're here. I will be done with my training on Friday. We will organize something good.

That would be perfect. Are you free tonight? I'd love to have dinner with you.

Angelo: Today I can't. On Sundays they are big days for family. It is always emotional on Sunday.

Ok I understand. I'm sorry you are going through this.

Angelo: Yes. Thank you. I will talk to you tomorrow. Maybe I can stop by after training.

That would be nice. I would really like to see you.
Angelo: Okay I will tell you more tomorrow.
Okay. Have a good night.

Well, I was hoping to go to dinner with Angelo, but this has to be very difficult for him. Should I just leave him alone? Maybe we would both be better off if I did.

With no good answer for myself, I shrug and plug in my phone to charge, turn on "Hymn for the Weekend" and think what my next step is.

I guess I should have told Sebastiano I was available for dinner tonight. I wonder if he is available? I pick up my phone again to message him, then I remember our day together: we never exchanged phone numbers or social media accounts. Ugh. I can't believe I did that. I remember now, I thought I would be seeing Angelo. Coming here to Sorrento, I was expecting to do most things with Angelo, otherwise I would have gone to Naples... like I was supposed to. I almost feel bad for meeting Sebastiano, but I shouldn't and really, I don't. Just wish I had gotten his number and now I'm sad I will probably never see him again.

I shake my head and the doubts of my choices fall away. I am here now. So... where will I go for dinner?

I find myself standing in front of Centauro Restaurant and Bar waiting to be seated. It's in the middle of the main square where the restaurants border the turnabout I had taken videos of earlier. Even on a Sunday evening, there's an abundance of people and an electrifying energy. I like it. It would be better perhaps, if I wasn't all dressed up to eat by myself, but then again, I need to get used to doing everything alone. I am of course, single now with very few friends. And that's what I get for allowing myself to be put under a rock for so long.

"Buonasera. For dinner or drinks?" the waiter, about my age, asks very politely. He is wearing an all-black, button-up long sleeve dress shirt with black slacks, a black apron around his waist and black dress shoes. Distinguished, but not exactly what I'm into right now.

"Yes, thank you... for dinner please."

"Sure. How many?"

"Just myself."

"Only you?"

"Yes." I smile. "Only me."

"Oh no. That's no good. No good to eat alone," he says and looks me up and down. "And you are very beautiful, why will you eat alone?"

Oh hell. I see the table nearest to us look up and give me the once over, and the couple that just walked up do the same. Oh, for the love of god and my own fading confidence, please just walk me to a table. I gather my scattered thoughts and square my shoulders that are threatening to give away my lack of confidence.

"Well, with someone or alone, I still need to eat," I say with a sweet smile.

"Yes, yes, of course. Follow me."

With a controlled sigh of relief, I follow the concerned waiter to a table. He asks if it matters for smoking section or not and I don't care, I just want to sit down.

"Okay good. A table in the non-smoking section would have been another fifteen minutes wait," he states as he takes off the top table cloth from the last patrons.

I'm surprised to see there's another identical table cloth underneath, ready and clean. I can't help but wonder how many are under there as I sit... finally.

I relax in the chair and decompress mentally from the short but bright spotlight that was just on me. Ugh. Coming out to dinner alone was worse than I thought.

A new and younger waiter brings a basket of three different types of bread, olive oil, butter, a small bowl of peanuts and asks what I would like to drink. I order bottled water and rosé wine. I have to drink wine with every meal here... because I can. I smile and thank him as he promptly brings the drinks and leaves me to decide on a meal.

The service is impeccable and I can't help but smile bigger when I see my order of flat pasta with a very red, spiky lobster placed in front of me.

"Is this fine?" the younger waiter asks. "Is there anything else you will need?"

I smile up at him and then back to my plate. "Oh no, thank you! This is perfect."

"Okay, enjoy."

And I do. My stomach is heavy and satisfied as I place my fork and knife into the empty plate. It was so delicious; it didn't take long for me to inhale my dinner. Okay, I guess this wasn't so bad. I settle back into my chair with my glass of rosé in hand.

"Scusami."

I turn and look behind my left shoulder and see a man in his early thirties. Ruggedly handsome, just the right amount of beard stubble and blue eyes that sparkle in contrast to his black hair and tanned skin. Oh. Maybe I won't be sitting by myself after all.

"Oh... yes?" I stammer a bit.

"May I use this chair?" he asks, steps around and pulls the other chair slightly from under my table.

"Umm, yes of course, please do."

"Grazie," he says with his smile sparkling too.

I hesitate; I don't know what *you're welcome* is in Italian. I need to learn so much... and fast.

"Oh, yes you're welcome," I say as invitingly as possible. I sit up straight in my chair and lean into the table; to hell with it, I'll try to be like the bold women.

"You are more than welcome to sit here," I say and smile up at him.

The handsome man smiles back and pulls the chair all of the way out. I watch as he takes it behind me, two tables away to where a very beautiful Italian woman sits down on it as he assists.

Ugh, I know my face is the color of my wine. No... darker, I'm sure. I turn back to looking out towards the busy street; I could die right now.

My small bottle of wine is empty and I'm pretty much over sitting here, still trying to not feel embarrassed. It's been half an hour, but for me, it's almost crippling; I need to get over this embarrassment thing. I know it's why I chose poorly when I met my ex. Never talking to people growing up and always feeling overly self-conscience is a recipe for disaster in life. To jump at the first person that gives you any kind of attention is not the right way, and now I need to reprogram myself.

The waiter stops by my table again and I ask for the check. This dinner adventure is over, but at least my first time out to dinner alone is done, no matter how degrading it was. Another box checked.

He is very prompt and brings the check on a small silver tray with a shot glass full of a bright yellow liquid.

"Excuse me," I ask looking up at the waiter. "What is this?" I point to the small glass.

"It is limoncello. You have not had this?"

"No, I haven't. But I've seen it."

"You must try it. It is made here in Sorrento and is very good."

With a huge smile of anticipation, I pick up the yellow glass. "Grazie."

Past my tongue and down it goes. A taste of hard lemon, sweet, but with a burn.

"This *is* very good. Thank you!"

"You're welcome." He smiles and picks up the small silver tray I've left euros on, then turns and leaves.

I gather my purse, walk through the maze of full tables and exit the restaurant. I wonder if heading back to my apartment is best for tonight? I wish I wasn't walking by myself. I look around and notice that I am literally the only woman in this square walking alone. Groups of friends comfortable with each other's company laugh and hang onto one another... the forever lovers around every corner, and families; big families sitting in the various restaurants sharing wine and conversations.

I've had a good day, I remind myself. I met Sebastiano. I smile at this and can see his face when we first met and instantly, I feel better.

Down the street and a left at the end of the little road, I walk through the narrow alleyway that leads to my apartment. I vaguely notice the people under red umbrellas eating their dinners as I reach the end, turn right and I'm in front of the distressed doors. My phone dings several times as I step inside. It's Angelo; he wrote fifteen minutes ago. I read all of the messages while I climb the stairs by the elevator.

Angelo: Babe what are you doing? I have some time I can stop by.

Angelo: Babe. Are you home?

I open the apartment door quick and throw my purse on the couch at the same time I kick off my shoes and respond to Angelo's messages.

Hi! Yes, I'm home now.

I wait and watch my phone in anticipation. I'd love to have some company.

It's been two minutes and I'm trying not to think I've missed my pocket of time with him, but I need to pee. Into the bathroom, I pull down my panties with my dress half up, still watching my phone. I sit down and relax just as it dings and the stream is interrupted as my stomach gets butterflies at the message he's sent.

Angelo: Okay good. I'm coming over. Where were you? I think I'll make sure to whip you tonight, just because you weren't home.

Angelo: And you want yes?

Yes, I do.

Angelo: Good. I will be there in 30 minutes.

Okay.

I finish as fast as I can, jump up and push the two buttons behind the toilet, into the wall to flush. Really, I want to know why there are two buttons when they both seem to do the same thing. Sidetracked... I need to hurry!

Quick into the bedroom, I throw open the closet doors and go straight to the back-left corner of my roll-on suitcase. I know exactly what I want to wear for him tonight. You know... since he's bringing a whip and all. I smile and am even more excited.

Thirty minutes on the dot and my phone dings again. Butterflies fill my stomach and throat. I grab my long, black, thin jacket from the coat hangers by the front door, whip it on, remember to take the keys and close the door behind me. There are several other apartments on this floor, and one apartment I pass on the corner as I try to quietly traverse the stairs in these high heels. Then there are several more apartments on the first floor. I love this place, completely enclosed on all sides but with a partially open roof towards the back.

The left, big wooden door creaks faintly as I slowly swing it open and I'm face to face with Angelo. Oh yes... excited and nervous at the same time; why do I always feel this way with him?

"Ciao," he says seductively, kisses my cheek and then the other and he steps inside.

"Ciao," I squeak.

I turn and start to walk back to the apartment. He is following extremely close behind and I can feel his eyes on me as we walk up the stairs. I reach up and adjust the front of my jacket; check to make sure I'm still fully covered, no spoilers for him yet.

"What do you have under that jacket, Mila?" Angelo growls in a low tone as his hand brushes over my ass.

I turn just enough to give him a small seductive smile. "You will see soon enough." I turn back around before I trip up the stairs and ruin all chances of being sexy. "But I think you'll like what I have on tonight."

Through the middle door, then my apartment door. I start to turn, to take off my jacket slowly, for him to watch, but his hand is around my throat instead. So quick, he pushes my body up against the wall. The keys drop out of my hand, landing loud on the tile floor. I gasp and feel wet at the same time. He holds me there, leans in and kisses me passionately. My hands press flat on the wall while his free hand roams my body, under my jacket.

Angelo pulls back with a look of surprise and curiosity. A small, devious smile crosses my face.

"Oh, Mila. What do you have here? Take off your jacket and let me see."

His hand slides from my neck and he takes two steps back. I follow his command, pull my jacket off of my shoulders slow and let it drop to the floor around my heels. My outfit is for his enjoyment. A black leather corset with no covering of my breasts, three silver buckles on black straps that tighten down the front of the bodice, a black lace garter belt with thigh highs and of course, black high heels.

"My God. I love it," he says, reaching out. His hand gently rubs one exposed breast and then the other. He watches my nipples harden.

A heavy breath escapes my lips as I feel his soft touch. Sensual and erotic, I stand with the most important parts exposed. His eyes and fingertips roam, each part of my body gets their own time for attention. My head falls back, lips parted, and my eyes close, heavy with the satisfaction of finally feeling him again.

His hand between my legs, runs up the inside of my thighs until reaching my clit. He lingers there, just barely touching me. My body reacts to his teasing; I'm soaked and every pore is yearning for more. One hand reaches up and tilts my mouth to his as he slides his tongue in, teasing mine. Just as they touch, his fingers slide deep into me and I gasp into his mouth. His kiss is harder, more urgent. The nice is over. Faster and deeper, his fingers penetrate me. My body spins with his, away from the wall; it's all a blur. His handsome face, his lips, his tongue. His hair is soft between my fingers as I pull it, grasping at everything I can while his fingers fuck me deep. I want him. I want to feel him stretch me... feel him fill me.

Angelo spins us to the couch. He guides the top of my body over with my hands on the cushions. My feet are still on the floor and my bare ass facing him. I look over my shoulder and I can see the want in his wild eyes as he unzips his pants and pulls out his hard cock. My body automatically reacts; I bend down slowly, making my breasts push outward and my ass tilt higher towards him.

I look back down at my hands on the couch; my head spins a little and I remember now, I had rosé with dinner. I'm still feeling the effects. It's good... I think.

A loud moan jumps from my throat as he brings me back from drifting thoughts. He thrusts into me fast and deep, my pussy clenches around him. Over and over, deeper and deeper I feel him. My skin tingles where his hands are holding my waist, pulling me into each push and I scream.

"Yes! Yes! Fuck me Angelo..."

"Si. You like my cock?" he growls in my ear, his body bent over mine.

"Yesss... I like your cock," I whisper, now breathless. "I want your cock."

His face is next to mine. I can feel his breath on my neck.

My head is suddenly pulled back and I'm looking at the ceiling.

Oh god yes. I close my eyes and the rest of my senses are even more heightened to his touch; his breath in my ear, his body in mine, fucking me like he said he would.

"You're my slut yes?"

He's finding my end over and over. My body quivers.

"You are going to come?"

"Yesss…" I moan.

"Good. Come. Cum now."

On his command, I do. I moan loud and gasp as everything is drenched.

"Oh, naughty girl… you squirt so much. You *do* like my cock."

"Yesss."

"Now is my turn."

Angelo stands up straight, his fingernails lightly claw down my back to my bum. Every part of my body is tingling, all nerves on edge and my mind is swimming in ecstasy.

He grabs onto my ass, tilts it up and slides in deeper. Faster and deeper, over and over and my insides are climbing again. He pushes in as far as he can go and holds me there. Moaning, we finish together.

We both collapse on the couch. He leans with his back on the pillows against the arm of the couch and I'm half on my stomach, facing the opposite end. I feel his hand on my legs, lightly rubbing up and down. He pulls away, stands up, slides the condom off and walks to the bathroom. I hear the water run then he reappears, collapsing again in the same spot.

"You feel so good, Mila." He pauses for a second. "I needed that."

"So did I," I say a little muffled, my face half on and half off of the couch cushion.

I slowly draw my knees closer to my body and turn over onto my back. Looking at Angelo, I see the stress in his handsome face. He holds my ankles and stretches my legs to rest across his. I don't know whether to ask why he needed me tonight or what's on his mind or if he's okay. Does he want me to ask? Or should I wait to see if he just tells me? I used to be able to ask him anything when we were messaging back and forth and talking on the phone almost every day. But that was before I got here. He would always answer... and in depth. He seems so distant now.

"Are you okay? Do you want to talk about anything?" I'm shocked to hear my voice say.

His face is blank. No emotion whatsoever.

"No."

Okay, shit. I hope I didn't just make this weird. I want to hold him, to console him and let him know it's still safe to talk to me, like he used to.

A few minutes pass.

"I destroyed my house," Angelo says, breaking the silence.

I sit up a little more. "Why did you destroy your house?"

He looks into my eyes. "Because I fought with my friends." He looks down at his hand on my leg. "They think I should do more. They say my sister would want me to live, not be so sad and angry."

"I'm sure they're just concerned. They probably just want to help." I reach down and gently rest my hand on his leg.

"Yes, I know." His hand runs as far up my leg as he can reach without sitting forward, then back down to my ankle. "I'm just tired of everyone telling me how I should be or how I should feel. They should know not to tell me anything. They have been my friends for a very long time."

My mind races with what I should say. He just told me his friends can't give him advice, so I doubt he'll be open to anything I say and I don't want to make him mad to the point where he'll leave. I want him to have me to lean on. I'm glad though; he's finally talking.

Angelo leans forward, off of the pillows. My legs; alive with his touch as he spreads them open, and his hands slowly run up to the top then split to either side, stopping on my hips. The pressure is seductive as he squeezes a handful of my flesh. His left hand moves to the back, caressing my ass. His right hand slides down between my legs.

Instantly, I'm turned on. My breathing is slower and heavier as he watches my breasts rise and fall. Slowly, his index finger runs down my clit and into me. I let out a breath through my open mouth and look into his eyes with want.

Maybe this is what he needs, I think as my body is on fire for him again. He pulls me down to lie flat under him, my legs spread wide open. Maybe this is how I help. With me, he can take his mind off of his sadness... at least for a little while.

My bare feet pad down the short hallway as I walk naked into the kitchen, flip on the light switch and open the refrigerator. Water. I need water so bad after the last three naughty sessions with Angelo. We never talked again about anything serious. Instead, he showed me his whip he brought with him. Actually, it was a flogger and it made our time together feel more purposeful, trusting and erotic. He definitely made my body shake and cum. So much so that I need to replenish the water in my body; I'm just a little dehydrated. I smile at the flashbacks.

In the cabinet, I take out a small glass and pour water, drink it all without a breath then pour another. Much better.

I turn off the kitchen light, take the glass with me into the bedroom and place it on the night stand. I had borrowed an adapter from Mario for my phone to plug into the European outlet and now my phone is being charged with no more stress. Mario has been very helpful since our coffee and naughty time. I feel much more comfortable asking him for help with directions or any random question. I'm glad Angelo told me to call his friends if I need anything. I suppose that's the way they do things.

I close the wooden window covers only halfway and crawl my tired body into bed. It's three in the morning and I'm exhausted.

10

Chapter 10

I wake to the sound of my phone again. It's 7:00 a.m. already? Damn if the nights aren't getting shorter and shorter.

Painfully, I roll over while my hand looks for the phone on the night stand. It's found and I squint. My eyes focus through the light and see it's only 3:30 a.m. Oh god, I've only been asleep for thirty minutes? I check why my phone woke me.

My daughter.

I sit up quick and turn on the lamp. The night shirt I was too tired to put on before I passed out is in reach and I slip it over my head. Having only talked to my kids one time since I landed in Europe, I need to see them. The combination of the kids being in school and the 12-hour difference makes it difficult, but I've missed them so. No matter what types of things I'm doing here, they are never far from my mind.

I call her back. Only one ring and she's smiling at me. Facetime is perfect. I'm loving the era we live in now; being able to talk to and see my kids this far away makes me feel so much better. When I was her age, there were only pay phones and phones stuck to the walls inside your house. When someone was gone... they were just gone.

"Hi honey!" I say with a huge smile.

"Hi Mom. I miss you." Her smile fades a little and I try not to feel it in my soul.

"How are you? How is your brother? I miss you too, baby."

"We're okay. Grandma is trying to make sure we're happy."

"That's good, honey girl. It's only seven more days and I'll be on the plane back to you guys."

"Ugh. Seven days is a whole week. That's such a long time." Her smile is gone now and her eyes are shiny.

"Oh, my love, it's not very long. You have just one more week of school and I'll be home. Thank you honey, I really needed this time."

Her eyes dry up a little. "I know Mom. It's okay, we just miss you."

"I know, I miss you and your brother too. I think about you guys all of the time. I need to bring you both here, I think you'd love it."

"Okay Mom, I have to go now, Grandma is taking us to get something to eat."

"Okay my sweet, I love you!" I blow a kiss and she blows a kiss back. "Kiss and hug your brother for me, okay?"

"Yeah, okay I will. I love you too. Hurry and come back."

All I see is her kissy lips in the whole screen; frozen. Then she's gone.

I can't go back to sleep, even though I need to. All I can think about are my kids. Is this going to put a wedge between us, me coming here without them? Is this an acceptable guilty pleasure?

Guilt.

I feel guilty for their unhappiness right now, while I'm here... indulging in my own wants and needs as a woman. Ten nights. Twelve days total with the flying. That's okay right; given that I've never left my kids even for one night in 14 years? Do you *deserve* to do something for yourself when you have children? What about the working business women who are also moms? Don't they leave their children often to make the money? Is that a more acceptable reason?

Well, it doesn't matter now, I suppose. I'm here and I can't go back for another week.

I dry the sides of my eyes, turn over on my stomach and force the thoughts out of my mind so I can find sleep.

I know it's 7 a.m.... really, this time. The light coming in from the window tells me so. I still have residual feelings of guilt from my daughter's call. But I decide it will be worse if I'm away from my kids and don't even enjoy myself. I grab my phone and text Angelo. He should be on his way to work.

Good morning! Just seeing if you made it to your training.

Angelo: Why are you texting me this?

Oh.

Only because you left here late last night. I'm just saying hi really.

Angelo: Then say hi. I have a mom.

I'm sorry. hi!

Angelo: What do you want Mila? I'm late for training. I don't have time for this.

Nothing. Never mind. Have a good day.

I watch my phone for a minute but he's gone. I guess I won't message him in the mornings anymore. Learned my lesson. I decide to overlook Angelo's mood swing, well... drown it out of my head is more like it, plug my phone back into the living room outlet and turn on Coldplay's "Hymn for the Weekend." I get ready for another day out in Italy and place my black wrap with white floral print on the bed. With it; my black slippers, a canvas tote bag, a loose, black beach pullover shirt and another new sexy one-piece swimsuit. It's time to relax in the sea.

Out of the big brown distressed doors, I always feel like I'm being teleported. In the safety of the apartment, I'm me, with my things and thoughts. But outside of these doors; I'm met immediately with a busy tourist street, people walking in all directions. Some meandering; deciding on whether they're hungry or curious what's in the next shop and some walking as fast as they can; I'm assuming late for a get together. Then there are the wandering eyes from the men in the restaurant right across from my apartment. Wondering, I'm sure, what the situation is when they see me with Angelo and his friends. They watched as I got lost on my first day here and watch as I learn which way is which. Today, I think is the first day they seem more like friends than prying eyes.

"Ciao!" the older restaurant man greets me with a wonderful smile.

"Ciao, Tommaso!" I say, satisfied with the fact I know and remember his name. They are all nice, but he is by far my favorite.

"And where are you headed today, bella Mila?"

"Oh, grazie." I smile at the compliment. "I'm going to jump in the sea!" I say, excited and spin once around to bring attention to my dressed down beach outfit.

"Ah yes, I see you are ready."

"Yes, I need the water today. Will you be here when I get back?"

"Yes. I just started. I will be here until we close."

"Okay good. I will tell you if I love your sea like I love the ocean where I'm from."

Tommaso laughs. "Yes, please do... but tell me, where are you from?"

"Hawai'i."

"Ahh Hawai'i! It is a dream to go there." His smile stretches even farther.

"Just as Italy is my dream, and here I am." I smile big. "You should go to Hawai'i."

"One day, bella Mila, one day." He smiles in a way that makes me think he will not, in fact, one day go.

"Well Tommaso, I hope so. I know you would love it. And now I'm off to enjoy your home." I smile all teeth and his relaxed smile makes me feel great about today.

"Enjoy and I will see you when you return."

"Grazie!"

I follow the now familiar cobblestones and past the other side restaurants; where I put up my hand a little and say "No, grazie" about a half dozen times. I already have my favorite restaurant on this street.

To the right, I walk a short distance then take a left after a horse drawn carriage and two small cars pass. I look up at the sky and feel more energized and euphoric with the sun beaming down, warming my face. I'm here. I've said this to myself often, at least three times a day so far. Like a pinch to remind myself I'm not dreaming, that I really came to Italy. I never thought this was something I would do, and the words *you're crazy, I could never do that* from some of my friends back home, resonate in my head. For me, it was only because I had never had the urge to before, not that I couldn't or wouldn't. Traveling alone doesn't scare me; what would scare me now, is never doing it.

A quaint little church to my right and a painter to my left, with an easel and colorful palette. He has several paintings around his feet to be sold, all scenes of Sorrento. They are marvelous, but unfortunately, I will have to stick to my own pictures with phone for memories.

Past a pretty, round area of bright green grass, several white benches for anyone to relax under the tall full trees' ample shade and then out to the edge. And here it is again the breathtaking view I saw on my first morning. Another amazingly stunning day with the sun shining bright; happily skipping and reflecting on the top of the vast blue sea. The sea. It's like home to me. Alive and moving against the world with its own rhythm, sustaining life inside and outside of itself. Now, it will help me to relax. I smile and mentally pat myself on the back for being here as I take my first of many steps down the long stone path built into the stone wall, that is itself, built into the cliff.

Zigzagging down the side of Sorrento, I'm sure no one can walk this path without constantly looking out to the boats and ferries coming and going, shuttling to and from Naples and the islands of Ischia and Capri. If you look down, you can see the people sunbathing far below on the wooden decks that stretch out, with Mt. Vesuvius across the bay in the far distance. I'm in love with this view.

To the left, I need to take off my sunglasses to walk through a cool dark tunnel, then out into the gleaming sun again and the last part of the walkway.

"Ciao bella!" I hear a voice below me and ignore it. I can't think every compliment yelled out is for me. How narcissistic would that be? And I definitely learned my lesson at dinner last night.

I make the last turn and finally land at the bottom. I see a cute Italian man of about 25 standing in front of the entrance to the restaurant where I ate my first breakfast.

"Ciao Mila," he says smiling like we both share a secret.

Oh, it *was* for me. "Hi!"

"Do you remember me?"

"Ahh, yes of course I do." I was so tired that day, I just now remember him. "You were very nice to me on my first day here. And... you even remember my name."

"Of course, how could I forget a beautiful woman such as yourself?" The corner of his mouth curves up in a small devious smile. "How long is your visit? You will save some time for me?"

My cheeks blush as two older women hear what he said and giggle as they walk past.

"Hmmm... maybe," I flirt and continue on my way, trying to make it seem like he didn't just throw me off and make me nervous.

I turn back and smile. He winks and knows he's the winner. Damn men.

There are long wooden piers that stretch out into the sea from the land, but those are guarded by the restaurants; like the one I just left. Then, there is one, shorter pier that is for anyone who doesn't want to pay to sunbathe. The coveted sunshine rises over Sorrento town, which is on top of the cliff I just walked down. Granted, the longer piers have the sunbeams touch down on them quite a bit sooner than the short pier does, but between not wanting to spend more money than necessary and trying to relax where there are no eyes on me the whole time, I opt to be with the locals on the short pier.

Not caring at all where the sunshine is hitting on the used and sun-bleached wooden planks, I drop my bag close to the edge, strip off my wrap and shirt and kick off my slippers. I see people walking down a set of metal stairs into the water and find my way down too.

Oh. Holy hell the water is cold. With a sharp draw of breath, I dive in from the middle stair. The sea shocks every inch of me, but so very quickly it changes to fantastic. This was the best idea.

I glide over onto my back and look up into the perfect blue sky. I realize it mirrors the sea I'm swimming in and the only sound is my own breathing, amplified. Inside my own head, with the unbelievable feeling of knowing I'm in another country all by myself, doing something amazing just for me, I'm slightly overwhelmed and very proud of myself. Even with the internal battle of leaving my children for 10 days, I needed this. I needed to take time for myself. If I don't know who I am, what I want, and how the world works, then how can I raise kids who will know themselves? I add a few more drops of saltwater to the Mediterranean.

Okay that's enough. I roll back over onto my stomach and dive under. The water is perfectly clear. I can see the huge stones far beneath me... and the arms and legs of a swimmer. Oh shit! I move quick before we collide, but then see something I have to do and swim under one of the long piers to get there.

At a thick, blue, floating chaise lounge, I kick as hard as I can to try and pull myself up. It's sitting high above, on the top of the water and I'll be damned if I don't get up there on the first attempt. Honestly, I don't think I'd have the strength for a second try.

Finally, I lie back into the contoured plastic, my energy spent. I really do need to rest now. I close my eyes to the bright sun and mentally slow my breathing.

Ten minutes later, there's splashing nearby and I wake to see another woman attempting the other floating chair. With her elbows bent outward, next to her ears, she kicks and kicks. The woman finally pulls the top part of her body onto the middle of the chair then slowly pulls the rest of her body up. A seal is the vision that pops into my head. Now I wonder if that's how I looked trying to get my body up here. I sit up and slide back into the sea; I need to eat. There's still only a certain amount of alone time, in the middle of the rest of the world, I can handle.

Slow and in complete peace with life, I glide gracefully toward the metal stairs. Under the long wooden pier, past a couple of teenagers play-drowning each other, avoiding the swimmer that almost did a hit and run when I first got in and I'm almost to the exit.

"Buongiorno," an older, stout man bobbing next to the stairs says.

I smile and stop. "Buongiorno."

"Come stai?"

"Oh, I'm sorry, I only know English," I giggle, embarrassed.

"Why? You look Italian. Like you are from Naples."

"I keep hearing that." A grin stretches across my face. "I'm loving that everyone thinks I'm from here."

"Well it's okay, I know good English," he says with a charming, crooked smile.

"Okay, perfect!"

"My name is Giuseppe. What is your name?" he says as he splashes a little water on his bald head.

"Hi Giuseppe, I'm Mila."

"It's very nice to meet you, Mila. Your name is beautiful like you."

I blush smile. "Grazie. You're very sweet to say so."

"Ah! You do speak Italian."

"Ha ha! Nooo, that's about it," I say swimming out of the way of a woman gliding into the water.

"What are you doing here? Where are you from?"

"I'm from Hawai'i and I'm here on my celebratory divorce trip." My smile is gigantic every time I say that last part.

Giuseppe grins. "Good for you!"

"And you? Do you come here often?" I smile.

"I live here. I am from Sorrento."

I let out a small giggle. "That must be amazing, I wish I was from here. But I mean do you come here at this place, in the sea… swimming."

"Yes. Every day. I used to be the captain of a cruise ship for twenty-three years. Now I am retired and I swim every day because I can." He smiles and swims a little closer. "Also, I come here every day to get out of the house and away from my wife for a little while."

We both break out laughing. Oh, I like him.

We talk for twenty minutes more. I find out he has three grown children, loved being captain of a cruise ship and he's still a big flirt, just like all of his younger counterparts.

"Well Giuseppe, I'm going to lie in the sun to dry off and then find something to eat."

"Yes. You should always eat."

"It was so lovely to meet you," I say.

"It was wonderful to meet you, bella Mila. I will be here every day. Come back to say hi."

"I definitely will." I look back and smile one last time before I reach the stairs and climb up.

Comfortable in the sun for about 30 minutes on the pier, I suddenly feel extremely antsy; I need to see more of Sorrento and to eat. I jump up, grab my things and back up the side of the cliff I go. It's so hot out with the sun directly above. Shit. I look down from the top and almost want to go back and jump in the sea again to cool off; but my stomach says no.

#

Showered and dressed in a long beige summer dress that shows off the tops of my still perky after-forty breasts, flat sandals and a smaller bag with a long strap to wear across my body, I'm ready for another adventure out. On my way down the stairs, I pass an older man with a little white dog.

"Buongiorno," I say, trying to find volume.

"Buongiorno," the man says in a much more relaxed tone than mine.

My phone dings just as I open the big distressed door. I step back into the court and let the door close again.

Angelo: Hello beautiful. What are you doing today?

Beautiful? He must have forgotten about this morning.

Hi! I went swimming but now I'm hungry and going to find something to eat.

Angelo: Yes. It's a perfect day for a swim. But you are done already?

Yes. I need food.

Angelo: Why haven't you gone shopping for food to keep at the apartment?

I don't know where the grocery store is yet.

Angelo: Just walk down any street and you will find people selling everything you could possibly need.

Oh okay. I'll do that right now.

Angelo: I will call Mario and ask him to bring you something. Wait for a minute.

Ok thanks!

Hmm, I guess he's not still mad at me. I wish I knew when to not worry about his moods. My ex would yell and be mad all day for the smallest, most minute things; leaving the door open while bringing in groceries, pouring the kids a little more milk than they'll drink, not being ready when he was, on and on so that I can't even remember the infractions. I spent so long hearing him telling me that I don't know what I'm doing that I started to believe it. So, if I could deal with my ex for fifteen years, I can deal with Angelo's mood swings... he does have a good reason to be difficult... right?

Angelo: I talked with Mario. He and the same friends are going for pizza tonight. He will message you soon to see if you want to join them.

Okay that's nice. What about you? Will you come too?

Angelo: I have to see my family first after I'm done with training. But I don't think so.

Oh. Alright.

Angelo: Don't make me feel bad. I just saw you last night.

It's fine. You are the one that's my friend. I just want you to know I would rather be with you.

Angelo: I'm not your boyfriend. I won't be with you every second.

I know that and you haven't been. But what we talked about before I got here... we haven't even had a meal together. I would like to just sit and talk over food and some wine.

Angelo: You have only been here four days Mila. You already know I have other things going on.

God, I hate when he adds my name to messages. A sassy undertone, I know he's getting mad again.

Yes, I do know.

Angelo: And stop talking about what we said before. It doesn't matter now.

What the hell does he mean it doesn't matter?! Everything he told me was the reason I came here instead of Naples!

I relent.

I will go with your friends if Mario messages me. If you find some time, it would be nice to see you too.

Angelo: Okay. Have fun.

Thanks.

11

Chapter 11

The chair is tall like the table. The off-white covering above diffuses the strong sun and stretches over the makeshift dining area surrounding a small wooden building. Inside the small building is a little kitchen, a tiny bar section and four men making magic happen in a cramped space. There are several people standing at the counters that hang off of the large openings on two sides of the building. The patrons can chat with the men inside, drink and be entertained while watching them turn out delicious food.

I order wine. Rosé as usual. That, and a plate of linguini with sautéed shrimp show up to my table only ten minutes after I speak with the waiter. The waiter... he's very nice, very professional. He brings warm bread wrapped in foil with a small bowl of peanuts, olive oil and a small plate of butter. I forgot I have to ask for water since there is a shortage here right now.

"Flat or sparkling?"

"Flat please." I smile.

He walks away but quickly returns with the water, places it down where there's room and checks on the other table, consisting of a man and a woman. The couple looks very relaxed, laughing and touching each other's arm from time to time.

It would be nice to have someone to share this meal with. Like Angelo. I guess I have to switch gears in my brain and just assume he's not about to spend normal time with me. I sigh; big inhale and long exhale. I wish everything was as people say.

My phone dings. Oh, I forgot I plugged in the Wi-Fi password when I was at Centaruro restaurant last night. It's right across the square and apparently reaches here too.

Mario: Ciao how are you today?

Ciao! I'm very good thank you. How are you?

Mario: Good. We are going out for bowling and pizza tonight. Would you like to join us?

Yes, I would love to come! Who is going?

Mario: The same as last time.

Okay great! Thanks. What time?

Mario: We will collect you at 6.

Hahah! *Collect* me. I love the way the English language is used here. I actually laugh out loud and accidentally get the attention of the people around me. I smile.

Okay. I'll be ready.

Mario: Perfect. I might have a couple of girls joining us too.

Okay. Friends?

Mario: I met one on a dating app and she is traveling with a friend. I invited them with us tonight since they leave tomorrow. And who knows, maybe something extra will happen for us all.

Oh. I re-read that last part and can only imagine what he means by it. We had a conversation covering this subject when we were all driving back to my apartment the last time. He knows I have never been with a woman. I don't actually know if I want to be. Honestly, it doesn't even turn me on when I think about it. So... I'm not quite sure how I'll feel if I'm ever in that situation.

117

Interesting. Haha, I'm not so sure I'll be up for that tonight.

Mario: Don't worry, I'm not sure if they will be either. Won't hurt to find out. But we will see you at 6. Now, I need to set the bar up for tonight.

Okay. I'll see you soon.

I put my phone down and dig into my lovely meal; a sprig of parsley on top, and it all looks amazing.

Six o'clock comes fast since I lingered at the restaurant during lunch. I watched the cars circling the square, tourists busily enjoying their Italian vacation and the steady stream of patrons coming and going from the little restaurant. Afterwards, I meandered down the streets, taking time to check out the other bars and shops I usually just walk past. I made it back, showered and changed my outfit three times until I decided on tight, ripped jeans, an equally tight black shirt with no bra and my short Converse. I am of course, going to the bowling alley so no heels. Right as I finish applying my lipstick and adding euros to the little purse, my phone dings.

Mario: We are downstairs.

Great! I'm on my way.

I open the big distressed door and have three handsome faces looking at me. We take turns with floating cheek kisses and as I look past Mario's shoulder, I see the restaurant men watching as usual. I smile.

The door closes behind me and I follow my three men down the street and down another road.

"Are we walking to the bowling alley?" I ask Marco.

"Yes. It's not too far from your apartment and it's difficult at this time of night to find parking."

There is a layer of clouds in the sky tonight and suddenly water starts to drop, prompting Marco to open an umbrella. I didn't even notice he had one. He is very tall and holds it over the both of us, but the trees decorating the sidewalk are short and keep running into the top of it. Marco instead, holds it over only me and ducks under each oncoming tree. Aww, he's a gentleman. I smile at the thoughtful gesture and love finding out something more about him; about his character.

The rain lets up and Marco closes the umbrella while we follow Mario and Federico to the right, around a corner and down another road.

"So," Marco looks down at me. "What is your age?"

Ugh. That damn question again. Mentally, I roll my eyes but make sure he doesn't see it.

"Hahaha! First tell me the age you think I am," I say, feeling sassy tonight.

He smiles. "I think… 37."

"Good. That's pretty close. I'm 42."

"Yes. Pretty close." He smiles again then turns back to looking at the road. "You are good for 42."

Those evil words strung together that are supposed to be a compliment, but somehow, sound less than one. *Good for 42.*

"And you?" I ask looking up at him. "How old are you?"

"I am 36."

"Hey you two." Mario looks back at us. "We're here."

I look up and notice, just a short distance in front of the other two men, a lit-up *BOWLING* sign on a small building. Cool. I'm thrilled they asked me to come here with them tonight. I love being one of the boys!

Inside, I follow suit and sit down at the table in the middle of the restaurant on the same side as Mario and next to Federico who's on the end, with Marco in the chair across from me. I know now, that

Federico will do the ordering for us, just like last time. I am however, the only one that orders wine with pizza. The men all order a cola, like normal people who aren't on vacation.

"So," I begin and look to my right at Mario. "When are your new friends joining us?" I smile.

He smiles back. "They should be here any time now. Oh, and Mila is one of us," he says, turning his attention to Marco and Federico. Then says the same thing in Italian for Federico. "She's like us, she's one of the boys."

How did he know that's how I want them to see me?

The other two nod their heads in agreement and Marco looks intently at me through his glasses. His gaze still makes me squirm in my chair.

The beautiful looking pizza arrives. Two different types and the aroma together is hypnotizing.

"This looks so good," I say, staring at it all but coveting the bigger of the two.

"Here," Mario says as he rolls two mozzarella balls onto a plate and pushes it in front of me. "You need the balls."

Marco, Federico and I burst out laughing.

"You're terrible. But yesss, I do need the balls. All of them." I give each man a look of intent.

Everyone becomes quiet for a second and Mario translates what I said to Federico.

"Yes," they say in unison.

"Mmmm, eat up then, Mila. We want to watch." Mario grins.

I pick one up and lick it slow and sensual, put it half way between my lips and slowly pull it back out, sucking it. Picking up the other mozzarella ball, I look around the table at each man, stare into their eyes and lick and suck each ball. But it's Marco I can't look at for long, so I pop the balls into my mouth and chomp down.

"Oh!" they all say. "Ouch!"

"Ahahaha! I couldn't help myself," I say, chewing the delicious cheese.

"I hope you can help yourself with us," Mario says with his hands now deep in his lap.

"Ciao!" A woman's voice comes from the right.

Two American women walk up and Mario stands to give them the standard hello; with introductions all around, they both sit. Tiffany, the one Mario connected with, sits across from him while her friend, Cara, sits next to him on the end.

As everyone is talking and teasing, I think of Angelo; I wish he were here with me. I quietly take out my phone and message him.

Ciao lover. I wish you were here. I hope everything is good at home.

Angelo: Ciao how is everything?

It's good. I just wish you were here too.

Angelo: I told you I might not come.

Yes, I know. I'm just checking in case you could. We'll be here a little longer, I think.

Angelo: Okay.

The night at the bowling alley is ending and I finally understand we are not going to bowl... we were never really going to bowl. I just love how I take everything at face value. Mentally slapping my forehead, I decide on another goal: stop believing everything I'm told. I also understand why Mario told the others I'm just *one of the boys* tonight... that meant I get to help pay for dinner. It's fine. At least this way, I don't feel obligated for anything.

"So, should we all go to a hotel and have some drinks?" Mario smiles, looking around the table.

"Umm... I think I'm done for the evening," I say.

My phone vibrates.

Angelo: Ciao

Ciao we are leaving soon.

Angelo: I may stop by then.

Okay let me know.

About ten minutes later, we all walk out of the bowling alley pizzeria. Mario, Marco and Federico are standing with the other two girls and I'm in no mood to play *whose pussy goes with which cock,* if that's even a thing. Plus, I'm obviously a little tipsy from the wine.

I walk over to Mario. "Grazie! I really enjoyed tonight. Thank you for inviting me."

He kisses my cheeks. "You're very welcome."

I say goodbye to the two girls and wave at Federico and Marco. "Ciao!" I say to everyone, turn and begin to walk back the way we had come... well, I think this is the way. Fuck it. I'm just going to keep walking until I see something I recognize. It shouldn't be too difficult... right?

I know I'm pretty abrupt in leaving and look back once to see them all with curious faces, watching me walk across the street; but right this second, I really don't care. I'm not about to wait to see if I'm propositioned with a woman in my mouth tonight. I know what Mario was hinting at earlier.

I cross the road and love that I just don't give a shit. The wine from dinner is holding its buzz and I'm feeling empowered with my decision.

"Hey! Wait! Mila, where are you going?!"

I turn to see Marco running across the street after me.

Oh my god. A man running after... me? I've always wondered how it feels to be chased after. It feels... amazing!

He slows and stops right behind me. "Are you okay? What are you doing? Where are you going?"

I turn to face him. Mmm why is he so delicious? Tall, handsome and ran after me.

"Oh. I'm just walking back home."

"Are you upset? Did we do something?"

"Oh no! I'm so sorry. Does everyone think I'm mad?" I say and turn quick to look back at the others, then back at him.

Marco nods his head a little.

"Nooo. Mario had mentioned all of us getting together with the two girls and I just wanted to leave before anything happened. I'm just not into them like that."

"Yes. I'm not either," he says with a serious tone.

Interesting... I had assumed the whole situation was already discussed and approved between the three friends. Three women... three men... it seemed to make sense.

"Come. I will take you home." Marco starts walking in the direction I was headed.

I follow and smile because I *was* heading in the right direction. But deep down, I'm so glad I don't have to find my way back; we all already know I have the worst sense of direction.

I hear someone yelling in Italian and quick footsteps getting louder, closer behind us. We both turn and see Federico catch up. Marco and Federico exchange a few words in Italian.

"Federico isn't into it either," Marco says, turning to me.

I smile and follow the two men to the right, across the street and to a cute little silver car. Marco opens the passenger door for me as Federico crawls into the back from the driver's side. Marco slides into the driver's seat and I'm quite surprised how perfect he fits, given he's so tall. He pulls the car onto the road and we pass Mario and the two girls. Hmm... he should have a good night tonight.

Marco looks at me. "So why did you just walk away?"

"I didn't want a discussion about it. Hey... but I did say goodbye." I smile.

He smiles back.

"Besides, I'm getting to where I make a decision and go with it," I say, turning to look straight ahead at the road and away from his intense eyes.

"I see."

We pull into the square closest to my apartment and I turn to look at Marco, our eyes meeting at the same time. I know I'm blushing and I'm thankful for the dark night. Quickly, I lean in and kiss his cheek.

"Thank you for bringing me home," I say. I lean in closer and whisper in his ear. "And I'll take you tonight, if you want."

I sit back in my seat. I can't believe I just said that.

Marco has a curious look on his face as I gather my purse.

"What did you say?" he asks.

"Message me. I'll tell you there." Federico is watching all of this interaction and I don't want him thinking it's going to be a free-for-all-tonight.

"I don't have your number," Marco says, picking up his phone.

I tell him my number as he enters it into his phone. Now it's official and I'm excited I gave my fear of rejection the middle finger.

"Ciao!" I say, waving at Federico. I close the door, turn and walk away with a little extra skip in my step.

The Blue Charter restaurant is all folded up and dark as I walk through the distressed wooden doors. Half way up the second flight of stairs, my phone dings.

Marco: What did you say in my car?

I said I would take you tonight. If you would like to that is.

Marco: Yes, I would. I will drop Federico off and be there in 15 minutes.

Okay perfect.

"Holy shit, holy shit," I whisper as I skip stairs, rush through the first door, then the second. I fling my clothes off into the closet and grab a little black lace outfit with thin pink ribbing down the front. It's on my body in a second and I make sure my breasts are covered... for now. I smile, run into the bathroom, quickly brush my teeth and make sure my makeup hasn't settled under my eyes. I find and slide on my black sexy heels I had left in here. I rush around as carefully as possible; grab all of the clothes I had littered the living room with when I changed earlier today and throw them into the bedroom closet.

I'm so nervous. Why do I get so nervous when it comes to Marco? My phone dings.

Marco: I just parked. When you open the door, I don't want you to talk. Okay? No talking at all. You only do what I say.

Okay yes.

Marco: Good. I'm almost there. Come open the door.

Yes sir.

Marco: Good girl.

I throw on my long black jacket just in case I run into a neighbor. I'm sure they've heard me during the naughty times I've already had in my apartment, but hearing and seeing are two different things. I grab the keys and quickly maneuver through the two doors, making sure to keep the middle door slightly ajar. I tiptoe down the stairs and open the big distressed door.

There he is.

His gaze; intense as he steps over the threshold. I close the door behind him and he quietly waits. I can feel his eyes on me. I turn, look into his face and instantly become wet. Through his eyes: I'm already undressed and in the most compromising of positions.

Without a word, I turn, walk up the stairs and feel Marco close behind me. I assume he's watching my ass as I traverse the steps; the steps that seem longer than ever tonight.

Through the door I left ajar, I find the correct key to my apartment. Inside, I turn to hang up my jacket and expose my sexy outfit while

Marco quietly steps inside and closes the door. In an instant, he has a handful of my long hair and pushes my body up against the wall so fast that I gasp. I can feel how hard he already is as he leans his weight into my thigh, his free hand roaming up my other leg to my ass then between my legs. His expert hands feel amazing on my heightened skin. Suddenly, I feel the absence of his body as he moves away, still keeping me pinned to the wall with one hand. His other hand slides up and penetrates deep inside me. A breath moves through my lips.

"You are already so wet, bitch," he growls in my ear.

I want to say something back, but remember his instructions.

Deeper and harder his fingers slide inside of me. Moans escape my lips and I move my body back on his hand.

"Suck."

He releases my hair and slides his fingers out of me. I turn around and see his hard cock already out. I drop to my knees, wrap my hand around it and slide him into my mouth, as deep as I can, down my throat. I want him to remember me and what I can do.

I feel his hands on the back of my head and his pulsing cock slide in even deeper. I gag and gasp for breath and pull my mouth back.

"Good, bitch."

I look up into his approving eyes and know I've accomplished what I was after.

He guides me to the couch. He sits, throws a pillow on the floor between his feet; his pants now around his ankles. I lick my lips, kneel on the pillow and slide him back into my mouth. Sucking and stroking him, I feel my other set of lips getting soaked.

"Are you more wet, bitch?" he asks after a few minutes.

I pull my head back. "Yes sir."

"How wet?"

"Very wet, sir," I answer, with my hand still slowly sliding up and down his shaft.

"Good. Come."

He finally takes his pants completely off and leaves them in a pile by the pillow, pulls me up and escorts me into the kitchen; my heels clicking on the black and white tile floor.

Unlike Mario and Angelo, Marco doesn't kiss me this time. He is in full character of Dom. He does it well. So well, in fact, that I want to follow him and do every single thing he says.

With only his intense fixed stare speaking volumes, he places his hands on my sides, helps me onto the kitchen table and lays me on my back. This is the second time I've been put on this table and for a moment, I find it funny that I'm never going to use it to eat my food off of.

My wayward thought is cut short as he spreads my knees apart and watches between my legs as he slides two, then three fingers deep inside me again. I can't stop my eyes from closing, my head presses harder into the table and a long moan emits from my mouth. His fingers know where to go; they hit the same spot inside me over and over. I feel the pressure and I can't stop it.

"Yes bitch. Squirt. Squirt for me now."

His Italian accent only turns me on more, mixed with his Dom demeanor, my body gladly obliges his command. Over and over I make it rain, drenching the floor and the plastic tablecloth. I feel a puddle forming under my ass as he continues to pleasure me.

I'm becoming spent. Finally able to take a breath, I open my eyes and watch him slowly slide his fingers out of me. Marco turns my head to the side, to the edge of the table, I open my mouth and take him deep. Oh, I feel so naughty lying in my wet pleasure, with his cock growing bigger as he slides it in and out of my mouth. I leave my hands down by my sides and let him fuck my mouth as he pleases.

Moans escape him, then he stops. I open my eyes as he helps me off of the table and into the bedroom. He sits me down on the edge of the bed and I look up into his commanding eyes. I've found this is what I like. I like to not having to think about anything... to just please and be pleased.

Marco never does fully penetrate me tonight. Strictly oral and squirting pleasure for another hour. I want more but I am satisfied I wasn't alone tonight. Very satisfied.

As I watch Marco pull his belt tight and into place, he looks up and walks over to where I'm now lying correctly on the bed. My parts are all back in place, barely hiding beneath the lace outfit, except for my right breast, that he pulls out to tease my nipple. It hardens quickly between his thumb and finger.

"Good," he says, turning his gaze again to my eyes. "Very good."

"Thank you, sir," I say with a slightly devilish smile. Whether he got what he wanted or not... I did.

Marco leans down, kisses my forehead, smiles, then turns and walks out. I hear the front door close and I can't help the grin growing across my face. I did it! I am never the instigator, but I was tonight. Elated at another goal accomplished, I swing my legs over the edge of the bed and jump up to go take a shower. I'm so happy I spoke up and made this happen tonight; slowly breaking out of my 42-year shell. I walk into the living room and finally remember where I had tossed my phone.

Oh no...

Angelo: Where are you?

Angelo: I'm driving by right now.

Angelo: I told you I was coming.

Angelo: Who are you with?

Angelo: Mila answer your phone.

Shit. Of course, he was trying to see me tonight. Story of my life.

Hi I'm here!

Angelo: You're at the restaurant? I drove by there already.

No, I'm at my apartment. I told you we were leaving there.

Angelo: I told you I was coming by.

I thought you meant to my place.

Angelo: But you had Marco there. So you really weren't waiting for me were you.

Damn they shared information quick.

You told me you might be by. But you also always tell me not to count on you to show up.

Angelo: Marco called me to ask if it was okay for him to go to your apartment. At least he's a good friend like that.

He's not here now, you can still stop by.

Angelo: I'm already on my way home.

Okay. I wish we had better communication tonight.

Two minutes later and still no reply. He's done.

I clean up the kitchen, straighten the couch cushions, peel off my naughty outfit and step into the shower. I wonder if Angelo would have really stopped by if Marco had not been here tonight? I decide on *no* he wouldn't have stopped by and I'm completely happy with the way my night went.

Finally, ready to sleep, my long satin nightgown feels like a soft kiss as I slide into bed, under the sheet. I turn out the light on the night stand and with the wooden shutters half open, I can hear the garbage trucks stealing away through the tiny streets, clearing away the day's trash. *I'm sure that should be a metaphor for something in my life:* my last half-conscious thought as my eyes flutter shut.

12

Chapter 12

"One ticket to Pompeii please."

"Three and a half euro," the ticket man says, seemingly tired. With deep wrinkles in his forehead, dark purple bags under his eyes and only one glance up, he looks like he's over the monotony. I wonder how long he's been sitting behind this scratched up, Plexiglas window, deciphering all different accents that slaughter his language.

I dig into my purse and hand him the euros. I'm still feeling bad about not knowing the language, so I don't say much back. After handing me a ticket and some change, he points to the left, behind where I'm standing in the train station.

Through the large opening to the outside, there are train tracks with one train sitting at the far end and another pulling up. The moving train stops and empties its large cargo of people. I hold my ticket up to see the numbers and look for a sign that corresponds with a specific track or train as the people all disembark and exit through the building behind me.

"Do you know which train goes to Pompeii?" a young man's voice asks.

I turn around and shade my eyes to see him better. "Um, sorry I'm not sure."

Suddenly, my arm is jerked downwards; my body flies forward. I barely catch myself, stumble a few feet and realize my wallet I was holding, along with my ticket, was snatched out of my hand. I look up and see the young man that was just talking to me bolt in the same direction as another boy the same age, and run away with my wallet.

"Hey!" I yell out at the two. My heart sinks further with each step they take away from me.

What the hell just happened?! My brain tries to grasp the situation as I'm still trying to catch my breath, when I see the boy in front suddenly get tackled from the side. He flies to the ground with a loud thud and the boy that was talking to me, still running, is soon out of sight. The young thief springs up and runs in the direction of his friend.

I watch, still dumbfounded, as a man walks up. He brushes the dirt off of his pants and shirt, picks up my ticket from the ground and hands it to me, along with my wallet.

"I believe these belong to you," he says.

"O-oh yes, thank you. So much," I say in awe of everything that just happened. I quickly put my wallet back into my purse, adjust my sunglasses and shade my eyes again to see him clearly. Oh my god… he's so handsome; sexy even after tackling a thief. "That was amazing," I manage to say. "I can't believe what you just did."

"It was nothing, really. I saw them walking towards you and had a bad feeling something was going to happen. They were very fast but at least I was in the right position to help."

He looks to be in his early 30s. A few inches taller than me, light brown hair, a slim muscular build that's visible through his tight, light green t-shirt and fitted dark brown pants; he's definitely from Europe. I feel a small smile emerge on my face. Americans don't dress like this.

"I'm so grateful you were. I don't even know how I can repay you.

You saved my vacation and I am so, very much in your debt." I don't do damsel in distress very well and fight the strong urge to roll my eyes at how lame I sound.

"Well, you could tell me which train is going to Pompeii... to start," he says with a sexy side smile.

Ugh! I can feel my shy self peeking through the curtains of my brain.

"I'm actually not sure. I was wondering the same thing right before all of that drama happened." With a little laugh in my voice, I nervously move a piece of hair from my eyes. "But my guess is this one," I say, pointing to the train that had pulled in a few minutes ago.

"I was thinking the same thing." He looks into my eyes and smiles.

All of a sudden, a rush of people starts boarding the train. I have no idea where they all came from.

"Suppose we should find a seat fast," Mr. Handsome Savior says.

"Yes!" I smile and follow his lead through the nearest sliding train doors.

He stops in front of an empty seat on the right and extends his arm out for me to scoot in first.

"Thank you."

We settle in and soon after, the train lurches forward; my body jerks back, then forward in the seat. His hand shoots out and holds onto my arm. It's warm and strong but still gentle and I'm trying not to react to the millions of butterflies in my stomach. I notice his eyes are deep green, sprinkled with intensity and concern. I'm almost lost in them.

"Are you okay?" he asks, slowly removing his hand.

"Um... yes... I'm okay. Still a bit shaken but I'll be fine. Thank you." I smile and realize I've been staring into his eyes for much too long. As I look away, I see the corner of his mouth slide up into a small smile. Well, his handsome self is definitely easing part of my frayed nerves but creating new ones.

"Where are you from?" he asks, readjusting himself in the seat.

I cross one knee over the other and relax again. "I'm from Hawai'i." I smile.

"Oh wow. I've always wanted to visit Hawai'i."

"Where are you from?" I ask.

"Switzerland."

"Oh, I hear it's beautiful there."

"It is, but very opposite of Hawai'i's beauty." He smiles bigger.

I turn and look out of the window, nervous. I can't look him in his eyes for long; he'll know too much of what I'm guilty of thinking.

"Have you been to Italy before?" I ask, turning back for the answer.

"I have been to Milan and Rome. Mostly with my father when I was younger."

"Very nice. So, this is your first time to southern Italy... like me."

He smiles. "Yes, it is. I like it. It's different from northern; it's more... relaxed. Well..."

"Other than what just happened," we say in unison and laugh together.

Our laughing is suddenly infiltrated by music. We look up to see a middle-aged man playing an accordion and singing. A woman is lightly hitting the palm of her hand with a tambourine behind him. They walk through the doorway from the train car in front of us, stop beside my new friend and the man says something in Italian as the woman presents her short top hat from off of her head.

"No. Grazie," Mr. Handsome says to the couple, holding his hand up.

They pause for fifteen seconds still playing, then continue on through the rest of our car, going from seat to seat.

"Gypsies," I say. "My friend told me."

"Yes. They are called *Roma* or in Italian, *Rom*. Most are like this, offering something for money. Some others are pickpockets. I see your friend told you well; you are wearing your purse across your body, not just on your shoulder." His eyes move to the strap lying between my breasts.

"Yes," I say, feeling like my breasts are exposed and I unconsciously adjust the offending strap. "He stressed to be careful on buses... and trains especially." I extend my hand. "My name is Mila by the way."

"I'm Julian," he says, stretching his right arm over.

My hand slides into his and I feel his warmth for the second time. He squeezes just enough and my mind instantly wanders to how his hands might feel on the rest of my body. His green eyes seem to know again what I'm thinking; I pull away to break the spell.

"What brings you to Italy?" he asks with another small, sly smile.

Shit. I'm ridiculously transparent. "Honestly?" I answer.

"Yes, of course."

"It's my celebratory divorce trip." I smile big, as usual.

"Congratulations!" Julian smiles back with a wide grin. "And how has it been so far?"

"It's been wonderful," I say knowing that's only half of the truth. Wonderful and stressful at the same time is what I really want to say.

"That's great. And now you're on your way to Pompeii... with me." His eyes sparkle.

"Yes... and why are you here alone?" I ask, feeling I need to put the spotlight on him instead. "You are travelling alone aren't you?"

"Yes I am. I always travel alone."

"This is my first time."

I look up at a group of boys in their early teens standing in front of the exit doors. They're having fun teasing and pushing each other and I wonder if Julian notices I can't look him in the eyes for very long.

Julian's attention doesn't waver from me. "That's very adventurous of you."

"I suppose so. A lot of people have told me this. But I don't understand, it doesn't seem that crazy to me." I look back at him

134

for a moment.

"A single woman traveling alone to a foreign country... adventurous. Not very many seem to do it."

"Well, I don't know why not. I feel if you want to do something, then just do it. If I waited for someone else to come with me, who knows when I would be here. Anyways, I have figured out it's very liberating to be in another country by myself. I get to meet interesting people... like yourself." I lightly bump his arm with my shoulder.

His smile is sweet and relaxed, and he lingers longer against me as he bumps me back. "Yes, that's very true. But you're a woman, you don't think it's more dangerous traveling by yourself?"

"It could be I guess, but this is why I made connections before I came here. People who can tell me where to stay and the places I should avoid. I feel you can't wait for everything in life to be perfectly safe; it should be an adventure." I smile.

"Too true." Julian returns my smile with perfect pearly whites.

The train car gets dark. I look out of the window to see nothing. We're going through a tunnel and my mind quickly jumps to naughty thoughts. Hmmm... what could we do in the time it takes to get through one of these tunnels? And just like that, I'm blinded by the sun again.

For the rest of the trip, we talk about life in Switzerland, Hawai'i and Europe in general. There is so much about the world that I'm just now finding out. Nothing about other countries were never explained in American schools, unless it was a special, one day report on where your ancestors came from. I'm feeling further behind the rest of the world in more than just in sex and social behavior. I feel I know nothing at all. So now, basically, I am like a toddler trying to soak up all of the information I can.

While talking, we pass through several towns. Through open fields of tall grass that quickly change to dilapidated apartment buildings with strings of colorful laundry hanging out to dry in the breeze. Old buildings, abandoned and broken; graffiti adorning each intact wall. Perfect. I can just imagine this as a beautiful photoshoot background for a magazine.

The train slows and stops for the fourth time.

"This is us," Julian says, turning to me and smiling. He extends his hand out again for me to exit in front of him.

The majority of the train empties here and Julian leads me across the tracks to the other side. We walk down a small road to the giant entrance of the Pompeii I heard about when I was a kid in school. Yes, this part of history was quickly covered. We stand in line for tickets and soon, are walking down the trail towards a history of devastation.

We meander to the right and see giant sculptures in the middle of an open square; at one end is a large building with amazing columns adorning the front. All of the structures still standing are part of what used to be a mind-blowing, intricately built city. Just the remnants alone are breathtaking and we take turns snapping pictures for each other; the contrast of our modern selves standing in front of ancient history.

Pompeii is a maze and I'm happy to have Julian here to explore it with. My eyes are filled with the preserved paintings on walls, stairs that now lead to nowhere, leaving me to wonder what used to be at the other end. I'm happily chatting with Julian and skipping over broken stones in the warm sunbeams. Somewhere between the beautiful square garden, an old well seen through a hole in the broken, ancient walls and a cherub fountain... he takes my hand in his.

"Come this way," he says, quickly turning a corner.

It's a small area that has no other tourists. I turn to mention how nice it is to see a place with no one else in it, when I'm cut short. He pulls me gently against his body, his green eyes mesmerizing.

"Can I kiss you, Mila?"

Butterflies are back to occupying my stomach and electricity shoots through my body, to the top of my head as I nod.

"Yes."

His lips are soft. His kiss; slow and long. Our lips part and tongues touch. He tastes sweet and our kiss is deepened. I feel his strong hands tighten around my arms and pull me closer into his body, making me let out a small squeak. I feel his mouth smile. I slide my hands down his chest, around to his back, pressing my firm breasts into him. The electricity is emitting from the both of us now. His hand leaves my arm and traverses up my neck. He takes a fistfull of my long brown hair and slowly tilts my head back, his kiss now even deeper and I'm addicted.

More passionate and frantic, my hands grab at his shirt to feel his skin. He holds me tight against the front of his hard, muscular body with his arm around my back and I can feel him growing against my thigh.

Footsteps and voices echo from around the corner and Julian reluctantly pulls away. I straighten his shirt while he readjusts mine and smooths my hair from my face. Our eyes meet. We can't help it and grin and laugh.

"Oh my…," I say as his hand rests on my lower back, as he escorts me down the path past other buildings with iron gates. "That was… very nice."

He smiles. "Yes Mila, it was very, very nice. The longer I'm around you… you have me so excited I couldn't wait any longer, I had to feel you."

"And… did you like finding out?"

"Mmmm so much. You feel better than I had even imagined." His hand lightly runs up my spine and I get goosebumps even with the sun blazing down on us. "And I had imagined quite a lot." His sly smile is back.

We continue our exploration of Pompeii. Every chance we get now, every empty corner or quiet pathway; our lips are pressed together. Our hands never leave the other's body, somewhere always touching; exploring each other.

"I think I found the bathroom," Julian says an hour later. "Wait for me?" He smiles sarcastically.

"I guess you'll have to see if I'm still here when you come out." My smile matches his.

A quick peck on my lips and he walks away, through a small doorway and out of the sunlight.

I wander a short distance, take a long breath in and look up to the sky. I close my eyes and let the sun warm my face, while I listen to birds chirping, a faint rustle of leaves in the slight breeze and the low roar of visitors. My purse vibrates, abruptly bringing me out of my serenity. I dig into my purse and find my phone.

Angelo: Hi baby. How are you today? What are you doing?

Angelo: Training is boring. Wish I was with you wherever you are.

I'm in Pompeii right now. Looking at history.

Angelo: How is it? Have you seen the naughty things that are all over?

What naughty things?

Angelo: There are carvings of men's genitalia all over Pompeii. Lol

Really?! That's wild! I will look for them.

Angelo: Let me know when you are back home and I will try to come see you tonight.

Okay. I have to go for now.

Angelo: Okay bella. Have fun.

Thank you. You too. Ahah!

"I'm relieved to see you're still here."

A warm breath whispers on my neck. Julian's pillow lips kiss my exposed shoulder and I stand still, under the one tree I had found. He moves my hair to the side and kisses the bottom of my neck, working his way up slowly to behind my ear. I turn and meet his lips with mine. Every part of me wants him so bad.

I pull myself away, making sure to lightly brush my hand across the front of his pants as I go. "Let's see some more," I say smiling.

"You want to see more of...?" Julian's eyebrows shoot upwards and his eyes dart to the bulge straining against the front of his pants.

"Ahaha! No! Well... yes, but I meant some more of Pompeii."

He chuckles. "Ah okay, yes let's go explore Pompeii my sexy Mila." He untucks his shirt and playfully smacks my butt to make me move.

We maneuver through the sea of people from around the world, laugh at each other's stories and stop for random pictures of the ancient city. Across a small wooden walkway, we come to one of the sites of bodies.

"It's interesting how this happened," I say, looking through the tall plastic walls surrounding the plaster-preserved, ash bodies of men, women and children. I hesitate. "But I can't look anymore."

I avert my gaze to look down at my feet. My feet that are standing in the same place these poor people died. This is making me so sad. How horrified and completely helpless must the mothers and fathers have felt, wanting only to protect their children. I instantly feel anxious that I left my kids so far away from me. I have to walk away.

After another half an hour of getting lost together, we're famished. We make our way out of the maze of astonishing stone walls and walk down the street towards the train station where we find a plethora of food vendors. We decide to look for an indoor restaurant.

At a corner table for two, our food arrives quick. Julian had ordered pasta with shrimp and I ordered a caprese salad. He looks at my salad then cuts his eyes up at me.

"Haha! I know what you're thinking," I say with a laugh and lean in with my right shoulder. "I actually love this salad and want nothing *but* this salad. I'm not being a *typical woman,* ordering this just because you're here Mr. Sexy Savior."

"Ahaha yes! That *is* what I was thinking." Julian gives his sly side smile. "Sexy Savior huh?"

Our meal is wonderful and filling, as is our conversation and company. The afternoon expires quickly and it becomes time to meet the train back. Julian insists on paying for lunch and I kiss his lips with a "thank you" on our way out.

"Mila, I wasn't expecting to enjoy this trip to Pompeii as much as I did," he says, takes my hand, holds it up to his lips and gently kisses the back. "It's definitely because of you."

A warm rush flows from his kiss, through my body and I feel my cheeks flush. "I've had the best experience here because of you too."

"I wish I didn't have to tell you this... but I have to catch a different train. The train to Rome. I won't be going back to Sorrento with you. This vacation is a working one for me." He pauses with a held breath. "I had a free day today and stayed in Sorrento last night just to come here... to Pompeii."

My heart sinks. I had, for some unknown reason, just assumed we would both be riding back together.

"Oh, okay," I say, trying not to show the enormous amount of disappointment growing in my mind and chest. "Well, I'm glad we met." I force a happy smile and look up into his concerned green eyes. "And I'm actually really happy those boys tried to steal my wallet."

It takes him a moment, then Julian bursts out laughing. "Yes! Otherwise I might not have had the courage to come talk to you." He smiles and kisses my lips gently and meaningfully. "You are a beautiful woman, Mila."

I have heard this said to me several times now during this trip and it is still difficult for me to accept. I really don't know how to act and always automatically look down, bashfully smile and say thank you. This time is no exception. I suppose after fifteen years of never hearing these words, I don't feel like I am beautiful. It's interesting, the different types of abuse we get accustomed to and accept.

We continue our trek to the train station, holding hands and flirting back and forth with a little teasing thrown in. At the station, his train to Rome arrives shortly after we do. The reality of *the end* is now prevalent.

"Arrivederci, my Mila," Julian says, turns to me and slides his warm hands up my arms and to my shoulders.

"Arrivederci Julian," I say and kiss his soft lips. "Can I see your phone? Open it up to the contacts?"

He gives me his phone and I enter my name and phone number. "There. Now you can always say hi if you want." I smile and hand his phone back.

"Thank you, I will definitely say hello." Julian smiles and kisses me one last time. A deep embrace with a kiss I never want to end.

The train to Rome opens its doors and I watch the light green t-shirt move through the cars. Julian finds a seat next to a window close to where I'm standing and blows me a kiss. I smile and blow a kiss back as the train slowly starts moving in the opposite direction to Sorrento. My phone vibrates.

Julian: You are the best thing that has happened on this trip. I will see you again my sweet Mila.

Thank you, Julian, for everything. I can't wait to see and feel you.

I watch until the last car of the train is out of sight.

I stand on the cracked white concrete, next to the now empty train tracks and try not to feel just as empty. Something wet hits my forehead. I look up and another drop hits my cheek.

Great.

The clouds I hadn't noticed forming while Julian and I were walking to the station open up. I look behind me and see a colorful array of umbrellas belonging to the prepared and everyone else moving under the lush trees for a drier wait. I decide to join them under a tree and find an empty spot. The rain only gets more intense. The trees, unable to hold the heavy rain, start losing the water that has accumulated and it all comes down.

Ugh. When is this train coming? My shirt is soaked, my hair is plastered in messy strands to my face and neck and I'm cold. I look and feel like an abandoned pet once again. Twenty minutes later, the rain finally subsides. Everyone under the trees moves closer to the tracks, the umbrellas close and all of the people waiting move to the edge. I follow suit, trying to smooth my hair back into place as I wait by the tracks too.

The train is a lovely sight as it pulls into the station and stops a few feet in front of us. I find a seat and finally exhale. I didn't realize I hadn't really been breathing. I look around the car and make eye contact with an older Italian woman that has apparently been staring at me. She eyes me up and down with a disgusted look on her face. I turn and look back in front of me. Yes, yes lady… I was not smart enough to buy an umbrella or get out of the rain. How can a day change from amazing to: *"oh my god, I just want to be in bed with the covers over my head"*, in such a short time?

The ride back to Sorrento is solemn. I stare out of the window and think about my time with Julian. With everything outside a blur; I focus only on what's in my head and not what my eyes are seeing. Why was something, someone, so wonderful handed to me, just to have it taken away so fast?

By the end of the line, I've decided to appreciate the unexpected connection I had with Julian. The sweet kisses and the best visit to Pompeii I could have ever asked for. Yes, I think I can feel good about this... if I try hard enough.

13

Chapter 13

The hot water is therapeutic as it cascades down my cold body. It warms every inch as I lean forward in the shower and feel the wet heat on my face. I've been thinking about Julian since I watched him leave Pompeii. I turn and bend my head back. The water hits the top, drenches my hair and descends down my face, my back, my breasts... taking with it the rest of my thoughts of him. I have to learn to leave feelings where they were last felt.

Happy to be back in my cute little apartment, I pad to the living room with bare feet and a towel wrapped around my hair. I plug my phone in to charge, turn on my music and "Hymn for the Weekend" comes on first. Perfect. This song always puts me in the right mood.

In black slacks, strappy black skinny heels and a long-sleeved, white button up dress shirt with a black lace bra peeking through, I'm ready for dinner. I am eating out again by myself and decide to wear my glasses instead of contacts. The naughty librarian look.

My phone dings.

Angelo: Beautiful how are you tonight? Where are you?

Hmm *beautiful*. I guess he's still in a good mood, but seems to have forgotten he said he may see me tonight.

I'm back at the apartment. Just ready now to go out to dinner.

Angelo: You are on a date tonight?

Nope. Going out alone... again.

Angelo: Oh, that's good.

No actually it's not. You can't come see me? Have dinner with me?

Angelo: No. I can't tonight. I'm not in the mood.

My eyes roll and I throw my phone back onto the couch. Now where is that lipstick I had earlier this morning? I hear my phone ding, ding again, then ding once more before my curiosity gets the best of me.

Angelo: I have a friend that would like to meet you.

Angelo: You don't have to eat alone.

Angelo: Hello? Mila don't be like this.

Ugh. I want to ignore him so bad. But... I could have some company tonight. Out in Italy with someone is so much better than out in Italy alone right now.

I'm here. Who is this friend of yours?

Angelo: Giovanni is his name. He is a good friend but I am the only one to share.

Share? What have you told him about me? What is he expecting?

Angelo: Don't worry, you don't have to do anything with him. It would be nice - but it's up to you.

So, what does he know?

Angelo: He knows only that you are a naughty woman.

And... what else?

Angelo: I told him how sensual you are. He's excited to see for himself. He doesn't believe.

Angelo: It would be nice. He is nice. You would have a good time. Maybe you could just show him a little bit.

Not eating alone sounds fantastic. I really want to say no. But once again, I feel I need to keep an open mind. And this is just too easy. I make a decision and write back.

I will go meet him. But only because I don't want to eat alone tonight. I'm not promising anything else.

Angelo: Okay, okay that's good. Go have a good time. He is a good guy I promise. I would not have you meet anyone that is not.

Okay. I trust you. Where do I go?

Angelo: The restaurant Sirena. It's across from Centauro restaurant that you know.

Okay yes, I do know which one. When do we meet?

Angelo: Here is his picture. He will be there in thirty minutes waiting for you. Are you dressed?

In the long mirror, I take a quick picture and send it to Angelo. Just as it sends, a picture of Giovanni comes through. Hmm, he's nice looking. Handsome in fact. Nice light brown eyes and a kind look, but with a deeper hint of knowing something you don't. He's also in good shape; I can't be mad about that. The picture is of him sitting on a fancy beige couch with his shirt on his knee instead of his body. A very touchable chest. Not so sure anymore that I don't want to show him what I'm capable of. There's still a lot of things for me to learn and he looks like he could possibly teach me something new.

Oh Mila, I scold myself, you really need to slow the hell down. I shake the naughty thoughts from my head... well... at least shake them to the back of my mind.

Angelo: Oh si bella. Very good! You are a naughty secretary! I sent this picture to Giovanni. He is excited to meet you.

Okay. I am grabbing my purse and keys. I'm heading to meet your friend.

Angelo: Yes, go. Have a good time and tell me how he is after. He says he is the best. I trust what you think, so tell me as soon as he leaves.

I told you I'm not trying to be naughty tonight. I probably won't find out anything.

Angelo: Whatever you decide. But just keep an open mind. For me.

Okay. You have a good night too.

My heels click on the cobblestones and the wafting culinary scents of the now familiar side street restaurants all smell so delicious. No matter if you just ate, you'll want to stop and eat more.

A slight, warm breeze and a smile on my face, I notice just how happy I am to have someone to spend time with tonight. I round the last corner from the little street and see the restaurant I'm meeting Giovanni at. My stomach is immediately in knots. My shyness is back, now that I'm so close to meeting a complete stranger, with who knows what kind of thoughts in his head. I don't think I want to know all that Angelo has told him.

At a small table outside of the half walls of the restaurant Sirena, I see a man sitting alone. He looks relaxed and I believe it's who I've come to meet. I can do this. My walk feels more uneven the closer I get and I'm concentrating on not tripping on these cobblestones. Why did I wear skinny heels?

The man suddenly turns and looks in my direction, stands and smiles. "Mila?"

"Yes. Hi. Giovanni?" I smile back, take my last few steps to close the gap between us and awkwardly extend my hand.

His smile stretches across his face. He bypasses my outreached hand, holds the upper parts of my arms and kisses my left cheek then my right. I really need to get used to this greeting and know this is how it's done every time, with everyone.

"Please..." he says, steps to the side and pulls out the chair next to his.

"Thank you." Nervous and with a smile pasted on my face, I sit.

Giovanni joins me, still with a megawatt grin. "Would you like something to drink? Beer? Wine? I think Angelo said you enjoy wine?"

"Yes. Wine would be lovely thank you." He has the best smile ever.

"Okay perfect. Red or white?"

"I just started drinking wine about six months ago. I don't know much about what I like yet." I smile and notice there's a platter of meat and cheese with little curled crackers. I'm so hungry.

"Is Chardonnay okay? It's a white wine."

I look back up. "Chardonnay is perfect!"

Giovanni raises his hand to get the attention of a cute young waiter. They talk in Italian and I can see by the body language he's asking for the wine. I hear the word "grazie" and the waiter walks away on a mission.

"He is a good friend of mine." Giovanni turns to me and pops a ball of cheese into his mouth. "So, I trust his judgement on wine. He promised me this wine he will bring us will be amazing. I can't wait to see if I will still be his good friend."

We laugh together and I relax a little; I didn't expect him to be funny. I've been watching Giovanni closely and notice he's very confident. He's adorable actually, always with a very sincere smile that makes his happiness infectious and has quickly put me at ease. He's also more handsome in person. Angelo was right, he *is* really nice. I can't help but smile continuously, just happy at my decision to be here.

The waiter returns with the wine, pops the cork and pours Giovanni a small amount in a large wine glass. The swirl, a calculated inhale before a small sip and Giovanni smiles again, nodding his head. The waiter pours more for him, then a glass for me. I try it. It's smooth and mellow.

"That's very good," I say with a smile.

The waiter smiles bigger then returns to his other customers as Giovanni picks up his glass and holds it in the air.

"Cheers," I say, meeting my glass with his.

"Cheers." He smiles deviously behind his sip.

"So… will you and the waiter remain good friends?" I ask with a knowing grin as I take another drink.

"Si. Yes. This is very good wine. He did what he said, and so he shall remain my friend," Giovanni says, finishing his glass. "At least for now."

We both laugh again and he refills my glass and then his.

"So, Mila, tell me how you came to be in Italy. Angelo said you are from Hawai'i."

I put my glass down and lean back against the chair. "Yes, I am from Hawai'i and it was a very, very long flight to get here." I smile.

"Yes, I'm sure it was. How long is it? How many hours?"

"36 hours with the layovers."

"Oh, no. That sounds bad and looks like I will not be visiting Hawai'i." We both laugh and I relax even more.

"But I am here on my celebratory divorce trip." I pause and pick up my glass. "I am trying new things." I smile a little naughty and take a sip of wine. Oh my god, why did I just say that?

"Oh yes …?" Giovanni picks up his glass, places his elbows onto the table and leans in closer.

"Yes. I have been under a rock for quite some time and feel it's time to find out what I've been missing." Ugh, I just keep going.

"You are an interesting woman, Mila. I will be right back and you can tell me of all the things you would like to experience," he says as he smiles and stands. He takes a half step towards me, bends down and plants a gentle kiss on my lips.

A surprise I wasn't prepared for, yet I kiss him back. He straightens up and walks down a narrow alley at the side of the restaurant. I wonder if I will be strong enough to not sleep with him. Do I want to say no? I drink the rest of the wine in my glass and try to answer my thoughts.

"Ciao!" I hear someone nearby say.

I turn to look and see a man walking up to the table with a grin. Is he talking to me?

"Ciao, are you here alone? May I join you?" He rests his hands on the back of the empty chair at our table.

"Oh... hi. Ciao. Umm no, I'm here with a friend. Sorry, but thank you." Where were these men on the days I've had meals alone?

"I can keep you company until your friend returns?"

"Davide! Ciao! Sit, sit and talk for a moment."

Giovanni shows up with the best timing. I watch as Davide smiles and sits. I feel Giovanni's hand move under my long hair and gently massage the back of my neck.

"Mila, this is another of my good friends, Davide. Davide, this is the beautiful Mila visiting from Hawai'i." Giovanni gently squeezes the back of my neck.

"Hi," I say.

"Oh, buonasera bella Mila!" Davide stands halfway, leans in and kisses my left cheek then my right.

Giovanni sits and asks Davide if he would like some wine, but he declines and the two go in and out of speaking English and Italian as I watch and enjoy listening to them switching languages. I'm fascinated by anyone who can. Why, oh, why didn't I continue with learning French in school? At least I would have known something more than just English. The two men move to talking about another one of their friends that, apparently, is getting married soon.

"One day perhaps," says Giovanni. "How is your girl?"

Davide's eyes dart to me then back to Giovanni. "Oh, she is very good. Out with some of her girlfriends tonight, that's why I'm here."

"Excuse me."

I hear a chair scrape against the cement and turn to see Giovanni stand again.

"I have to talk with my friend once more, I'll return in a moment."

He bends down, his hand slides behind my hair, grasps the back of my head and tilts it up to meet his lips. The kiss is longer and deeper. Giovanni straightens, smiles and walks off towards the inside of the restaurant. I'm left feeling embarrassed. With Davide watching, this kiss felt like either a dog marking his territory or a show of naughtiness... like I'm open game. I grab my glass and drink the rest of the wine Giovanni had given me, then pour another.

"So, Mila," Davide starts. "You like Giovanni? Have you been out with him before?"

I swallow my sip of wine before I choke on it. "Umm, well no, tonight is the first time of us meeting. I'm friends with Angelo. I didn't want to eat alone." Damn, I think that was too much information.

Davide sits back in his chair and I think I see the glimmer of a shit-eating grin on his face.

"Oh really? I know Angelo," he says, still with that disturbing smile. "And I know Giovanni... very well in fact. We are good friends and share a lot."

Fuck.

"So, tell me, do you think I'm cute? Maybe I could come with you and Giovanni tonight."

The last of the wine I had just poured goes down my throat in a gulp; I can't believe this. Where is Giovanni? I look in the direction he had walked. He had to know how his friend is, and *no* I don't find you attractive and even less now that you've approached me in this way. I want to say all of this... so bad.

"Didn't you just say you have a girlfriend?" I reply instead and pour more wine.

"Oh... yes. She's my fiancée actually."

This time I do choke on my wine.

"Are you okay?" Davide asks, concerned, and sits up closer to the table.

151

"Y-yes. Thank you." I cough a few more times on what I inhaled. "If she's your fiancée, why would you ask to go with me and Giovanni tonight? I'm pretty sure I understand what you're asking."

"Well, I'm still unsure if I want to marry right now."

"How long have you two been together?"

"Four years now. I love her. I think I love her... she is a good woman."

"And do you two have an open relationship or are you being a bad fiancé right now? Would you be okay if she did the same thing you're trying to do right this very second?" I think I've thrown him off a bit.

"No. She thinks I am a good and honest man."

"I see," I say and lean back in my chair. The focus needed to be moved onto him.

"No, I don't think you do," Davide says, leaning in closer. "I don't do this. I am very loyal to my fiancée for the years we've been together. It's when I saw you sitting here, sweet Mila, sitting alone looking... well, looking how you look."

Instantly, I'm irritated. "So, you're telling me... it's *my* fault that you want to cheat on your good fiancée. Is that right?" I take a quick drink of my wine.

"Well, yes. Look at you." He motions with his hand in the air from my shirt to the ground then back up to my face. "You just look like sex."

"Hmm, I understand." I bite my tongue, holding back all the things I want to say right now.

"So, what do you think? Can I join you and Giovanni tonight? I promise you will not be disappointed." He smiles like he has a secret.

Fuck no! I want to scream. I was feeling confident in my choice of outfit tonight, but now I'm feeling like a piece of meat they hang here from ceilings.

"No, you cannot join us," I say dryly.

"Why not? Isn't that what you're meeting Giovanni for? I can join and give you an even more pleasurable time."

Holy shit! I can't believe how he's talking to me. My graciousness is gone.

"Do you talk to every woman this way?" I seethe. "Does this approach usually work for you?" My eyes can't help but shoot daggers.

"No bella Mila, you are special. I think you understand."

That's it. I can't sit here and let him make me feel uncomfortable anymore.

"Well, Davide, I *don't* understand and I *don't* find you attractive." I set my empty wine glass down and lean forward. "Since we're being so straightforward, I don't want you to get any more wrong impressions about me. So... you will not be joining Giovanni and myself tonight, or any other night. For you to assume the only reason I'm here meeting Giovanni is to fuck, you are the rudest man I've met here. What you need to do is go home and wait for your fiancée. Maybe even stop at a store on your way to buy her something nice just for talking to me like you have. Either that, or you should end it with her until you know what you want."

Davide's mouth opens slightly but nothing comes out. His eyes look a bit dazed at what I just said, like he's trying to process it all.

"But it's only one night."

Oh my god. A sharp inhale and I open my mouth...

"Ciao!"

I look to my left and see Giovanni saunter up to the table and sit. All smiles. He has another bottle of wine in his hand.

"Sorry it took so long, I thought we might want another," Giovanni says placing the wine on the table. "So, Davide, are you sure you don't want to have a glass?"

"Um no, grazie. I was heading to my friend's house actually, I'm sure he's there now." Davide stands, leans over and kisses my left, then right cheek. "Ciao gorgeous Mila, it was wonderful to meet you." He smiles.

"Yes, it was quite interesting meeting you," I respond.

We watch as Davide walks away, through the scattered crowds of tourists and locals, down the little street and out of sight. I'm relieved to see him go.

"Davide is very nice, yes?" Giovanni pours the last of the wine into my glass.

"I suppose he could be."

The smile leaves Giovanni's face as concern replaces it. "You didn't like him? Did something happen?"

"He wanted to come with us tonight. He was under the impression I was a guaranteed night of sex because I'm out here with you."

Giovanni's smile returns... with an extra vengeance. His head falls back and he breaks out in laughter, then steadies himself. "Aha, I see. Davide is funny. I do have a reputation among my friends, so I can see why he would think that." Giovanni stops laughing and looks at me with sincerity in his eyes. "I assure you, Mila, I am here only to meet with you. I have heard of an exotic and very nice woman from Hawai'i for months and wanted to meet you for myself. If something more happens between us, it will be your choice."

I believe him.

We finish the second bottle of delicious Chardonnay and platter of meats and cheese with fun, comfortable conversation. I'm so relaxed with Giovanni now, whether it's the wine or his personality, I'm not sure, but we decide to order a third bottle of wine and walk to my apartment.

14

Chapter 14

Giovanni also knows Lorenzo, the owner of this Airbnb. I slip off my heels and head to the kitchen for two wine glasses.

"This is nice," Giovanni states with an impressed tone as he walks to the long windows at the end of the living room. He parts the red sheer curtains and looks outside, down at the little alleyway.

"Yes, it's really cute and perfect for me," I call out while walking back into the living room. "Here, follow me and I'll give you the quick tour."

We walk the short distance to the kitchen as I point out the bathroom and bedroom on our way. Two wine glasses from the cabinet, a pop of the cork and then back to the living room.

At some point, between normal conversation of life in Hawai'i, being a single mom, his life as a travel agent and how I met Angelo, we have run out of wine.

"May I kiss you, Mila?"

Finally. I had decided I wanted to give him more of me after the second bottle of wine, but I do appreciate him being a gentleman. "Yes, Giovanni, you may."

His kiss is soft with passion. It feels so good. As he starts to pull back, I move forward and kiss him again; harder, deeper, and longer.

This kiss doesn't stop. From the couch in the living room, down the short hallway and into the bedroom as he lays me onto the bed. He finally pulls away from my lips and looks at me.

"Oh Mila, you are a very nice woman. Angelo was right." We both smile and I giggle because the way he said that sounded silly. His eyes move to the top of my shirt, where it's unbuttoned. "May I see your breasts? I have been curious all night with the tease of seeing a hint of this black lace."

His fingertips run softly over the contour of the top of my left breast, following the edge of the bra. I reach up and slowly unbutton my shirt halfway. I push the bra down and expose my right breast for him. He covers it with his warm hand, gently squeezes then leans down.

"Mmmmm." My eyes close as his warm mouth covers my nipple. I feel it harden while his tongue flicks slowly back and forth. My back arches slightly, pushing my breast against his lips. Giovanni breathes harder, wraps his hand around my breast and engulfs it. Instantly hot, my nipples are a direct line to my sex and make my whole body move. I want him. I want to feel him everywhere. He must notice my angst as he pulls my other breast free and makes love to them both.

"Oh my… God," I moan, feeling his hot breath against my skin and my breasts massaged into his mouth.

Giovanni reaches down and starts unbuttoning the rest of my shirt.

"Wait," I say breathlessly. "I have a thing with my stomach. Let me put something on for you."

He looks a little puzzled. "Okay, bella. What do you have for me?"

"Just wait one minute, you'll see." I smile. "I won't be long."

I scoot down the bed, grab something black from the closet, and quickly skip into the bathroom. In two minutes, I return to the bedroom.

"Oh… you are amazing." Giovanni moves off of the bed, meeting me halfway. He runs his hand again over my breasts, that are now partly exposed through the strips of black material. My nipples harden again. He takes my hand and turns me around so he can see the entire outfit. He stops me when my back is to him.

"Mmm. How did you get this ass?" he says, sliding his hand down the strips of cut material from the middle of my back to my ass, gently squeezing my cheeks. I feel the fabric against my skin as he moves it up, exposing my right butt cheek. He gently coaxes me to bend forward, just a little at the waist, lays the palm of his hand on my ass, rubs in a circle once, and suddenly I feel a sharp sting. It doesn't hurt... it excites me. He slaps my ass again and I let out a breath. Giovanni lifts the other side, exposing all and repeats the slaps on the left cheek. My eyes close, my head falls back. I love it. Nothing is said. I feel his hand slide between the top of my legs and his fingers lightly touch my pussy from behind.

"Oh Mila... you are very wet," he whispers in my ear.

"Yesss. That's your fault." I push my ass out towards him and his fingers slide inside of me.

In and out, he slides more of his fingers. I can hear how wet I am. It sounds and feels amazing. With his fingers deep inside of me, he grabs my shoulder with his other hand and guides me quickly to the end of the bed. He bends me over roughly and I catch myself on the bed with my hands, my feet slightly spread apart on the floor. Five more deep quick thrusts with his three fingers, then he's down on his knees behind me. He spreads me open, his wet tongue now inside, licking and sliding in, moving back and forth from the inside... to my clit and sucking. I'm going insane. I was not ready for this.

"Oooh my god. Giovanni."

"You like what I do to you, puttana?" he asks, leaving me needing him.

"Yes... please, don't stop," I moan breathlessly, my eyes closed, my brain still imagining the feeling of his hands and tongue on me... in me.

I feel my ass spread and I gasp as his whole wet tongue licks me. I can't help but lean forward, my back arching, pushing upwards and into his tongue.

"Ahhhh," I breath out loud, the tip of his tongue penetrating me. I am extremely relaxed from the wine; I don't care what he does. It all feels so good and I'm drenched from pleasure.

Over and over, Giovanni slides his tongue around and inside of me. I feel his fingers slowly slide in. His tongue teasing my ass and his fingers pleasuring my pussy. I'm cumming.

"Uhhhhmm...yes!" I say in a cracked voice, louder than I thought would come out. I can't catch my breath as I feel the warmth and quickening. Giovanni says nothing. He doesn't stop or slow down.

"Oh my god!" I scream and cum again.

His fingers are out quick, he stands, grabs my hips and plunges hard, deep inside of me.

"Mmmmm..." we both moan.

Hard and fast, he only comes out of me halfway each time. My pussy is clenching around his cock. My breasts bounce forward with each determined thrust and he reaches up to touch them. Faster and harder, I can't help but make a noise each time he finds my end. I can feel he's close to finishing and I cum again.

"Oh, fuck. Yessss..." I cry out in ecstasy. Giovanni shoves in as far as he can then pulls out quick. He rips off his condom and I feel his hot cum cover my ass.

I collapse on the bed, my body still feeling the aftereffects of passion. Giovanni walks into the bathroom. I hear the water run and then he returns, falling onto the bed next to me. The wet towel he brought from the bathroom is warm on my skin as he cleans me up. He lies down with me, wraps his arm around my body and kisses my head. I turn and look at him, our lips so close.

"Thank you, Mila. You are a very exciting woman," he says with a soft kiss on my lips. "But I hope you know I'm not done yet." He smiles.

"Oh, dear Giovanni, I was hoping to hear you say that." I lean closer and kiss him. Deep and passionate turns into desperate and naughty.

My body is pushed further up the bed. He's over me, his tongue dancing with mine; forcing me to crawl backwards, toward the pillows I grab and throw to the floor. With Giovanni now on his knees between my legs, spread open wide, he slides his fingers into me. My eyes close and my head falls back. It doesn't take long before he gets what he wants.

"Yes puttana, squirt. Squirt for me now," he commands.

I can't help but do as he says. My body responds to his touch. The excitement builds and I feel the release.

"Yesss puttana, yes. More. Keep cumming for me."

I do. It's so much, I can't stop. It feels so good as he's hitting the same spot inside of me over and over. With every stroke of his fingers, my entire body tingles.

"Oh...my...god," I'm finally able to say between gasps of breath. My head is spinning from the alcohol and the pleasure, my body building over and over again.

He pulls his fingers out and rubs my clit quickly back and forth. I continue to make it rain.

I have no more left to give. I'm spent. Giovanni slides on a condom and enters me, fast and deep. "You are such a sensual woman, Mila," he whispers in my ear between slow deep strokes. "I love how much you came for me, tesoro."

It feels wonderful with him inside of me. My body is tired but my want is very much awake. Giovanni makes love to me for another hour. From being on my back, taking him deep and slow, to him flipping me over and taking me from behind. Fast and wicked. When I lie on my stomach, I push my ass up, offering myself to him to do as he pleases, and he leans over my back and whispers naughty things in my ear, first in Italian and then in English. I feel him push into me, his hot breath teases my ear and his words fuck my mind... it's incredible.

"Mila, did you enjoy what we've done tonight?" Giovanni asks, moving my long hair away from my breast and cupping it in his warm hand. We've taken a break from the extreme passion and I'm appreciating the soft touches with kind kisses.

"Yes, I've loved it all, but what does 'tesoro' mean?" I say, as I watch my fingertips lightly run over his chest and down his stomach.

He inhales sharp as I near his pelvis. "It means treasure."

I smile and love how sweet that sounds.

"Tell me, what else have you done?"

"Done? Sexually?"

"Yes. Anything really kinky?" He smiles a small crooked smile.

"No. I'm just now getting out here. I don't even know what I might like to do."

He bends his head down and kisses my nipple that he's been teasing. "Have you ever had a golden shower?"

I *do* know what that one is. "No, I haven't."

"Do you know what it is?" he asks, slowly sucking and licking my nipple, then does the same to the other one.

My back arches a little, my breast pushes against his soft lips. "Yesss," I whisper. "I do know what that is, but I've never thought of doing it."

"Will you tonight, with me?" Giovanni lifts his mouth off from my breast.

Hmm. Do I want to go that far? That deviant? Well, to me it's deviant, but to others I'm sure it's low on the scale of things that could be done. But I AM pretty drunk and what the hell, I'm here to try new things... right?

"Yes. Yes, I will do this with you," I say before I think too hard and change my mind.

"Great!" Giovanni grabs my hand and leads me off of the bed and into the bathroom. "We will go in here," he says, pulling back the shower curtain. "That way it won't be a big mess to clean up." He turns to me and smiles.

"Ah yes, this is a good place. I don't think Lorenzo would appreciate if we did this anywhere else." We both laugh, but mine is a bit nervous. We better hurry and get to it before my mind changes.

Giovanni bends a little and slips my left nipple back into his mouth. His right-hand slides between my legs and I feel my clit stimulated. He pushes one, then two fingers inside of me, I gasp and my eyes close. His mouth, off of my breast and onto my lips, our tongues touch and now I'm desperate. Desperate to do anything naughty. I step into the little shower and turn to face him. Giovanni steps in and he's already half hard.

"Kneel down," he commands gently.

I kneel down facing the shower wall and turn my head to look back up at him. He's standing with his feet close, on either side of my bum.

"Close your eyes."

I close them. It's quiet. Then I feel wet, very warm wet on my face. It's surreal. I'm inside my own head; it's interesting. I can't see what's happening, so it's not what I expected. I expected I would feel degraded, but it's not like that. I'm mostly surprised at how warm it is and with my eyes closed, it's just like warm water. I feel the warmth on the top of my head, penetrate through my hair, on my shoulder and then on my back and breasts; hitting in-between the straps of my naughty outfit. I feel the warmth back to my face and then... it's done.

"Keep your eyes closed," he instructs.

With my eyes still closed, I turn and feel for his cock. I'm turned on and want him in my mouth. I want to feel him grow because of me. I wrap my hand around it, slide him into my mouth and instantly he grows. I slide him in deeper and anxiously move my mouth forward and back, making him fill and stretch my mouth.

"Oh Mila."

Giovanni turns on the shower, pulls me up by my hands and wipes my face with a washcloth. My eyes open to see the want in his. He spins me around by my shoulders, pushes me up against the shower wall, slides on a condom and plunges into me. Yessss, this is what I wanted.

After another quick but naughty session, we wash each other's bodies; with me finally taking off my outfit.

"I love this outfit," Giovanni says and hangs it on the curtain rod. "I have never seen anything like this."

"Thank you." I smile. "It's one of my favorites too."

"Thank *you*," he says turning me around and looking directly into my eyes. "You were amazing. Really, you have never done that before? Because you did everything just perfect."

I smile again. "Yes Giovanni, I'm definitely sure I have never had a golden shower before now." What a strange thing to be complimented on doing well. And even stranger; to be proud of such a compliment.

We finish our shower rather quick and it's a little after four in the morning... but we're both hungry. Giovanni offers to take me to one of the only places open at this ungodly hour, so we leave my apartment and walk ten minutes in I don't know which direction to his car. It's not too far of a drive after we find the car and we park against the curb, in front of a bakery. The smell of freshly baked pastries, chocolate, cream and coffee slams into my senses the second I walk through the doors. Three men in uniform turn around in unison to look at us, take a long glance, then turn back to continue their conversation with the man behind the counter.

"What would you like?" Giovanni asks me.

"I'm not sure, they all look so delicious. Could you just get me what you decide to have?"

"Of course." He walks between the men and orders for us.

Giovanni escorts me outside to a table with two chairs on the sidewalk in front of the store.

"See the man there?" He nods as we both sit. "The one talking to himself at the other table?"

I turn to my right and see a man who looks like he's in his early thirties. And yes, he's having a long conversation with just himself… out loud.

"Yes, I see him. Is he okay?"

"He was a normal kid before, you know. One day, he found out that his mother is a whore and he truly lost his mind."

"Oh my god, that's terrible."

"Yes, it is. You see, mothers here in Italy are everything, especially to sons. When he found out about his mom and that everyone already knew, his mind went. He was devastated and has never recovered."

"That's such a sad story." I turn and look once more at the man, with a new feeling of wishing for him. I hope one day he can come back from this.

"Excuse me, I'll go get our pastries." Giovanni stands and walks back into the bakery.

I look at my surroundings. The man has stopped talking to himself and is now speaking to the uniformed men that were inside the bakery. To my left, I finally notice the other cars that are parked along the curb. Police cars.

Giovanni returns and hands me a huge round pastry that smells of chocolate. "Police here in Italy eat at donut shops… just like the police in America!" I say with a laugh.

"Ha ha! Yes, they do."

We eat the pastries and talk about our lives. I love that we're really getting to know each other more; after the fact. Kind of backwards but I appreciate that he's genuinely interested in my story. Not like the American men I have met through my years, who seem interested until they have sex with you... then you really do feel bad about the whole situation.

"So why do you do this?" Giovanni says all of a sudden and very vague.

"What do you mean?" I take another messy donut bite.

"Why are you having sex here with a lot of men?"

Instantly, I'm mad. I'm mad that I have to explain myself. One of the most amazing feelings when I divorced was the realization that I don't have to explain myself to anyone. Not where I've been shopping, not why it took so long at the dentist or even why I bought myself a new pair of socks. But this question; I think I am more than going to explain.

"What makes what you do so different than what I'm doing?" I ask dryly. "If I wasn't this way, then you wouldn't have just had a great time, right?"

"Yes, but why do you need to do this?"

"Is it so strange that I have the same wants and desires as a man? I am a woman, yes, but I'm also a human just like you." I take a drink of his water and calm down a little. I look back up at him. I want him to understand. I exhale. "I was married for fifteen years. I was a loyal wife with most of those years filled with an overlord, shitty sex and trying to raise happy children the best I can. *You* do the same. *You* be loyal for fifteen years with the same person, raise children and do nothing else for yourself. Have terrible sex and never cheat... *then* come and tell me I shouldn't do whatever I want with my body. Tell me I don't deserve to have pleasure and seek out what I may enjoy in life and in men. Tell me *then*, that rules apply to me but not to you."

"I see," he says. "I apologize. You should be able to do as you wish. There is no difference, except you deserve to do what you want... even more. I never thought of it in this way and as a man, we usually do have double standards."

I'm kind of shocked he understood so quickly and I smile. "Thank you, Giovanni."

15

Chapter 15

L ots of love and missing as I wake up to messages, pictures and a video from my kids. A smile stretches across my entire face while I read my daughter's updates on the rehearsals she's doing for a local play. My son tells me very dramatically about the new Xbox game he wants. Though my heart hurts every time they ask when I'll be home, I sit up in bed and message them back. It's dinner time for them, but at least they will see it afterwards. I keep imagining how wonderful it will be to see their faces looking at Italy for the first time.

I jump out of bed, since I need to do some laundry, and remember I had seen a washer behind the bathroom door. I grab some clothes, the other dirty sheets, strip the bed, take it all into the bathroom and toss them into a pile on the floor. I close the door to access the washer, but stop. Oh no… why didn't I think about this? It's all in Italian.

"Ahaha!" Of course, it is. Silly me. "Hmmmm. I can figure this out," I mumble, turning the knob like I would at home. It looks about right and I pull on it. Nothing. I look at the other buttons, push one and pull on the main knob again. I hear the drum of the washer start turning so I quickly push the knob back in and find some laundry soap under the sink. I start it again, with all of the laundry in and smile at feeling accomplished for having done such a menial task. But I did this task in another country, in another language. Sometimes, it really is all about the little things.

Francesco: Hello my love. How are you?

I heard the ding of my phone and luckily, I'm at lunch with free Wi-Fi. Oh my… it's my very sexy, sexy in Naples… just across the bay. I'm happy to hear from him and I know we need to see each other.

Ciao lover. I'm very good, thank you. Just now having lunch out. How are you?

Francesco: I am good too but missing you. When will I get to see you? I can come to you, to Sorrento. I have my bag ready to bring.

Mmmm… his bag. He's told me of the things he has in there.

I'm not sure when. You know I'm here seeing a friend.

Francesco: Si amore. I know, but he is not your boyfriend and I only have to stay one night if you wish. I just really want to meet you in person.

Yes. I want to see you too. How about tomorrow night?

Francesco: Yes amore! I will be there tomorrow night after my work.

Okay good I will see you soon then.

Francesco: Si! I need to go back to work now but I will see you tomorrow night. Have a good day amore.

Thank you handsome! Have a good day too.

It's day six. Wednesday afternoon. I have two more nights until Angelo will finally be free. I'm so looking forward to having a nice night out with wonderful Italian food, wine and mostly, a relaxing normal time with Angelo. It's what we've been talking about and planning for over five months now. I know he told me to forget what was said before, but I have been longing to do these things. It's hard to plan for so long and not still crave his company in a restaurant; have a nice time in town, and then...

My phone dings again. I smile and wonder what else Francesco must want to say about tomorrow night.

Angelo: Good afternoon beautiful.

Oh. Angelo.

Hello sweet. How is training today?

Angelo: It is good. Boring, but only two more days after today. What are you up to?

I'm out having lunch, then I will finally look at all of the little shops for souvenirs to take home.

Angelo: Very good. You should have done that already for food.

Yes, but I found the grocery store the other day! I'm going there too after the shops.

Angelo: Brava! I have to go. The break is over. Have a fun day.

Thank you, I will.

I'm thrilled I found the grocery store... finally. Having a full kitchen in my apartment, I've been dying to cook, so I finish up with lunch and hop off of the bar area I was eating at. A brilliant and bright hotel restaurant overlooking the sea, but now it's time to explore.

My phone dings again.

Angelo: I will probably be able to come see you tonight.

Really? That would be very nice. Message me when you get home?

Angelo: Yes, I need to check on my mom first. She hasn't been feeling very well.

Oh yes, okay of course. I would love to see you though.

Angelo: I will let you know.

My day is brighter now. I would love to hang out with Angelo tonight.

The first shop I come to has an eclectic mix of toys, tourist souvenirs and Christmas ornaments. Perfect! Roaming through the cute shop, I find a tiny music box with an Italian tune written on the bottom. I crank the little handle and love the melody. This one will be for my son. I find another one I like just as much for my daughter, then a few magnets for my mom and one for myself. The next few shops have purses, scarves, men's handmade leather shoes, and one shop with large oil paintings. I find a scarf for my mom since that's what she requested I bring back for her. It's pretty with shades of brown, tan and cream. Perfect. I walk into a small shop with wooden boxes next. They have exquisite, intricate drawings on the top and sides. With several different designs and sizes, I decide on a medium size, light tan box with a drawing of the Sorrento coast. The same view I had on my very first morning in Italy. This will be for my daughter. I hope she likes it.

"Buongiorno! Come stai?" says the middle-aged man behind the cramped counter in the back corner.

"Oh, hi. Umm... Buongiorno! I'm sorry," I say embarrassed. "I don't know Italian, only English."

"No problem," he says with a smile. "I said, how are you?"

"Ah, yes, thank you. I'm very fine. I love your store. Very unique boxes."

"Grazie. Thank you. I see you found one you like the most?"

"Yes." I smile and place it on the counter.

"You are not Italian? Not from Naples perhaps?"

"No, I'm sure I'm not Italian... unfortunately. I am from Hawai'i."

"Hawai'i! Oh, that's very exotic... but you still look as if you are from Naples. With wavy hair and tanned skin. There must be very beautiful women in Hawai'i." He winks.

I feel my cheeks blush a little from the roundabout compliment. "You should travel to Hawai'i and experience it," I say smiling, but avoid directly acknowledging his comment.

"Yes, I think I will. Do you have a lot more shopping to do today?" he asks as he rings up the twenty euros for the box.

"I do. I still have a few more things to buy for my children."

"Well I'm happy you stopped in my store, and if you have any questions about Italy or where to go in Sorrento, please be sure to come back. I will be happy to help you in any way." He bags up the box carefully and hands it and the receipt to me. "Really, anything I can help with."

"Thank you... grazie. That's very kind of you and I will be back if I have any difficulties." I smile sweetly, turn and walk towards the door. I stop at the door, turn and wave goodbye. He was very nice. Actually, everyone I have met has been very nice, helpful and amazingly sweet.

A few more stores, including a cute, tiny store that sells only limoncello and I've accomplished my goal. All of the souvenirs I needed are bought, so I decide to walk down one last random little side road full of shops. There is a small group of people standing in the middle of the little street, about halfway to the other end; three men and two women, having what looks and sounds like a fun conversation. I can't understand what they are saying, but they're laughing and playfully pushing the shoulder of the man in the middle. Suddenly, his eyes meet mine and his voice gets a bit louder. Is he talking to me? Yes... he's looking right at me and now so is everyone else. Still reverting back to my shy self in times like these, I feel like my legs have become stiff and heavy; comparable to the stones I'm walking on. Again, the man in the middle says something in Italian and in my direction. Finally, I am face to face with the group. In their thirties, it looks like; the two women are very beautiful and dressed smart, in flowing pant suits with the men in colored, tight slacks and dress shirts. I smile.

"I'm sorry... I don't know Italian. I can only speak English."

"Oh yes, but you look Italian," the middle man says.

I giggle a little. "I guess I must, I have heard that I look like I'm from Naples quite a bit."

"Yes! This is where I thought you were from too! You are exquisite and I saw you from far away. Where are you from?" The rest of the group is watching me intently.

"Well, thank you. That's very sweet of you to say. I'm from Hawai'i, here for a few more days."

"Very wonderful! Hawai'i is amazing, I would love to visit there." Middle Man sweeps his hand from right to left and introduces everyone in his group. "So, bella, tell me what is your name?"

"I'm Mila. It's very nice to meet you all." I smile.

"And Mila, now you must guess my name," he says.

My mouth drops open a little. "I wouldn't know where to begin."

Everyone laughs. "I will give you a hint. It is a common Italian name."

At this point, I've decided he is the jokester of the bunch. "Mario," I say.

"No. It does not start with an M. Another hint for you. It is the same name as a famous man."

I guess a few more times; there's no way I'm going to get it.

"Bruno! My name is Bruno... like the famous singer Bruno Mars," he finally says.

There is no way *Bruno* would have ever entered my mind. His group laughs and disburses to their own shops, waving as they leave.

"Come Mila, come see my gorgeous shop," Bruno says, suddenly taking my hand and placing it in his arm to usher me there.

Sure, why the heck not. We walk into a bright and colorful shop a few feet away. It *is* gorgeous. All one-of-a kind pieces, very eclectic but stylish. One wall is covered in plum colored paisley wallpaper. The adjoining wall is white with thin black stripes and a medium sized dot of plum color that breaks up the stripes randomly. The third wall has hand painted scenes of Italy in black and white. All of the vases, statues and accents are bright, colorful pieces. A lavender blown glass bowl, a lemon-yellow vase that holds freshly cut white daisies, a deep red, abstract sculpture and a few hand drawn sketches of naked women are scattered throughout the boutique.

With my arm still in his, Bruno shows me all of his favorite pieces of women's clothing. "And here, my beauty, is what I see enhancing your brilliant curves." He pulls out a white piece of material from the center of the rack. "Now, take your time, bella Mila. I will go help this woman and be back for you," he trails off as he walks towards the door to a woman in her 50s. I didn't even hear her come in.

I pull out what Bruno had handed me. Wow. It is very pretty. A bright white dress with an oriental neck clasp, form fitting in the bodice and hips then flared in an A line just above the knees. There is a small print design on the right shoulder in red that meanders down and across the front, to the middle, then down to the left hip. As the print descends, the color slowly turns to a deep mauve at the end. Underneath the top material from above the knees, overlapping layers of white chiffon cascade down to the ankles. Just gorgeous.

"What do you think? The most stunning yes? Perfect for your lovely body." Bruno is suddenly standing behind me.

"Yes, it's perfect." I turn to look at him, then back to the dress. "But I have nowhere to wear such an amazing dress."

"Oh si, but you do."

"I do?" I ask, turn around and see the huge smile on his face. A bit of a scandalous smile, I decide.

"Yes, you come to my house tomorrow night. I am having a party and would love for you to attend."

I feel my eyes twinkle with the excitement of being invited to a party in Italy and a huge smile extends across my face. "Oh Bruno, that would be lovely." I hesitate only for a second. "Okay, I would be happy to attend."

"Perfect, my bella Mila. Here is my card. It has all of my personal information on it for you to get in touch with me. I will message you the address when you are ready to come by." Bruno extends a very monochromatic business card. I was expecting a loudly colorful card.

I buy the dress and he sweetly imparts the local discount since he still swears I'm from Naples somewhere in my family tree.

The day has been eventful and wonderful. I have food now in the refrigerator, all of my souvenirs are bought, extra wine for my expected company and an invitation to a party tomorrow. Tomorrow. Oh my god... tomorrow I'm supposed to see Francesco! I can't cancel on him again. I wonder if I can change it to tonight? Oh, but Angelo may come over tonight.

I jump up from the chair at the table in the living room, head into the kitchen and pour myself a glass of Chardonnay. Back in the living room, I plug my phone into the charger and flop my butt onto the couch. What am I going to do? I tuck my left foot underneath my right leg and stare at my phone. Okay, pros and cons. Angelo, is who I've come to Sorrento to see. I feel he needs my time when he's available. He's been frustrating but he's still my friend. Francesco, is nice and ridiculously handsome, but he did say something when I was still in Hawai'i that I just can't forget. Who actually tells someone they can't be seen in public with them because they're too old?

I'm mad all over again. I can hear Francesco say it like he's right here, standing in front of me. *"I know too many people, amore, you are too old. We can stay at the place you're renting. We will have a great time and I can bring pizza for dinner. We don't need to go out."* Okay, my blood is boiling again, just thinking about when he said that to me. He is one of the reasons I'm so concerned about my age. Sometimes age really *is* about the number because I sure as hell don't look or feel old.

Alright, I can't do it. I can't use the little time I have left for someone that won't be seen with me because *I'm too old.* I open the message app and write to Francesco.

Hi... I'm sorry, but I forgot I have another commitment tomorrow. I won't be able to see you.

I close the app and feel better about my decision. Another sip of wine, I plug my phone into the speaker, turn the music up loud and go into the bathroom.

With only a towel on after my relaxing shower, I pad around from room to room dancing with another half glass of wine. I'm loving the feeling of independence; taking control of my life has been exceptional. Granted, I don't feel a hundred percent in control, but I think I'm getting the hang of this.

My phone dings.

Francesco: Amore! Are you sure? It will only take me an hour and a half to come to you. Would another day be better?

I only have a few days left. I don't want to keep you waiting and not be able to meet.

Francesco: No amore, I will wait. Let me know when you are free even if only for a short time.

Well I'm not going to argue with him. I don't hate him, he's just not up on my scale of people to see since *'he can't be seen with me.'*

Okay, I will let you know when I am free.

Francesco: Si amore, I hope you do have time. My bag is here packed to see you.

I do want to see the contents of your bag. Okay I will message you later and let you know.

Francesco: Okay amore. I will hopefully see you. Have a good evening.

Thank you! You too.

Okay, I feel better. But now, I should find what I'll wear tonight in case Angelo comes over.

16

Chapter 16

Five-thirty p.m. and Angelo usually messages me when he's done with training. Nothing yet. I look at my phone just to make sure I didn't miss the ding. Nope, nothing.

Since I'm bored as I wait to hear from Angelo, I open a dating app set to maximum: ten miles away. I sit down comfortably on the couch with both of my knees to the side and my feet tucked underneath my butt. I'm in a tight, short, black leather skirt and a cream-colored tank top tucked only in the front, and of course, with no bra on. I'm ready to go whenever he calls. Sipping at a half glass of Chardonnay, I haphazardly swipe through the pictures of men of Italy. I'm not interested in adding any new men, I'm only window shopping when I swipe once more and then go back. The profile pops back up and I read the bio. Hmm, interesting. I think this is one of Angelo's friends he told me about. Not only did he tell me about him, he sent pictures before I got here to entice me to be with them both. Christian. He's handsome. I find the pictures Angelo had sent me. Yep... the same Christian; eight pack abs, sexy smile and what's not on the bio pictures - how well-endowed he is. One of those photos where the whole scene is very nice, but you just can't look away from a particular part. I smile.

I just can't pass this up. I press the *like* button and it matches right away; he's already *liked* me too. I wonder if he knows who I am? My phone finally dings.

Angelo: Hi. My mom is not feeling very well. I won't be able to see you tonight.

Oh. Okay.

Angelo: Don't be mad. I told you my family always comes first. You are lucky I see you at all.

I didn't say anything Angelo. I said okay.

Angelo: Yes, but I know you enough. I know you are mad.

I am disappointed. I was looking forward to having someone to have dinner with.

Angelo: I never said we were having dinner. Go out. There are lots of women who eat alone here in Italy. It is the best place to do so.

It's fine, really. I will find something.

Angelo: Yes. I will talk with you tomorrow.

Okay, good night.

And just like that, he's gone again. My phone shows it's now 7:00 p.m. I think of Francesco, but change my mind since I just told him I had plans. Also, I'm still sore about him not wanting to be seen in public with me. So now what should I do? Make dinner here? No, it's depressing just thinking about another night in the apartment by myself with all of Italy right outside of those doors. Go out by myself again? I don't really want to sit and watch everyone else with someone, having great times and conversations. I need to though... I can't stay in here.

I stand up slow, unplug my phone, grab my purse and put the house keys inside of it. I walk into the bathroom and check my makeup; it's fine. In the bedroom I find my black heels with skinny straps. If I'm going to do this, I'm going to look great doing it. As I fasten the second shoe, my phone dings with a different sound.

176

It's the dating app.

Christian: Hello beautiful how are you this evening?

I smile at the timing and sit back down on the couch for this conversation.

Hi. I'm very well thank you. Nice to meet you, but I think we have a friend in common.

I'm just going to get right to it. It's dinner time and I don't have the luxury of playing cat and mouse right now.

Christian: Oh, is that right? Who would that be?

I believe it's someone you work with.

Christian: That's very interesting, tell me more about yourself. Maybe I've heard of you.

Okay. I am from Hawaii, 42 and here for a little over a week.

Christian: From Hawaii. Yes, I believe I have heard of you. How is your time in Sorrento?

Really? You know about me? Sorrento is amazing... Italy is amazing!

Christian: I'm happy to hear you are enjoying your holiday. Yes, from Angelo. This is your friend si?

Yes! You two are good friends I understand. I believe I even have a picture of you.

I can't help myself. I have to bring up the picture and get this conversation to move along even faster.

Christian: Oh you do? Which picture? Now I'm nervous what it could be.

It's a very good picture. It does show what you have to offer.

Christian: Send it to me. I want to understand what you mean by that. Here is my number let's meet on the main messaging app. 39 333 211 5555.

I add him and send the picture right away.

Christian: Oh yes that photo! Ahaha it doesn't leave much for the imagination. But tell me, do you like it?

Yes it's a very nice photo. I was definitely interested in meeting you after seeing it.

Christian: What are your plans for tonight Mila?

I was supposed to see Angelo tonight but he said his mom is not well and needs to stay home.

Christian: Ah yes, his family has had a difficult time recently.

Yes.

Christian: I am on my way out to restaurant Sirena. Do you know where this is?

Yes, I do.

Christian: Great! If you are not busy, we can meet there tonight. I will be about 15 minutes.

Okay perfect I will see you soon.

Christian: Ciao bella see you soon.

I have someone to go out with! I grab my purse, check the straps on my shoes to make sure I had finished fastening them, I add a touch of lipstick after running into the bathroom to re-check well... everything and I'm closing the front door on my way out.

I'm becoming proficient at walking the cobblestone streets of Sorrento in skinny high heels and I feel so good about tonight. I do wish I could feel just as wonderful going out alone. Soon hopefully; baby steps.

I turn the familiar corner to the bustling opening of Sorrento square, weave in and out of the crowd and find myself face to face with Christian.

"Mila?" he asks with a sexy smile.

"Yes. Christian?" I respond without much volume. I wasn't quite ready.

"Yes, yes," he says leaning in with a kiss on my left cheek and then my right. "Come, let's find a table."

It's a very busy night all over Sorrento. We walk together to a high table with tall chairs; the only empty table the restaurant has to offer outside of the half walls. Christian pulls a chair out for me and I hop up on it as gracefully as possible. I see his eyes wander the length of my body.

"You can walk in these heels on our streets?" he asks smiling and slides onto the chair next to me.

"Yes!" I smile big. "I feel very accomplished because of it too."

"Ahaha very good! And you should feel proud, it is quite a feat." Christian pulls his wallet out from his pocket. "So, tell me Mila, what would you like to drink tonight?"

"I usually have wine, but I'm pretty tired from my long day of shopping." I smile. "I think I need a vodka and Red Bull to start with."

"Vodka Red Bull. Okay, I'll be right back. Wait for me?" He winks.

My smile hasn't gone away. "Yes, of course."

Christian walks into the restaurant, towards the bar and my attention turns to the street as usual. Watching the orchestration of so many people walking to and from the square, in and out of the circle of restaurants around the outer edge, the traffic carefully moving around the sea of people and a horse drawn carriage, it's easy to get lost in it all.

"Are you warm enough?"

I look up as Christian slides a tall, skinny glass in front of me. I take my liberties and examine his sexy, compact body as he glides onto the chair. A tight and untucked, dark blue, long sleeve dress shirt that showcases his biceps, light grey slacks that fit *just right* and black velour dress shoes. Yum.

"Yes, I am warm enough, thank you."

"We've been having a bit of wind in the evenings this month. Let me know if you get cold."

I nod my head since I'm taking a gulp of my drink. I think I'll need to stay quite awake for tonight.

"So, Mila, how long will you be visiting?"

I wipe the corner of my mouth carefully, so as to not disturb my lipstick and I readjust my naked bum on the hard, wooden seat. Why, oh, why did I wear such a short skirt?

"I will be here until Sunday night. I leave very early Monday morning from Naples."

"How will you get to Naples for your flight?" he asks, taking a sip of his whiskey on the rocks.

"Angelo is taking me."

"And have you done everything you've wanted here in Sorrento?" Christian says with a hint of a naughty vibe.

"Everything as in… sight-seeing? Food and wine tasting?" I cut my eyes to look into his as I pick up my glass for another gulp. "Or sex?"

He smiles and laughs. "Sex, my beautiful Mila. Have you done everything sexually you wanted to do?"

"No. I don't think I have."

He laughs again. "You're not sure?"

"Well, I just started having good and very different…" I hesitate. "Experiences. So honestly, I don't know everything I might want to do. These are the things Angelo was going to show me. Why I came to Sorrento, specifically."

"And has he shown you a lot?"

I pause. I need to word this right. I'm still confused, a little bit hurt and somewhat angry at the way things have been going with Angelo. It's not what I was expecting and not what I was promised. But then, I have to remember what he's going through.

"Um, not as much as I thought it would be by now, we'll just say that." I smile over the edge of my glass.

"Ah, I see. Maybe after our time out tonight, you'll let me show you something you haven't experienced yet."

Oh my… just the words I was hoping to hear. "Yes, maybe I will."

The evening has turned into late night. Spending this time with

Christian has been comfortable, fun and a god-send. Not only did I not have to spend another evening alone in Italy, but I've made a new friend. A few of Christian's friends passed through when they saw him sitting here with me; stopping to talk for a spell and find out who the visitor was. I do enjoy how curious they all are, but I'm beginning to imagine this sort of meeting is a popular pastime. I'm such a long way from the rock I've been under and living on for the last fifteen years, I'm enjoying anything I can learn tonight. And now, I'm curious to see what gems Christian can teach me.

We take the last sips of our third drink. "Mila, are you hungry? Would you like to get a bite to eat? This restaurant is about to close, but there is another place that has wonderful sandwiches."

"Yes, please. That sounds perfect."

"My car is right around the corner. We'll take that."

"Yes, that sounds perfect too," I say with a giggle. "I think after three drinks, I don't feel quite as confident on these streets in these heels."

A quick laugh and glance at my shoes; Christian agrees.

My body slides down into the black leather seat of his glossy black sports car and it feels like a warm embrace wrapping around me. The wind is instantly cut off and only the illumination of the dashboard allows me to see him slip gracefully into the driver's seat. Christian is small in stature but big in personality and looks. Handsome, suave, thoughtful, respectful, gracious... or I could just be really drunk.

Only five minutes and he's backing into a parking space, getting out, walking around the car and opening my door. I remember now why I wore such a short skirt; I feel extremely sensual in it and these high heels. And stepping out of this sexy car with the help of a gorgeous man, I mentally pat myself on the back for being here... better late than never.

The restaurant is quaint and comfortable. Almost like a part of someone's home; meat hanging from the ceiling to cure, picnic style tables and a butcher/register in the middle by the front of the restaurant. Christian doesn't hesitate and leaves me to find a seat while he orders for us. I'm feeling good about my decisions tonight. I take a seat, relax a bit and look around the room. I see a couple of Christian's friends I met earlier tonight. I smile and wave and they return the hello. I wonder if a lot of places around the world are this easy and this friendly; would I have just as fun of a time? I think I'd like to find out.

Edgy as a black and white photo blurred in just the right places, the darkness surrounds us like a sheer black curtain; still slightly seen, but feeling hidden enough that anything can happen. Christian and I are sitting close again in his car; his hand wanders and feels its way up my inner thigh as we head to my apartment. My right hand is on top of his, as it slides slowly up my leg. My left hand; wrapped around his upper arm, exploring the delicious muscles as they flex with each movement his hand makes on my leg.

At the restaurant, we sat closer and closer. His knee touching mine under the table, his hand on my thigh slowly moving up my leg, under my skirt and lightly brushing against my panties. We quickly ate our meal and left. And here we are, on our way to my place to see what he can teach me.

Through the three doors and into the apartment, Christian is more reserved than his friends. It's a nice change; I don't know what to expect. I walk into the bedroom and he follows, close behind and silent. Will I need to initiate the start of him showing me something new? I stop at the end of the bed and turn.

His hands suddenly on my shoulders, his lips on my half-opened mouth, his tongue touching mine. I melt into his hard body. I've decided I love a man who knows I want him. A man who lets me know he wants me; I don't want to ask for anything. My mind, thinking these things until it catches up with my body, feeling no gravity as he picks me up and tosses me onto the bed. His strength is shocking and instantly I'm wet. Oh, this is going to be fun.

He takes off his shirt slow; one by one, his buttons open, exposing his perfectly sculpted body. I slide my index finger into my mouth and suck it. His pants are off quick, then his designer underwear, letting his impressive cock spring free. Holy shit. Now I'm second guessing if I'm ready for this. With no more hesitation, Christian kneels on the bed, crawls on top of my body, lays me back and pins my wrists far above my head with his left hand. I feel how hard he is on my inner thigh as he slowly moves up between my legs and pushes against my wet panties. A quick, sharp tug on my hip and my panties rip, my wrists are readjusted... and tied.

"Now you be good and keep your hands above your head. I have both of mine now to do whatever I want with you." Christian sits up straight and looms above me, the dim light from the long, open windows makes him look ominous... I need him inside of me.

"Yes sir," I squeak out, squirming a little underneath his naked body.

"Good," he says, bending down, his hot breath warming the inside of my left leg as he slowly slides my skirt up to my waist, exposing everything beneath it.

Christian's tongue is soft as it glides between my lower lips, stopping at my clit and teasing with the tip. I squirm again as he leaves it, moves up my body, pulls my tank top collar down and exposes my breasts. He licks one nipple then the next. They both harden in his mouth, my pussy gets even more wet. He leaves my breasts; his hot breath slowly drifts down to the top of my skirt. He plunges two fingers deep inside of me, with his mouth and tongue back to my clit.

"Uuuhhhh... my god," I moan.

183

Christian moves his fingers faster and deeper, hooked inside of my quivering body; I begin to make it rain for him.

"Yesss " he hisses while rubbing my pussy with one hand and making me squirt forever.

I'm turned on more with my hands tied above my head, but I move them over my face to touch him.

Christian grabs my tied hands and pins them back. "Leave them here. Don't move," he says with force.

Mmmmmmm. "Yes sir."

He gives all his attention back to between my legs, making me squirt and cum over and over. He slides his skillful fingers out of me, grabs my body with one motion and flips me over onto my forearms and knees; my hands still tied together now in front of me. No words. I open my mouth and he slides his big... very big... cock inside. So naughty. So good letting him fuck my mouth this way. I can't move, can't hold his cock to make sure it doesn't go too deep. Bent over, my naked ass up, my mouth is stretched as wide as possible. And he's deep; the tip hitting the back of my throat and this makes me ache to feel him somewhere else, just as deep. Happy with the choice of drinks I had tonight... I do feel as if I have wings.

Christian unties my wrists after another hour of me learning what naughty things I like. He had pulled out of my mouth, gotten behind me after rolling on a condom and made my eyes roll into the back of my head. Filling and deep, he took control of my body. He manipulated me in different positions and plunged into me over and over; his hands held down my tied wrists while he was in-between my open legs, kissing and gently biting my neck; his hand on my throat, with me on my back, perfectly pressured for more ecstasy. He flipped me over again on my knees, my head down on the bed as he grabbed handfuls of my ass and he found my end each time. I lost count of how many times he made me cum. It really didn't matter anymore; I was happily exhausted at the end.

Christian slides off of the bed. I hear him in the bathroom and then open my eyes again to see him buttoning his shirt. He walks over with a smile, leans down and kisses my forehead.

"Goodnight, sweet Mila. I hope I showed you something new."

"Yes Christian, you did," I say through half closed eyes. "I enjoyed tonight very much. Thank you."

"Perfect. Get some rest and maybe you'd like to do this again. I still have some other tricks you may like."

Thoroughly satisfied and sprawled out on top of the covers, I smile and pass out.

17

Chapter 17

I stretch and survey my surroundings as my eyes blink open in the morning light. Oh, right… Christian. A small, naughty smile crossing my face, I notice the pillows strewn on the floor, look down and see I'm still in my clothes from last night… sans panties. Mmm yes, my panties. Definitely something to repeat. I roll over and notice my phone is stuck to my hip. With a little laugh, I unstick it and see there are messages from my kids. Sitting up quick, I read and answer them, hoping they'll see my replies before they go to bed.

It's interesting to me right now how I can switch mental states; that of being a loving, caring mom and also be true to my own needs as a woman. It's so foreign; something I've never done all of these years. I've always had the idea I didn't need or even shouldn't need to have my own desires after becoming a mom. It was easy to focus only on my kids and keep a marriage together; to tell myself that's what a *good mom* does, that no matter how unhappy the marriage is… a *good wife* stays together; makes it work. I'm sure it didn't help my womanhood any; the disdain created over the years for my ex-husband made me not even want intimacy. After years and years of never being told I'm beautiful or sexy… or touched in a sensual way; that part I think, just died. But I did it. I'm taking my life back. I can do it all. Have happy, healthy children and a happy, healthy me. Mind, body and soul.

I roll out of bed with motivation from my morning thoughts. Oh yes! And a party! Tonight, is the night of my new friend Bruno's invitation. I pull the covers and sheets off of the bed and onto the floor as I walk over to the closet. There's my stunning, new white dress. I take it out and hang it on the front of the closet door, ready for the festivities. But oh... I need shoes to match. I turn my attention back to the task at hand, grab all of the linen and add the comforter to the washer first. Note to self: Lay towels down on the bed from now on; so much easier to wash.

I feel like a pro with the washing machine, take a shower and soon, I'm walking out of the apartment into wonderful Italy. First on the agenda a bottle of wine. I read that *no one* shows up to *anyone's* house here without bringing a gift of some kind. Wine is on the top of the list, but even before that, I need something to eat.

I find a small café that has a wooden swing hanging from the ceiling in the front, where their wall to the street is all glass. The aromas in this café remind me of Giovanni, and when he took me to the bakery in the early hours after our night together. I should see how he's doing.

"Buongiorno," says the woman behind the counter.

"Buongiorno." I smile. "May I have two of these please?" I say, pointing to what look like small chocolate eclairs.

"Yes," she says. "Anything else for you?"

"No, thank you. That's perfect."

I sit near the swing with my deliciously naughty breakfast at a small, round table with two black metal chairs. My phone dings just as I fish it out of my purse.

Angelo: Hello love. How are you today? I heard you met Christian.

Hi! Yes. He is very nice.

Angelo: Why didn't you call me?

My face wrinkles up. What is he talking about?

You told me you were busy at home and couldn't see me.

Angelo: Yes. But you could have told me you were meeting with Christian. I might have been able to leave for a little bit.

Oh my god.

I'm sorry, I thought you weren't leaving your house. Next time, if it can be a possibility for you to see me, let me know.

Angelo: I don't like hearing from my friends about meeting you. I should hear from you. Marco is the only friend of mine that asked me if he could see you the other night before he went, not after.

I still don't understand. You tell me to meet with your friends because you don't have much time for me now. Then when I do, you get upset that I don't tell or ask you first.

Angelo: You should see this as we are swingers. They need to ask my permission first before coming to see you.

I bite the shit out of my pastry, put my phone face down and take a deep slow breath. Okay. So, does this mean he's crazy or more invested in me than I thought? All of these situations are foreign to me; does it mean I just don't understand this way of thinking? Is he being greedy? What the hell? How the hell *does* he think?! I pick my phone up, pause for a second and text back.

You should tell your friends this. Not so much me, I think. I don't understand what you want. I'm here to see you but you barely have time. I understand why... I just don't understand you telling me we are like swingers.

Angelo: I told you to come here to see me. I feel responsible for you and you are so needy. But you are here with me and I am allowing you to meet my friends because I cannot give you time. But you are still here because of me and they are still my friends. I'm just saying if they ask to see you, you tell them to ask me.

I cannot continue this conversation. I'm starting to feel like I was wrong to have an amazing night with Christian, even though I know I wasn't. I don't understand how Angelo expects me to act like he is my boyfriend. He's constantly reminding me I'm not his girlfriend. I'm confused and getting irritated… and I'm *needy*?!

Okay fine. If any one of your friends happen to call me again, I will tell them to call you. It doesn't matter for tonight though; I will be busy.

Angelo: Oh? Busy with who?

I was invited to a party thank you.

Angelo: Perfect. I am busy tonight anyways. It's good you will have something to do.

Yes. I need to go now.

Angelo: Okay message me later and don't forget what I said.

As I finish my pastries, I'm trying not to think about Angelo and the crazy things he just told me; but it's no use. Is it me? I keep trying to understand being back out here in the dating world after so long. Even when I was out here before, I don't remember being this confused. But then again, I have never been in these types of situations. Ugh. Fuck it. I need wine and shoes.

I make my way back to the apartment loaded down with shopping bags. I close the door with my butt and drop the bags on the couch to look at my treasures: a new white lace bra, a bottle of Chardonnay and a pair of gorgeous, mauve colored high heels. A bit of a hiccup with the sales lady at the shoe store though. Note to self: just try what's available, you never know what might work. A 36 in EU shoe size *will* fit a U.S. size seven. No matter what the internet says. But they are divine; slim, pointy toe, a skinny, very high heel and two thin straps that fasten around the ankle. I'm still not sure if I'm going to wear a bra with the new dress. You can just never have too many pretty lace bras so I bought it anyway. I take my findings to the bedroom, hang the washed comforter over the shutters to dry in the sun and breeze, then take a shower.

I step into the hot water. What the hell is wrong with Angelo?

I shampoo my hair. Swingers?!

I rinse my hair and apply conditioner. And I'm needy, huh?!

I rinse out the conditioner and lather my body with soap. Maybe I wouldn't be so needy if someone hadn't promised me so much.

I shave all of my *parts* and decide to be excited about the party instead of angry and confused... to hell with Angelo tonight.

Oh. Wow.

As I stand in front of the long mirror, I love what I see. Bruno was right; that sneaky devil. This dress of his is perfect, like it was made for my body and I feel amazing in it. I didn't want the outline of the bra showing through the material so I'm going without. The dress is not too tight or too loose; it's perfect. The shoes I bought look incredible with this dress and I just happened to bring lipstick that matches. I grab my phone, find Bruno's card and message him.

With only my new heels and matching mauve-colored panties on, I'm clicking around the apartment getting used to walking with the extra height. I don't want to mess up the dress so I took it off while I get everything else together, which was smart, because my phone dings and I click quick into the living room to see who it is.

Bruno: Ciao Bella! So happy you're coming. Here is the address. I am over the moon with excitement to see your amazing body showcase my dress tonight! We will begin at 20:00 but please come whenever you are ready.

Thank you, Bruno. I can't wait for you to see the dress... I'm in love. See you soon!

It's 8:30 p.m. Or rather, it's 20:30. I've always sucked at *military time*. Although, just like using the metric system, this is how the rest of the world tells time normally. So many things are coming to light on this trip. It's true what they say about travel being an eye-opening experience, and I'm soaking it all up like a sponge.

I decided to take my time getting ready, assuming parties really get stated an hour or so after the posted time, but now my taxi is here. Not bad really. I was only standing on the corner of the street for about ten minutes and I definitely wasn't bored while I was waiting. A couple of gentlemen stopped to talk and invite me to dinner, which of course, keeps making me smile. I've come to the conclusion, if you need a boost of self-esteem… take a trip to Italy. Several women even commented on my outfit, so I can't wait to see what Bruno thinks.

I slide into the back of the taxi, show the driver the address (it's easier to show him since I'll destroy the language and get nowhere fast) and I sit back to watch Italy pass by through the windows. Satisfaction blankets my entire body. The power of wearing exactly the right outfit, mixed with the realization… again, that I'm out in the world making connections and finding my way through a new life. I'm pushing my own boundaries and learning on the go. I wonder what else will come my way before I leave here.

"Are you sure this is the right place?" I ask the taxi driver.

"Si. It is the address on your phone."

"Okay, thank you."

I pay him the fare plus a tip and hesitantly exit the cab. It took about half an hour to drive to this location. I noticed during the drive that we went out of town and to a higher elevation. And there's not much in the way of houses or stores where he's let me out. My happy feelings go with the taxi as he speeds off, leaving me in the dimly lit and loudly empty street. Why didn't I tell anyone where I would be?!

"Wow, Mila what the hell?" I mumble. I do so good... then do some stupid shit.

I don't even know Bruno... really. Ugh, the trusting. The taking everyone at face value habit I have; it has never served me well. I don't even know why I haven't learned this yet.

I take a deep breath, clutch my small purse tight under my arm, readjust the thin handles of the bag holding the bottle of wine and grasp my phone in my hand even tighter. I look all the way to the top of the castle in front of me. Yep, an actual castle. I can't imagine Bruno really lives here, so I pull up Angelo for a quick dial. The surrounding darkness is starting to suffocate me and I can't make it up the long, wide walkway quick enough. Finally, I've reached the end and now I'm in front of two huge wooden doors; do I knock? Do I try to go in?

"Buonasera. Come ti posso aiutare?"

A not smiling man emerges from the dark corner of the massive stone wall and the door, in a black three-piece suit and a black shirt. He has broad shoulders and is very... very tall.

I look up at him. "I'm sorry, umm... I only know English."

"Good evening," he says with no change of expression. "How can I help you?"

"I was given this address... I'm looking for a party... I was invited by, uh - Bruno?" Great job, Mila. Way to sound confident.

"Your name please."

"Mila. My name is Mila."

The tall disconcerting man smiles. "Yes Mila, welcome. Bruno has been expecting you. Please, come with me."

Not even knowing I was holding my breath, I exhale and let out a nervous laugh. "Thank you."

He opens the two large doors and escorts me into the vast foyer of the castle. *A castle.* My mind is short circuiting and tries to grasp going from a small island in the middle of the ocean, to being invited to an exclusive party... in a *for real* castle. Is this a normal occurrence here? Should I not have my mind blown right now as I ascend the wide staircase? Wide enough to drive two cars up side by side and with a chandelier hanging high above us, being its exceptionally splendid self, sparkling in its own light.

I'm still impressed at how tall the doorman is as I follow close behind him and soon come to another extremely tall door. Adorned in gold filigree and worn, pastel rectangle borders, he pushes it open, cutting the silence with the sounds of a party. Eclectic music, fascinating and elegantly dressed people cover almost every inch of the large room, with servers dressed just as sharp in black and white suits or skirts and ties for the women. Oh. Yes. Only black pants and white ties for the male servers, black skirts and white ties for the women servers... no shirts for either.

"Godere," the statuesque doorman says with a small, wicked smile. I give him a curious look as he bows a little, steps backwards once, turns and disappears into the crowd. What does *godere* mean?

In the middle of the sea of people, I'm not ready for this. I need to ask more questions. Why didn't I ask Bruno questions? I grab the closest glass of champagne from a sexy male server and make my way through the moving bodies in sharp suits, tight cocktail dresses, gowns, shined dress shoes and all styles of amazing high heels. At the far back wall, I find a long, glass bar and spot one open chair. Everything from the floor to the bar, the fancy chairs and columns in the middle of the enormous room are black with gold accents. Even the majority of the party guests are dressed in black. I feel more out of place than I thought I would; dressed in white, I'm like a beacon just asking for attention. I love attention, but not when I'm this far out of my comfort zone. I wish going to new places was easy for me.

Completely pushing my boundaries, but with a place to sit and survey my surroundings, I feel like I can breathe a little better now. I'm startled by a deep voice; my body jumps and I turn towards the bar.

"Buonasera. What can I get you this evening?

The bartender with perfectly coiffed hair, except for a few strands that have gotten away, and hangs lightly in front of sex-whispering, smoky grey eyes. Is everyone here ridiculously gorgeous? I adjust my body to sit facing the bar, untuck my dress from under my butt and let it fall with the slit fully exposing my legs as I cross one over the other. I fix the bag with the wine I brought on my lap and place my little purse on the glass bar top.

I look directly into the bartender's gorgeous eyes. "Sparkling rosé please."

"Perfetto. I have a wonderful rosé from northern Italy."

"That sounds lovely, thank you." I smile.

He walks to the other end of the bar and promptly returns with a pink bottle and a large wine glass.

"You wouldn't happen to know where Bruno is, would you?" I ask as I lean in and yell a bit to make it over the music.

"No, sorry. I haven't seen him since we started," he says, sliding the glass in front of me. "Where are you from, if I may ask?"

"I'm from Hawai'i, here for a few more days."

"Wow. You are very good at traveling to be invited to this party." His smile; one of curiosity.

I giggle, knowing I definitely am *not* good at traveling, but I'm flattered. "I met Bruno near his shop. He's very sweet... and I bought this dress from him." I move the tops of my hands down the length of my bodice to showcase it. "He invited me so I would have a place to wear it. Though I think I would have chosen a different outfit had I known everyone would be in black." I blush a little, but try to hide it with a quick sip of my wine.

"It is an exemplary dress but not as exemplary as the woman wearing it." He smiles with one side higher than the other and his smoky eyes dance in the compliment.

I don't know what to say.

"You have picked the perfect dress for tonight." He smiles. "Scusa."

The charming bartender pushes away from the bar and walks off to attend to the rest of the people. The wine is delicious and exactly what I needed. I turn back to the throng of over-the-top bodies to scan the room for Bruno.

Soon, I finish my rosé and another appears in front of me. The hand that pushed it to me is still holding onto the stem of the glass. I turn and come eye to eye with Bruno.

"Bruno! You found me!" I squeal and hug his neck.

"Ciao, bella Mila! I could find you in any crowd, in any place, anywhere in the world. You are one of a kind and may I say, amazing in this dress." Bruno takes my hands lightly in his and spreads my arms out to the side as he takes a step back to get a better look at the dress. "Incredible. Marvelous. Stunning."

I feel my face warm with his unfounded compliments; still not used to all of this attention. "This is a very impressive party," I say to change the subject. "Thank you for inviting me."

"Of course, my beauty." He smiles big and lets me have my arms back. "Have you seen the entertainment for the evening?"

"Uh, no I haven't."

"Come with me."

I finish the glass of rosé in two gulps, grab my purse and hand him the bag with the wine. He looks inside and smiles sweet.

"Grazie, my Mila. This is very thoughtful of you. You *are* Italian, I just know it!"

We laugh and Bruno leads me by my hand through the crowd, stopping periodically to kiss the cheeks of various partygoers. Weaving our way to the back corner of the room, we exit through another set of tall doors into a dim, red-lit room. Victorian style furniture randomly adorns the stone floor. Set up like a plush lounge, there are men and women enjoying each other's company. This room is very different to the first. Here, it is more intimate, a sensual vibe I immediately feel. He walks us through a curved stone doorway and down a short corridor that opens up to another room colored in crimson. Sensual music plays from speakers in the top four corners.

Oh.

There are plush lounge sofas here too, oversized round chairs and large ottomans spread throughout this smaller room. Adorning most of the furniture are couples, two women and one man, one man and two women, a group of mixed men and women... every combination you can imagine are touching, kissing... slowly fucking.

There is a small stage against the far wall, only about twenty feet away from us. Instantly, my mind thinks between my legs; I can't help it. The energy in this room easily engulfs me and my face becomes hot.

"Do you like?" Bruno asks with a small knowing smile.

"I do Bruno, though I wasn't expecting... *this*." I pause as I watch the *entertainment*. "I've never seen anything like it."

On the stage are four people. Two men and two women. The women have on only garters, stockings and high heels. The men... nothing at all. Slowly, in rhythm with the music, they are touching, licking and kissing. Arms, legs, breasts, cocks... all intertwined and shared. The women are kissing and licking between each other's legs, their hands on the men's bodies, mouths on their dicks. The men's hands are on the women's breasts, fingers inside their obviously wet pussies; they slide their large cocks into the women as they moan in ecstasy, their heads falling back. The red lighting makes it all the more intimate and arousing. The audience watches. The groups of lovers periodically look up from their own enjoyment. Others watch while sipping wine and soon, are slowly touching each other.

"I think you will love this, but I do have to meet with a friend soon in the other room, so I will leave you here to enjoy. I will come find you when I am done, my Mila." Bruno flags a waiter and shows me to a couch towards the front. "Come and go as you please. But there is someone I want you to meet before you go for the night."

I sit down and smile up at him. "Okay, yes, I think I will be here for a bit. Thank you, Bruno."

"Prego. I will return soon to check on you."

"Okay. Oh, wait! I have a question."

Bruno stops and turns back around with a curious smile. "Yes, bella? What is your question?"

"Right before your doorman left me in the first room, he bowed just a little and said 'godere.' What does that mean?"

His curious smile becomes bigger and turns a little wicked. "It means enjoy, but not in the traditional sense. It means more of… intense pleasure." Bruno raises one of his eyebrows. "My doorman must have liked you quite a bit, he is more the strong, silent type."

"Oh," I say, embarrassed again. "That's a good word to know."

Bruno laughs, tilting his head back as he does. "Si, bella Mila. And now you know what he meant," he says, directing my attention back to the stage.

"Ah yes." I smile and look at the naughty stage.

Bruno kisses my forehead and leaves. Shortly, the waiter returns with a bottle of the rosé I was drinking at the bar, sets up a small table on the side and pours a glass for me.

"Thank you."

"Prego amore," he says seductively.

I lean back against the couch. My right elbow rests on the soft arm as I hold my next sip of wine and watch the provocative shape of the waiter walk away. Oh, my goodness... are these men hired on how sexy and seductive they are? Is there an agency only for this type of man? If not, there should be.

He exits and I see another gorgeous man enter; a fully dressed, beautiful man. I wonder who he's here to see? Tall, dark and handsome. The epitome of what you expect in romance novels and love movies of Italy, and he's walking this way. Hmm, he must be with someone sitting close to me. I look behind my sofa to see if I can guess who it is.

"Scusi," says a deep soothing voice.

I look up to see Mr. Epitome leaning down, looking right at me.

"Um..." I squeak and clear my throat. "Sorry, yes? Can I help you?"

"I think you're the woman I'm looking for."

Holy hell. I *must* be in an Italian movie. My face heats up again as those words bounce around my head; echoing just to savor them for longer. I'm sure he can see I'm a deer in the headlights.

"You are Mila? From Hawai'i, si? Bruno told me where to find you."

"Oh, yes! Bruno. He said he had someone he wanted me to meet." I finally snap out of my stupor and smile. "Please, have a seat."

The waiter brings us another glass and Mr. Epitome and I share the rosé over conversation. I find out he is Bruno's best friend and his name is Michele. Michele is satisfying to talk to, easygoing, kind and with a quick sense of humor.

"How do you like the entertainment?" he asks me with a small smile behind his wine glass.

"I do. I'm still getting used to it... but I'm here to see and do new things, so it's perfect."

Michele's smile is like the other men's here; seductive and naughty behind his eyes. I like it though. I'm getting to know what they want... for the most part anyways and I'm learning to just take each moment as it comes.

We talk about Hawai'i and my failed marriage. He tells me all about his five-year-old son from a previous relationship. I love that he understands about being a parent and we connect deeper because of this. I don't see his outward beauty as much now as I see his marvelous soul. Periodically, we both turn and watch the entertainment. It has now changed to bondage... with one woman and three men. I watch more closely. I wonder how it would feel being up there, with everyone watching me?

"You can join in you know."

"No, I didn't know that," I respond without looking away. I study the woman. She looks perfectly submissive and in ecstasy on her knees, her hands tied behind her back. My *want* remembers when Christian had tied my wrists with my own panties. But no... I don't think I'm ready for a complete audience.

"Hmm, tempting," I say, smiling back at Michele. "But funnily enough, I'm enjoying our conversation more than the entertainment."

"Follow me," Michele says, stands and extends his hand for mine. "I want to take you somewhere."

I take his hand and he leads me out of the two red-lit rooms and up a winding stone staircase.

"Oooh my god. Michele, this is just... wow," I gush in complete awe.

He has taken me to the top of the castle, into one of the two large towers. I look out towards the sea, over Sorrento and all of the town's lights shining through the dark night. I jump out of my skin when suddenly there's a loud bang. The sky explodes in brilliant colors! It's fantastic!

"Pinch me," I say watching the fireworks.

"Ahaha, why?" Michele asks with his hand slowly inching towards my arm that's resting on the stone wall.

I move quick. "Ahh! I was joking!" I laugh. "I'm just amazed I'm here... in Italy and enjoying such a glorious night with a wonderful person. I'm really happy I came. Thank you, Michele, for showing me this."

"Mila, you're sweet, I'm happy we've become friends. And I've been meaning to tell you... this dress you're wearing is absolutely stunning!"

With a permanent grin, I spin once around with my arms bent upwards. "Thank you. It's so much fun to wear. It's one of Bruno's you know."

"Yes, I do know; he was excited to see you in it. It's all I've really heard about for the last two days." Michele makes a sour face then smiles.

"Ah it makes sense then, why he was so adamant about me meeting you. Well, I'm glad; this is a perfect night for me."

The fireworks show goes on for fifteen minutes; past Sorrento City and over the Gulf between here and Naples. Somewhere during the middle of it, Bruno pops up and the three of us talk and laugh like I've known these two men forever. Interesting how one path... one decision can change your whole life. I had been so stuck on the bad decision I made 15 years ago, I'm thankful I'm able to step back now, see and make good decisions. I am treasuring this moment... right here... right now.

Michele walks up as I dance to the music drifting up to us from the DJ down below, takes my hand and twirls me twice. My body lands softly against the front of his. He is an incredible dancer, leading perfectly, especially since I don't really dance. Smooth and graceful, we move across the top of the castle. Bruno dances around us and soon I'm dancing back and forth; from Michele to Bruno and back again. Tonight is magical and exactly what I needed.

We've danced our way down the stairs, danced to several songs in the first room with the bar and have gone through two more bottles of wine. I feel great and completely satisfied. I've met so many people tonight that, at three in the morning, I'm ready to go back to my little apartment. I kiss the two men and gush a ridiculous amount about how completely perfect they are. This was by far the best night I have had in Italy. Bruno and Michele will be traveling to Milan tomorrow. I'm not sure if I will see either one of my new friends before I leave, but we all joined each other's social media.

I think of how many fascinating men I've met. Each has taught me something; information or feelings that have made me more of a whole person... ultimately, helping me piece together who I am, who I've always been deep inside and who I want to be.

I meet my taxi driver with a permanent smile on my face that comes from replaying the night in my head. Earlier, I saw I had messages from Angelo, but I'll look at those tomorrow. For now, I look out of the window; dark and quiet are the old buildings we pass. The sporadic street lights again remind me of an old film. My perfect night in Italy.

18

Chapter 18

I roll onto my stomach and message my daughter; tell her to hug her brother for me and to kiss his face. They are out at a restaurant again with my mom and I miss them so much. I can't wait to show them the world one day. Now that I've had a small taste, I know they need to see all of this too. God, I wish I had done this in my twenties; my kids would probably have been half Italian. I laugh at my random thought and get out of bed. I start to cook up a small meal for breakfast and finally take a look at Angelo's messages from last night.

21:00 - *Angelo: Hello beautiful. I hope you're having a wonderful night. If you are free, I can see you for a couple of hours.*

22:10 - *Angelo: Hello? I am going out with Mario to Centauro bar if you want to meet us for a drink.*

22:45 - *Angelo: We are here at the bar. Message me that you're okay.*

23:50 - *Angelo: Mila. I'm getting worried. Tell me where you are and if you are ok.*

00:56 - *Angelo: I hope you are okay. You're making me very worried. We are going to the Centauro club at 1:15 come see me.*

03:00 - *Angelo: I can only hope you are okay. I miss you. I'm going home.*

That's the last message and now I feel bad for not answering him last night. I could have at least told him I was safe. I start to message back. But what the hell?! Of all nights he's available? It had to be the night I finally had my own plans.

Hi! Yes, I'm okay. I got home very late and passed out. Just saw your messages.

I've finished cooking and take my plate with a small glass of orange juice to the table in the living room. I love how the morning light bathes this room in pink through the red sheer curtains. As soon as I sit down my phone dings.

Angelo: Good morning! Great I'm glad you're at the apartment safe. I was worried about you.

Yes, I could tell, sorry I didn't write back last night. It was an interesting time.

Angelo: Well today is my final test and I'll be done with all of this training. I'll be free to go out with you.

I'm really excited! Can we do what we talked about before? Go out to a restaurant, have dinner and wine? Then maybe have naughty fun after?

Angelo: Yes, I will be done here around four thirty or five. Then I'll go home to change.

Perfect! Let me know how your test goes. Good luck!

Angelo: Thanks. And I will let you know when I'm going home. Have a good day beautiful.

Thank you... I will. Can't wait for tonight!

Finally, the day is here! I missed the first Friday because I was passed out from jet lag and crying. Ugh. How I wish I could go back and change that night. Live and learn I suppose, but I have a feeling about tonight; all of this waiting will be worth it.

My phone dings just as I finish washing my breakfast plate. I dry it, put it away and pick my phone up from the kitchen table. I smile again with the visions of what I've done on this table, then look at my messages.

Francesco: Ciao amore. How are you?

Ciao! I'm good thank you. How are you?

Francesco: Good amore good. Are you busy tonight? Maybe I can come over?

Sorry, tonight I already have dinner plans. I want to go out in Italy and see things.

Francesco: Yes, okay I understand. But you will let me know if you have any free night for me, yes?

I smile at his message. He had made me so mad and feel unbelievably bad about myself... about my age, but I do love how persistent he is; still never seems to get annoyed by me putting him off every time.

Yes. I will let you know. I leave very early Monday morning so I will have only two nights left after tonight.

Francesco: Si amore. I hope to see you before you leave. Have a good day and I will wait to hear from you.

Thank you handsome. You too.

With elation as my companion today, I explore more of Sorrento town; one eye constantly on the clock, counting down to dinner with Angelo. I stroll through the little shops on my way to the sea and buy four packets of the same seasoning I had found in Lorenzo's apartment. After I sprinkled it on my breakfast this morning, I knew I'd have to bring some home with me. The street restaurants I pass daily have the same greeters standing outside, but now they just wave, no longer trying to get me to come in since they know the Blue Charter is where I go. I stand at the top of the stairs that lead to the sea and the lookout point is still absolutely amazing. Exactly like the first day I arrived. I wonder if anyone gets tired of such a view? I take my phone out of my purse, not missing what the time is, flip the camera around and take a selfie.

"Ciao bella. Would you like me to take a picture of you?"

I turn towards the voice. Blinded by the sun, I shade my eyes with my hand and it's like deja vu. Sebastiano! The ridiculously yummy personal trainer I met in Positano is standing in front of me again. Mmmm... him and all of his glory. My goodness, this man is perfectly sculpted.

"Sebastiano!" I stretch my arms out wide. "Oh, it's so nice to see you!" We kiss each other's cheeks and he wraps his arms around my entire body with a long tight hug.

"Mila. It's wonderful to see you again," he says as he pulls away, still holding onto my shoulders and smiling like the hero in a movie.

"It's so wonderful to see you too. What brings you to Sorrento?"

"I had a small meeting here today and now another, back in Positano. Tell me, what are you doing tonight?"

"I actually have dinner plans. I've been waiting all week for this dinner with my friend here in Sorrento."

"Ah yes, I should know a woman such as yourself would have plans."

I playfully smack Sebastiano's delicious, tattooed bicep. "Stop." I smile. "I've eaten alone here many times."

"Why didn't you call me?"

My shoulders slump in exaggeration. "We never exchanged information, remember? I forgot to get your number. I remember being a bit distracted." I smile.

"Okay, yes. Here's my number now." He takes my phone, enters his number then calls it. "There. Now we can be in touch." He hands my phone back with a satisfied look.

"Perfect!" I say perking up. "Thank you and let me know when you'll be back in Sorrento, yes?"

"Yes, I have to leave here soon for the meeting in Positano, but I will be back in the next few days."

"Well, I leave very early Monday morning. I hope we can find some time before then, maybe go out for a drink or something to eat?"

"We will figure it out," he says, matter of fact, and kisses my forehead.

We walk for another fifteen minutes, talking and teasing innocently. He stops and leans on a car in St. Antonino square. I realize it's *his* car and I'm sad it means he's about to go. A kiss, a hug and he slides into the driver's seat, starts the car and backs out. He blows me one last kiss as he turns the corner and drives out of sight. As suddenly as he appeared, he's gone.

I'm close to my apartment now and decide to get a new bottle of nail polish for tonight. A burgundy, I think. I have been passing a nail salon for the last seven days, so I find it quick, buy the perfect shade and happily make my way back to the apartment. Tommaso is working at the Blue Charter tonight; we kiss cheeks and I wish him a nice night at work.

Now inside the foyer of my apartment building, I check to make sure the huge distressed door has closed and revel in the fact that I am now walking around Sorrento, knowing my way and even knowing some people. Being comfortable and having a sense of belonging are things that have been missing in my life. Today just made me really see this. My phone starts dinging; catching up with messages received while I was out of Wi-Fi range.

Angelo: Taking a little break before the test. I can't wait for this week of training to be done.

Angelo: I hope you're having a good day out in Sorrento. I better go back in the class and get this test over with.

Angelo: It will be nice to go out tonight. Celebrate.

I don't message back. It's been twenty minutes since he wrote so I know he's busy with the test, but his messages have me skipping steps up to the apartment to start getting ready for tonight. So excited!

I've only had one glass of wine while painting my nails and they're flawless. Prior to that, I took a shower, ran Tahitian coconut oil through my wet hair so it wouldn't poof out when dry, straightened the apartment and picked out an outfit. I admire my nails once more and message Angelo. He should be done with the test soon.

Hi! I hope the test is going well. I did have a nice day today, thanks.

I decide it's better with Angelo to keep it short and sweet. It's been difficult this week with him, but I think we're past all of that. Plus, the reason I came to Sorrento instead of Naples is finally happening. My phone dings.

Angelo: The test went well, I passed of course. It was easy and now I'm finally done.

Angelo: I will drive home now and get ready. I'll let you know when I'm heading that way.

Okay! I'm almost ready.

I bounce into the bedroom and slide my tanned, lotioned body into a white summer dress that's too fancy for the beach. Sleeveless, but with a high collar that wraps around the neck in a thick lace material, covering to just above my breasts. The rest of the dress is double layered chiffon with an empire waist and hangs three inches above my knees. I have on the black skinny heels with ankle straps and my very long, thin black jacket. I do love the feel of wearing this raw silk jacket since it hangs down to my ankles and moves freely in the wind. Everything is in place; my hair, makeup, outfit, the wine and the apartment. Now, just to wait for Angelo's call.

Thirty minutes to drive to his house, then he needs to get ready and another thirty minutes for him to drive to Sorrento town. It's been two hours since our last messages. I don't want to harass him... I'll wait a little bit longer.

I look at my phone again. Light up, damn it. It's been another fifteen minutes. I message him.

Hi, I'm ready whenever you are. Are you close?

Another ten minutes pass. What is taking him so long? I look at the time again and I'm about to just go to the restaurant Centauro and wait there. My phone dings.

Angelo: Hey I'm at the bar. I met someone.

What the...?! I bring the phone closer to my face. Did I read that right? I read the message again. *I met someone.*

Instantly, all of the stress and bullshit I have been suppressing about Angelo over the last week comes rushing to the fore.

So it's fuck me then? A big finger for Mila after everything.

Angelo: No babe. I just met her here at the bar.

I've been waiting for you to message me, you said you would let me know when you were near.

Angelo: I don't know why you didn't just come out by yourself. She did. She's traveling alone too and see she met me.

I can't believe this. I've waited all week to do this with you tonight. You said you would call.

Angelo: Babe, just come out and join us. It's not a date with her.

Holy fucking shit. I toss my phone onto the couch and pace back and forth in the living room. Am I overreacting? Is he right? Should I have just gone out and not thought about our plans? Who fucking does this? Is this the way twenty and thirty somethings are? Is this the way all men are? Am I supposed to be like this? Was I kidding myself, thinking we were actual friends? Am I supposed to be happy and go with the flow... just accept any situation when it arises? Should I be the bigger person and join *them* or go do my own thing? What the hell would *my own thing* be...? It's too late again to make new plans. Am I taking this too personal? Okay. Get your shit together, Mila, make a decision.

I take a deep breath; bigger person. I guess this is the way it is out here. I pick up my phone and message back.

Okay, I'm on my way.

I'm already out of the three doors and walking down the street when he responds back.

Angelo: Okay.

On the cobblestones; I'm walking with a mission. I can't get there fast enough. I'm still upset about this change of plans, but trying my damnedest to get over it. "It will be fine," I whisper as I turn the corner to the street that connects with the square. "He said it's not a date with her. I can do this," I say quietly, trying to feel better about the situation I've been thrust into.

Fifteen feet from the restaurant, I message Angelo and ask where he's sitting.

No response.

I walk up to the opening and the host of the restaurant greets me. I think he's asking how many in my party.

"Oh, I'm meeting my friend that's already here. Thank you."

"Very good. Do you know where? At the bar or table?"

I scan the tables in this outside seating area and finally spot him in the far-left corner.

"I see him there," I say pointing so the host will let me in.

"Ah, very good. I will send a waiter over shortly."

"Thank you." I'm already three steps in and have a feeling I'm going to need that waiter quick.

Not a date my ass. I'm close enough now that I see them clearly. I see the whole scene. Angelo, on the corner of a four-person square table; so close to the twenty-something-year-old dirty blonde, sharing the very same corner, that no one would ever think they are not on a date.

My heart sinks so far my stomach eats it. What have I just done to myself?

Fuck it. I can do this. I straighten my shoulders, walk up to the table and smile. The pale girl looks up in between him explaining something about the forkful of pasta she's happily about to stick into her mouth.

"Hi," I say as positive as possible, with my hands on the back of the chair across *their* table.

Angelo slowly turns his head towards me. "Hi." He looks back at the girl. "This is the one I was telling you about." The two of them look at each other so close that they're sharing the same oxygen. Both let out a little laugh.

What the…? Did they just laugh about me? I look quick to my right. Where is that waiter?

Maybe it's me. I'm just seeing things, right? I pull out the chair and ease into it. The girl turns back to me, finishing the bite of pasta, that I can't help feel she just ate off of my plate.

"So, you are from Hawai'i, yes?"

Her accent, right at this moment, is like biting into a ball of aluminum foil. I can't think of a sound that I've hated more… than hearing her voice right now.

"Yes. I'm from Hawai'i. And where are you from?" I force a smile the best I can and look around again for the waiter.

She takes another bite of pasta after a look and smile at Angelo. Angelo – sitting there, shoulders slumped slightly forward, no expression on his face except the occasional smile at his newly found *non-date*. I realize he never stood up to greet me. No hello, no kisses on the cheek.

"I'm from Sweden," she says cheerily.

Again, my entire body cringes at the sound of her voice. Why does it irritate me so much? Maybe it's the whole scenario. She is the complete opposite of me. I am not European; she is. I have brown hair; hers is dirty blonde. She is very pale with blue eyes and I have an olive complexion with brown eyes. I am dressed up and she looks like she put on her mom's oversized office outfit. Honestly, it looks like she didn't even try. Now, I'm wondering why I did. Giving a fuck doesn't seem to matter. Oh, and she's twenty something… I definitely am not. This very second, I'm feeling my age more than I have on this entire trip.

"Ah, that's nice," I reply, not knowing what else to say. I want to talk to Angelo, not this girl stealing my night. It's not even her fault really, it's the choice he made and I want to ask him why. But I'm not going to have that conversation in front of her.

I wonder, is this how European women are? How I'm supposed to be? Promises and plans broken for another and still be happy to accept and enjoy?

I look around again. Where is that waiter? I absolutely need a drink… or five.

The two of them start talking again about the food as she joyfully eats another forkful and sips the glass of wine… I just noticed they are sharing. I feel flushed… hot actually. I see little black spots floating everywhere and I'm about to lose my shit. This is not the time or place, I remind myself.

I watch as they whisper to each other, smile and giggle.

I can't. I just can't.

Slowly, I push my chair back, force a half smile and stand. They both turn to me with the same nonchalant look. I have got to go. I force a few more words out to exit with a little bit of dignity.

"You two have a wonderful evening. I'm going to go." I almost choke on the words.

I look towards Angelo for some type of reaction; anything. Tell me no, he wants me to stay… tell me he and I are going to go somewhere together… say *"go to hell, Mila!"*… say *anything*. But no. Nothing. Just the same deadpan stare. I don't even look at the girl again. I turn and walk through the restaurant full of people happily enjoying each other's company.

19

Chapter 19

P lease legs, don't fail me. I feel faint. The little black spots I've been seeing have multiplied and I'm having a hard time breathing. I've walked around the corner to one of the little connecting streets where there are only a few people. Oh god, concentrate, Mila. I don't need to pass out here in the middle of Italy. Shit, I *am* 42. Could I have a stroke right here on the sidewalk?

I'll be damned. Fighting back the tears that are trying to breach my bottom eyelids, I wipe the corners and breathe deep. Do *not* cry. And do *not* show your age and have a freaking heart attack. I roll my eyes at the terrible thought and concentrate on calming down.

There's a small warm breeze; couples and groups of friends pass by me on the street. Leaning against the front wall of a closed shop, I try to look like I'm here on purpose. I feel like they are all staring at me and honestly, I wouldn't blame them. I *am* standing alone on the half empty street all dressed up in front of nothing. I feel like a fool and turn around to face the opposite direction, open the messaging app and type to the first person I can think of.

Ciao! How are you tonight?

Immediately I get a response.

Giovanni: Ciao Mila! I'm very good thank you. How are you?

I'm fine thanks. I was wondering if you were free tonight.

Giovanni: Oh, I'm sorry bella. I'm in Napoli picking up my friend from the airport. If I were there, we would definitely go out. But unfortunately, I won't be back tonight.

Ah okay. I met your friend Christian by the way. He's very nice.

Giovanni: You did? He's with me now. I wish I had been with you two that night.

That would have been fun. Well, I'll let you go. Have a good night.

Giovanni: Yes bella Mila, you have a good night too.

Damn. Two men off of the list, now that I know Christian is with Giovanni. I need to find someone to do something with tonight. This feels terrible. I'm hurt... so naïve. Here I am, standing alone on a sidewalk in Italy with nowhere to go. I feel so stupid. The tears threaten to roll down my face as I pace back and forth. I can still see the look on Angelo's face when I left. No message from him and he didn't come after me. What happened? We had plans. Do people do this? Is it my age or because I was waiting for him to call? Where did I go wrong? Am I not supposed to take people at their word? Is it really me being naïve or him just being a dick? Fucking hell... fuck this!

Opening up the app again, I find Marco.

Hello handsome.

In two minutes, he responds.

Marco: Hello. How are you this evening?

I'm not very good actually. I was wondering if you are free tonight to see me?

Marco: What's wrong?

Your friend was supposed to see me for dinner tonight, but now he's having dinner with another girl he just met instead.

Marco: I'm sorry for him he's done that. Right now, I'm at a meeting in Pompeii. I won't be available until 1 a.m.

That's fine. I would really like to see you. I need to do something tonight.
Marco: Okay. It will take me an hour to get to your apartment. Will you still be awake?
Yes. I will be happy to see you whenever you can come.
Marco: Do you want me alone or would you like me to bring someone?
It is up to you. I just don't want to be alone tonight. I need some fun.
Marco: Okay I will see you at 2.
Okay perfect. Thank you.
Marco: You're very welcome. See you soon.

I look at my phone it's only 8:30 p.m. ... 20:30. Now what? I have a long time to wait until Marco arrives and going back to my apartment is not an option. There's no way I'm going to sleep another weekend away in Italy.

I can't believe I'm here again. The same man... again, I'm crying about! All of a sudden, my shock and self-pity shifts to anger.

Why did he say we were going out together? If he didn't want to... why did he say it?! Not a date with that girl? What is his issue? Why did he lead me on? I gave up Naples and so many men to be here... for this. He didn't look very upset about his tragedy like he has told me all week; no problems being with another woman. Why did he think it was okay to treat me this way? Ugh, it's like he slapped me in the face.

All of these thoughts are in my head as I lean against the stone building, but the last one has me stop; stop questioning everything... even stop breathing for a moment.

Slapped me in the face. What a brilliant idea.

My long black jacket flies behind me as I walk with determination. I have put so much effort into trying to be *exactly* the *friend* Angelo has wanted me to be. And where did it get me? Embarrassed and made a fool of. If it wasn't for his friends, I would not have had the type of fun I wanted on this trip. Why did he promise me so much? Why did I care so much about doing what he said?

The last five months of conversations and this last week of confusing times with Angelo are running through my head, a thought for each click of my heels on the cobblestone. I turn into the restaurant. It sounds like the greeter is trying to say something as I walk past him and beeline through the full tables of patrons.

I stop right behind the dirty blonde and watch as Angelo slowly raises his head and looks up at me. No hesitation. No more thoughts. The whole palm of my right hand connects with his left cheek. The sting on my hand isn't nearly as satisfying as the complete look of shock on his face.

"Oh my god!" The irritating voice, again, of his *non-date* rises over the sudden silence of the restaurant.

I want to pull her hair; pull her head back and tell her to shut the fuck up. That she has no idea what I have been through with this man for the last five months and a week. That she is intruding and has done nothing to deserve this meal. Yes, I am feeling entitled. I also feel lied to... deceived... betrayed. I feel like a fool. Baited just for the sick pleasure of a man wanting to control me. I've been there already... for fifteen long years. What was the point of all of this? Talk to me or don't. Playing games is unnecessary and mean. I wish I was the type of woman that could just walk away from this gracefully; not let it upset my soul. But I also wish he was the type of man that could be respectful.

I turn and walk out of the restaurant, striding with my head held high. Yes. I smile with my mission accomplished. The mission of making a point and doing something selfish for myself; I couldn't let him think how he's treating me is okay. I see this happen in movies all the time and now I know why. So dramatic. Just like my jacket right now; flying behind me as I turn the corner and disappear out of sight.

At a bar across the street from where I left Angelo and his *non-date,* I'm enjoying a glass of rosé… finally. I wonder if I would have dealt better with that whole scene if I'd had a drink first.

Still, with several hours until I see Marco, I'm finally calming down. I look out into the crowd of people ambling through the square and take another sip of my wine. The breeze is warm and perfect, my mind has stopped overthinking and the spots disappeared as soon as I confronted Angelo.

Another sip and I haphazardly watch the crowed road continuously shift.

Yes. That should put a little damper on his night. At least she should wonder why I slapped him.

The crowd shifts again and creates a hole in the sea of bodies. Oh… god… is that…?

As the crowd splits open, I see the man's arm draped behind the girl's neck while they walk in the opposite direction from me. She moves her dirty blonde hair to accommodate his being close and he turns his face to hers. He leans in and kisses her lips. Angelo.

It's like watching a train wreck. Horrific, upsetting… and I should turn away, but can't. I'm stuck, as they stop and turn towards each other. They embrace and kiss deeper and longer. My stomach turns and my mind quickly brings to the fore the night when he made it perfectly clear to me that he doesn't hold hands or kiss in public. That night was my first Friday in Italy and here I am, repeating history. My age. I know now, it really is all about my age.

His arm around her neck again, they walk on, soon lost in the crowd and finally, out of my sight.

I drink the rest of the wine in my glass and try to control the downward pull. I look up again and see Angelo's two friends, Mario and Federico. I toss money on the table to pay for my wine and quickly catch up to them.

216

"Hey! How are you?"

Both of them turn and smile. "Ciao Mila!"

"What are you doing tonight?" Mario asks.

"Hmm... well I was supposed to have dinner with your friend, but he's found a new girl to be with tonight."

"Ah okay."

"Okay?" I say a little irritated. "He made plans with me but basically stood me up."

"So?" Mario says, the air around us quickly changing. "You're not his girlfriend, are you?"

"No, I'm not his girlfriend... but..."

"Then what's the problem? He can do whatever he wants, yes?"

"I suppose... but he made plans with me. That's not right, it's not nice."

"Not nice perhaps, but the way you're acting is like he's your boyfriend. You need to find something else to do. He can do what he likes."

Mario is cold and distant. I'm feeling like a fool again; why did I think his friends would care about my side of things? Why am I even looking for validation?

"Where is he now?" Mario asks.

"He went with her that way," I say and point in the direction they were already heading.

"Okay. Have a good night, Mila," Mario responds nonchalantly.

"Okay," I say with no more emotion. "I will."

Mario and Federico turn and walk away. What was that? Mario wasn't even a shell of the person I've talked to all those times before. What the hell is going on tonight?

Quickly, I find somewhere to be. I'm not going to be left in the street, in the middle of Italy again. I walk to another restaurant bar through a small alleyway, in a stone building and down stone stairs. It's empty.

None of the bars with music have begun yet, not for another couple of hours I'm told from the singular bartender inside. I make my way back to the bar I was at when I saw Angelo in the street. At least I have no more worries that I'll see him again.

There is a table next to bushes set in big pots and it's perfect. I don't want to see anyone or be seen. I've had enough cold shoulders for the night and I just need to make it to two a.m.

The waiter brings the same rosé I was just drinking before I saw the boys. I exhale slowly, lean back against my chair and sip the wine.

"Buonasera."

"Buonasera." I hear again and ignore it.

"Buonasera… bella. Hello?"

I give in and look up to see who is being ignored. I see a man; older than thirty, looking down at me through the bushes. The bushes, I now realize, are not tall enough.

"Hello. May I join you?" the man asks.

"Umm, no I'm okay."

"Okay?!"

"What? No, not okay… I said *I'm* okay."

"Ah, okay!" The man makes a little hop, turns and walks down the length of the bushes.

Damn deceiving bushes.

"Thank you," says the man, now standing beside the chair next to me.

I notice the waiter give the scene at my table a strange look but my attention goes back to the man, now pulling out the chair. Halfway to sitting, he asks if he can.

"Is okay?"

"Uh, yeah… okay, go ahead." He's basically already sitting. Whatever.

His jacket is thick and long. A bit too warm for this August weather, I think. It reminds me of a military coat for winter and looks like it

218

hasn't been washed in some time. With his hair cut very close to his head, his clothes mismatched and his fingernails dirty, he looks like he's homeless. I stop. I'm not one to judge tonight. You know... since I've obviously been a great judge of character so far.

"How are you?" the man says.

I take a sip of wine, lean back into my chair, and slowly place the glass back onto the table. I think for a moment how to answer that.

"I'm not very good right now, but thank you for asking."

"Oh... but you are very beautiful, you shouldn't be unhappy ever."

"Thank you for the compliment," I say without much emotion.

"You are very welcome. But tell me, why are you not happy?"

I take a breath and pause... should I tell him to F off?

"Oh, well that's a long story and a lot of complaining. I'm sure you don't really want to hear about it."

"Yes. Please. I do want to hear what made a wonderful woman as yourself upset." The man readjusts himself. He lays his jacket across his lap and rests his elbows on the table. He is all ears.

"Okay then, if you really want to know..."

"Oh wait! My name is Simone." He smiles and extends his hand.

I hesitate... but what the hell, right? "Hi Simone. I'm Mila." I reach out and lightly shake his hand.

The waiter, still with the weird look on his face, asks Simone if he would like to order anything.

"No, no. I'm fine," Simone says. "So, Mila, back to why you are having a bad night."

I smile at the waiter as he turns and leaves, still with that look.

"Let's see... where to begin?" I say, turning back to the strange man at my table. "I'm on holiday. I came to Sorrento specifically because a man promised to show me things here. Tonight, he broke our plans to be with another girl and I just saw them walking away together."

I drink some more wine, feeling irritated all over again as I hear the recap.

"Ah, I see. But this is not because of you," he says. "It's because of him. Do you understand?"

I think about it. "Yes, I understand what you mean, but it *is* about me. *I* made the decision to come here, *I'm* the one that's older and should know better. I'm also the one that's sitting here getting sympathy from a stranger." I set my empty glass down and scoot it in from the edge of the table; focusing on the trail of water it's creating.

"But you are only in control of your own actions," Simone continues. He bends his head down to find my eyes. "So, what someone else does is not your fault. If your heart is in the right place then that is what you focus on, not the negative of what someone else does. Peace comes from within. When you find that, it does not matter what other people do. And remember, everyone has their own demons to fight, so as long as you are at peace with yourself and your decisions, no one can hurt you." He pauses and stares deeper into my eyes for confirmation that I understand.

I relent. "I do see what you're saying. It's right actually." I pause and with a long breath out, I relax my muscles that have been tense all night. "It's not what I was expecting you to say at all." I giggle, a bit embarrassed at the implications of my statement. "Thank you."

"You are very welcome, pretty Mila. I saw you sitting here with a mad look on your face, but you should be happy here in Sorrento," he says, moving his hand in the air to everything around us.

"Ahah! Yes. You are right again; I should be happy here in amazing Italy."

"To be angry about someone else's actions is giving them the control over you. Life is too short to not be happy. Do you not want to be happy?"

"Yes, of course I do."

"Would you like to go for a walk? Talk more? I don't really like sitting in these restaurants."

I pause again for a split second and question whether it's a good idea to leave with him. But the things he said were much more insightful than I would expect from a not well man. What could really happen? It's a small town with lots of people walking around.

"Okay, sure. Where will we walk to?" I grab my purse.

"Just come with me, I will show you the most gorgeous place to be at this time of night in Sorrento."

I pay for my wine and leave a big tip. Somehow, I feel responsible for the strange look that's still stuck on the waiter's face.

Simone and I walk and talk, which is making me feel better about tonight. I'm not thinking as much about being passed up for a younger girl; well, maybe a little, but this is a good distraction.

The street lights are giving the night a golden glow, and the breeze is still warm, as Simone tells me of the beauty of the place he's taking me. I recognize this path, though, as we pass the church, where every day I see a local man painting outside of its doors. I know where we're going.

The moon; full and hanging low, right above the Mediterranean Sea as we walk up to the scenic point. The place I've seen and loved since my first morning here. It is extraordinary. The moon is bright and reflecting off of the small, slow-moving waves, dimly illuminating the side of the cliff and all of the buildings still clinging to it.

Simone walks me to the beginning of the stairs and we stop side by side. I rest my hands on the metal rail attached to the top of the rock wall; a hint to not go any further. I lean over just a little to look down into the darkness. In the night, you cannot see the bottom, where the path down the side of the cliff ends.

I stand straight again, a sudden apprehensiveness surging through my entire body. What am I doing? I'm in the dark, next to a stranger... at the edge of a cliff!

I now realize it's different to if he was introduced to me by someone I already know. Or even to Bruno's case; someone who I met as a reputable owner of something... anything. This man saw me at my weakest, saw me distraught and suddenly showed up out of nowhere.

The waiter's look. I can remember the strange look on the waiter's face. Now I understand; it was one of concern.

Oh my god, what am I doing?

"The most beautiful place, yes?" Simone says and turns to look into my eyes.

I can't tell if he feels the change in my energy. Can he see it in my eyes? Don't panic. Play it off, Mila, slowly... calmly... get out of this. My instincts kick in. I just need to get back to the square.

I survey my surroundings and see there are two other couples here. They are spread a little too far apart from us for my comfort, but at least I'm not completely alone with him.

"Close your eyes."

"What?" I say and whip my head back to look at Simone.

"Close your eyes." His mouth turns up into a crooked smile on one side. "Do you not trust me?"

Shit. Can he tell? Easy, Mila... take it easy.

"Ah... I did just meet you. Why would I already trust you?" I force a little coy smile.

"True." Simone's smile relaxes. "Just close your eyes. What could happen?"

The way he's challenging me makes me more uncomfortable. But maybe if I do this, just this one thing, he'll be satisfied and we can leave.

"Okay then, I'll close them."

Slowly, and against the will of all of the fibers in my body, I close my eyes.

Silence.

A split second – my eyes pop open. Again, that unsafe feeling; an overwhelming panic deep inside that I would suddenly feel myself weightless, falling over this cliff.

"You don't trust me," Simone says, a step closer.

"Sorry, I'm really not a very trusting person." Lie. "But I did come out here with you. I don't even know you, yes?"

Automatically, I tense up as Simone takes another step closer. I can't control my body and I take half a step back. I turn to look behind me; the stairs are right there… one more step and I'll fall.

He stops. I watch as he takes a moment to think.

It seems as if the wind has left, and taken my breath with it.

"Okay, come," he says finally. "Let's go back."

Simone extends his hand for me to move in the direction of the square and my soul is relieved. Was I being overly freaked out? Was I overreacting?

I'm about to scold myself for dramatically thinking bad things about Simone, when, to the left of us, two teenage girls walking together catch my eye. Their reaction tells me everything.

The girls; locals, I assume, look as terrified as I felt seconds ago at the cliff. I can see the whites of their eyes even in the dim light as they look at us, then at each other. Quick whispers. They make eye contact with me and look back at Simone. Huddling closer to each other, they quickly pick up their pace and hurry around a corner… out of sight.

Shit.

Simone doesn't seem to have noticed the reaction of the young girls. Good. But I need to keep him talking. I need to make it back to the square.

"So, Simone… how long have you lived in Sorrento?"

"Oh, I've been here all my life. I know this town inside and out," he says as he turns us down a small street, different from the one we walked to get here.

"Where are we going? I do need to get back to the square. I'm meeting a friend there soon."

My mind; racing with all of the possible scenarios of walking down this dark street.

"Oh Mila, trust me. I know every street here. I like to take the paths where most people don't go." He smiles.

Shit… shit… shit.

The walk down this street is narrow and empty, save for a couple of cats that run across our path. The lights here are even more dim. The sound of my heels; loud on the uneven cobblestones, reminding me of so many scary movies. This is the time and place, the singular sound; click. Click. Click… and the dispensable character doesn't make it to the other end of the dark road.

I shake the thought from my head. I can see it! The other end of the street! I will not complain anymore about being by myself once I make it out of this.

"Thank you, Simone," I say, looking down at where I'm walking, then back up at him. "Thank you for taking the time to talk with me." I need him to feel good… appreciated even. I'm almost safe.

"Of course, I'm happy to spend time alone with such a beautiful woman."

The end of the street opens into the bright and bustling square. I exhale and am suddenly in love with being a part of the sea of people.

Just a few more feet. I urgently feel the need to break away from Simone. Right now.

"Well, this was nice. I should probably get to where I'm meeting my friend." I smile and take a step away.

"Oh. Okay, but I can come with you… help you find your friend," he says with a step towards me.

"It's fine, thank you." I smile without showing my panic. "He should be messaging me soon."

"Oh, it's another man?" Simone says with a hint of disdain.

"Just a friend. I called him after I left the other restaurant."

We've walked right to the entrance of Sirena restaurant. I feel safe now, but still, I don't want any kind of scene. A clean break is what I'm looking for. Not him following me to my apartment or even finding me again because he has some kind of grudge. This would be the perfect ending.

He pauses, with a very serious look. Then, as if a switch is flipped, Simone smiles big.

"Okay then, give me a kiss goodbye and have a lovely night."

Yes! I made it unscathed. I lean in and kiss both of his cheeks, like it's done here in Italy.

"Have a wonderful night, Simone," I say, relieved.

"No. On my lips."

"What?"

"A kiss. On my lips," he says, more demanding.

"Ahaha!" I laugh, not able to control myself any longer. "Umm no, sorry but I'm not going to kiss you."

"Just one. I helped you tonight... showed you nice things."

"Yes, you did. And I thank you very much for that. But I'm not the girl that's going to kiss a stranger." This is the first time he's heard the solid *fuck no* tone in my voice.

"Okay, yes. You are right," Simone says. His face relaxes, his body shifts as he takes a step back.

"Take care and thank you again," I say, much sweeter.

"Grazie bella. You take care too and don't worry about another's poor decisions." Simone turns and walks out into the street and disappears into the crowd.

Again, tense throughout my whole body, I look around to see if anyone noticed this awkward exchange. I don't think anyone did, but I'm quite the idiot for even going with him. I'm glad no one else knows.

Some places are *mostly* safe... but nowhere is *completely* safe. I would do well to remember that.

I walk to the closest bar where you can stand at the small building's window opening. I order a glass of Chardonnay and down it immediately. Leaning against the edge where the window is cut from the wall, I finally, completely relax. It's been an emotional day, so I order one more glass.

I finish the wine, thank the bartender and click my way back to my Italian home – jacket flying in the wind behind me.

20

Chapter 20

R ed satin and black lace lingerie... black lace garter belt with stockings pulled up my thighs... sexy black high heels... and I'm ready.

Music is playing through the little speaker connected to my phone and I have just finished the bottle of Chardonnay I started earlier tonight. Now I'm feeling sexy in my outfit and opening the next bottle of wine.

I hear my phone ding through the speaker as the music fades for it. Marco!

My heart races, or rather, frazzled nerves jump through my body as I run to see my phone. Yes, it's Marco. He's here... downstairs at the distressed door waiting and with a little reminder that I am not allowed to talk; only to obey. Yum.

Right on time at 2:00 a.m.

I throw my long, black jacket around me and quietly race down the stairs, passing the doors of my accepting neighbors.

With the huge doors in front of me, I stop to smooth out my naughty outfit, tame my hair and hold my jacket closed around me.

Slowly, I pull open the door.

The sight of Marco standing in front of me is exactly what I need. In the dark, his crazy hair glows with the backlight from the faint streetlights. Sexy but serious. Seeing him now, I'm even more excited about tonight. Movement behind the other door grabs my attention as Marco turns his head slightly, breaking our eye contact as another man appears beside him; smiling.

A surprise for me. He opted to bring someone with him and I'm dying to ask who this new handsome man is but the rule; I cannot talk. I can't help but notice the two men have similar eyes and they wear their hair in almost the same style as they enter through the threshold and join me in the foyer. My jacket slips open as I close the door behind them. A flash of red and black and Marco's eyes widen for a quick second as I grab the jacket's edge and cover up again. I look up at him with a small devilish smile and seeking his approval. He nods his head once and I walk ahead of them, up the stairs.

Halfway up the stairs, I let go of my jacket; on purpose this time. I want to tease them as they're following me; give them a glimpse of my gartered legs around each corner. We reach the top and I hold the door open for them to enter my apartment. Still without a word, I close the door, turn to face the men and slowly let my jacket drop into a pile on the floor. I love watching their eyes wander down my body.

"This is my coworker... and cousin," Marco finally says, breaking the silence. "His name is Andrea."

Ah, this is why I can see similarities. "Hello Andrea, I'm..."

Marco, quick and calculated as a leopard, is against my body. His tongue on mine. One hand yanks down the top of my lingerie; my right breast pops out and immediately, his mouth is on it.

Between gasps, my nails lightly scratching Marco's back under his shirt and my head falling to the side from the extreme sensation of my nipples being sucked and bitten... I see Andrea. He's watching Marco against me; hands roaming my body, the want in my eyes as they meet his. I love Andrea watching... watching me aroused, fondled and moans of pleasure I can't stop from escaping my throat.

My body is yearning to be penetrated; being used for their pleasure will erase the bad choices of earlier this evening which will bring me extra pleasure. I'm lost in Andrea's gaze. The electricity in the air is thick and bold.

He takes a few steps forward and touches my body. The bare skin between my stocking and garter belt tingles as he gently slides his fingers from the front to the side. He softly runs his hand up to my waist, over the lingerie... then down again, around to my bare ass cheek. He makes this his home; lingering longer, feeling all of my ass. He slides over to the other side, moving in the same pattern to feel everything. My eyes close, my head falls back; a breath escapes my mouth from the pure pleasure of two men appreciating my body.

Marco has reached up between my thighs. Slow and steady, he slides his hand further up until his fingers move between my soft lips. Further still and they slowly penetrate me; moving up until his knuckles are pushing against me. His fingers deep and moving... I moan louder.

"Shhhh." Marco covers my mouth with his other hand. One hand making me moan and the other to muffle those very noises.

His fingers slide out, his body moves away from mine. As I'm opening my eyes, his fingers return and slide deep inside me again.

My eyes; now fully open and focused. Oh, god... it's Andrea's fingers inside of me. Instantly, I'm soaked. His fingers are making so much noise as they slide in and out. His lips touch mine. His tongue is soft... then hard and deep in my mouth. I suck it. I want him to feel and imagine how much I want what's between his legs... what I can feel growing as he leans in and rubs his body against mine.

Past Andrea's shoulder, I see Marco; his pants down, his cock hard in his hand. I watch him stroke it while he watches me enjoy being finger fucked by his cousin.

Marco's tall body... his intense gaze behind gold wire-rimmed glasses... the dominance over me; I am his right now to give to whom he wants. He's here to watch me enjoy being fucked and he came to give me what I want and what I need.

Marco steps up and Andrea moves to the side while unzipping his pants. Just one look from Marco and I know what he wants. My eyes don't leave his as I slowly lower my body and kneel on the floor. I wrap my hand around his hard shaft and a little smile crosses my face; I open my mouth and slide him inside. Deep and slow, wet and passionate, I suck him. His eyes close for just a moment... I look towards Andrea. Seeing him watching me suck Marco makes the want between my legs unbearable.

All of a sudden, society's views on what I'm doing, swamp my mind. I hesitate, with a feeling of shame about to wash over me.

NO.

That society has nothing to say about my life. Where were they when I was being mistreated by my husband? Where were they when I had no self-confidence or when I was physically and emotionally ignored? Nope. Society can worry about what they do. And I will not worry about society.

The thoughts of anything other than the three of us, evaporate from my mind and I give myself fully to the night.

Marco pulls me up, spins me around and bends me over ever so slightly as I hold onto the wall. Filled and stretched and finally content as he pushes all the way inside my yearning, wet pussy.

"Ohhh my god..." I breathe out slow.

Still inside of me, Marco takes me by the hips and turns my body away from the wall to where Andrea is waiting. Without hesitation, I open wide and Andrea slides into my mouth.

My body; excited and tingling all over. All of my nerves; heightened with both men inside of me. Marco slides out; slowly and reluctantly I slide my mouth off of Andrea and Marco leads me to the couch. I sit down with my heels on the edge, my knees up and spread open slightly. I slowly rub my wet clit for their enjoyment while I watch them take off all their clothes. Mmmm, why are they so sexy?

Marco sits on the couch next to me, grabs my arms and pulls my body on top to straddle him. My knees on either side of his long, thin body as I reach behind me and hold his hard cock. I raise my body a little more above him and rub the soft head slowly back and forth between my wet lips. I can't wait anymore. Holding him still, I slowly slide down, filling myself with him once again. I exhale and my eyes close. I arch my back and my hair falls further down my back to the top of my ass as my breasts are pushed towards his face. I ride him slow and deep and he rubs and sucks my breasts. I feel Andrea close behind me.

Marco pulls my body forward against his chest as he continues sliding in and out of me. I feel pressure against my ass and Andrea's hands rubbing and squeezing all of it. More pressure… then even more. I hold my breath… the tip of Andrea slides in. I'm completely transfixed. I let out a moan and rest my forehead against Marco's shoulder as Andrea slides even deeper inside me. I feel his pelvis push up against my ass as he buries himself in me.

My mind spins with all of the sensations as Andrea slowly pulls my head back by my hair. Marco makes love to my breasts and nipples again with his mouth and hands and I scream in pure pleasure with them both moving inside of me.

Marco covers my mouth quick. I'm there… my body building faster… "Oh my god!" I let out my screams of ecstasy, muffled into his hand.

For the next two hours, the two men fuck me from the couch, over one of the chairs in the living room, to the bed and on the tile floor.

Both inside me simultaneously... one at a time with the other watching... or one inside me while I stroke and suck the other. At one point, Marco has me pleasure myself so they can watch. The only time we stop is to drink the bottle of wine I had opened before they had arrived. The night is perfectly exhausting, and is most definitely, exactly what I needed.

On the couch again, now perfectly sated, I watch as Andrea dresses. Marco zips up his own pants, walks over, leans down and kisses my forehead. I grab the front of his dress shirt, pull him to me and kiss him deep.

"Mmm, thank you Marco." My smile is huge and genuine. "Thank you for coming over tonight." I slowly release him and he smiles down at me as he straightens.

"You are very welcome, Miss Mila." His smile turns slightly wicked. "It was only right to come say goodbye to you."

I just love how naughty he is.

With the men gone, I've cleaned up the empty wine bottle, washed the glasses and straightened the couch and bed. I turn off the lights in the living room, walk into the bedroom and crawl under the sheets. They're cooled from the air conditioner and feel amazing against my freshly showered skin. I'm finally ready to sleep.

My last thoughts pat me on the back.

Good job, Mila. Finally able to take a miserable situation, a miserable night and find something... someone to help make it a tremendous experience instead. Slowly, I think I'm learning.

21

Chapter 21

S unbeams find me through the window panes. It looks like it's a gorgeous day out, so I think it should be a sea kind of morning. I roll onto my stomach, then my back... stretching my entire body and it feels so good. I lie on my pillows, look out at the beautiful Italian sky and realize that even my stretches feel amazing since I've been divorced. It doesn't seem like that would be a thing, but I've been noticing little differences like this. I suppose I'm free now; my mind is free to appreciate and enjoy life fully, even the tiniest details. It matters... exponentially... who you choose to spend your life with.

Angelo pops into my mind and a pang of guilt from last night hits me.

Fuck this! I'm sure women have slapped men for more minute reasons than being stood up for another woman and having it flaunted in their face. I'm still confused by how he thought that was okay to do. Maybe, on the other hand, I should be more confused by how I thought I meant more to him as a friend. At some point I do expect a hint of decency, as I too have feelings and I am not going to be mistreated or disrespected anymore. Being *a man* is no excuse for shitty behavior and I shouldn't have to be *the bitch*.

Okay. That's enough.

As I hop off of my mental soapbox and out of bed, I'm done thinking about this… done thinking about Angelo and, instead, get dressed for the sea.

The morning is smiling back at me as I make my way happily through the little streets, packed as usual with tourists and locals. I cruise down the path on the side of the cliff to the water's edge. The cliff looks much more inviting than it did last night. I shake my head at the memories of Simone and Angelo. I'm so grateful Marco came to save my night - and my sanity.

"Ciao bella!" I hear as I step off of the stone path and onto flat ground in front of the first restaurant I visited here.

"Ciao," I say, stopping in front of the cute, twenty-something blond I always see.

"Please, you can lay in the sun here. Free for you… you will not have to pay."

I look past his extended arm directing my attention through the restaurant. The wooden walkway does extend much further out over the sea than the free pier I usually lie on. It takes a good half hour longer, at least, for the sun to rise high enough to warm the short pier.

I think for a moment of my options when a friend of his, with a nice smile, walks up. Oh god, it seems as if they've discussed this.

"Thank you, really. Thank you for the offer, but I think I'll just go to the other one," I say with a shy smile.

"Oh, but this one is much better. We want you to come and enjoy. Free for you, we promise."

"Yes! Come relax in the sun… on the chairs. It's much better here, the sun is already shining on it," his friend says.

They are exceptionally cute this morning.

"Thank you, really. I appreciate it but I won't be here very long today. I'll see you boys later. It's very nice of you."

"Okay, we will see you later then." The blond smiles. "Enjoy your morning."

Still smiling and with a little wave, I turn and walk down the dirt path towards the short pier. It was tempting to take up their offer, but I need peace this morning. I would have only been thinking about them watching me, and I don't want any men right now. I'm here today for me. The sun and saltwater always heal my mind.

I'm early enough to find a small spot on the worn wooden planks where the sun is barely shining. I lay out my towel, take off my pareo and stick in my earbuds that are already playing the music on my phone. I turn on my cellular data in case one of the many men I've met here decides to message me. I don't want to miss an opportunity on my last two nights. I have turned it on from time to time but now it will be worth the extra money. Exhaling slow and long as I lie down, my body relaxes in the beginning warmth of the sun.

I stir and realize my phone has dinged several times; I must have dozed off, perfectly relaxed. I shade my eyes from the sun, now fully over the cliff, and look at my phone to see for what good reason I was awakened... oh, hell.

Angelo: So, I bet you're feeling bad about last night.

Angelo: I'm sure you want to apologize.

Angelo: I was going to take you on the Amalfi coast today.

Did he just write that I should be feeling bad about last night?! I read his messages again. Yep. That's what he wrote. He's got to be kidding me.

I do not want to apologize. I feel just fine about last night. You slapped me in the face first by being with that girl when we already had plans. Maybe it's you who should apologize.

235

Angelo: You are crazy! You are not my girlfriend and I can do anything I want. You are here as a guest but instead, you do things to embarrass my whole family.

Angelo: I am from here and could have had you arrested for what you did but I didn't.

Angelo: You should be grateful.

Being slapped may have been embarrassing but maybe next time you should think about not doing what you did. You made me feel like complete shit.

I know I'm not your girlfriend, I was never trying to be your girlfriend and you should stop saying that. I was only expecting what you had promised me.

Angelo: My sister died. It does not matter what I promised you before.

I'm sorry, I really am sorry you lost her. You should not have told me we would go out last night if you didn't want to. There is only so much bad treatment you should expect me to take.

Angelo: I did so much for you. You should not be mad at me for anything. You should be thanking me instead, not embarrass me.

I can't do this; not here, not now. I'm here to relax... to clear my head and to forget all of the maddening feelings I've had during this last week.

I'm sorry we can't understand each other. We can just agree to disagree.

Angelo: You were wrong. You had no reason to do that to me last night. I told you it wasn't a date with her.

Oh my god.

Not a date? Then why did I see you kissing her in the street? Please, just stop bullshitting me. I only wanted to be your friend... I thought I was until last night.

Angelo: You are overreacting. We didn't do anything last night. She didn't want to do anything. We only walked around and talked.

Well, you chose poorly then.

I can't keep doing this with him right now. I turn the sound for my phone off, pull out my earbuds, get up, walk to the stairs and into the sea.

Yes. This is what I need.

Finally, lost in no thoughts at all, I slowly swim to the huge rocks that make up the barrier between the swimming area and the rest of the open sea. Earlier, there were a bunch of kids climbing on the rocks and jumping off into the water; I decide to climb too.

Since I still haven't mastered the skill of not giving a fuck what other people think, I make sure to get my body out of the water and up the side of the rock in one attempt. I make it and find a nice spot to sit. The top is smooth and wonderfully warm; almost hot, but I'm happy how satisfying it is on my cooled butt and legs. Scooting back into a nice spot to lean, I close my eyes and fade out again to recharge my internal battery.

Ten minutes later, I wake to the sound of splashing and playful yelling. It's the group of kids; back to jumping off of the rocks across from me. I watch for a few minutes as they play… but it's making me miss my kids. So back into the water I go. It's shocking to my heated skin as I slide back into the clear blue sea and all the way under. As the cold water penetrates my hair to the scalp, it's wonderful and awakening; washing away all of my stress. I feel alive and energized again. Alive and still so very happy to be here.

I climb up the stairs to the pier and see the captain I met last time, standing near my towel.

"Ciao Captain Giuseppe!" I wave and walk up to him, leaning on the wooden rails that overlook the water.

He turns and beams an electric smile with his wonderful crooked teeth. "Ciao! Mila from Hawai'i!"

We give cheek kisses and a hug.

"This is my nephew and his wife," he says, introducing the two people he's standing next to. "This is Mila from Hawai'i. She is very sweet and traveled here all by herself."

His words make me blush as his family and I exchange pleasantries.

"The Captain here is the most wonderful," I gush and gently touch his arm. "I will have to come back to see him."

"Yes! You must! I will be here waiting for a swim with you."

We all giggle and I kiss them goodbye. "I will definitely be back, but I do leave Sorrento tomorrow."

"Oh, that was very fast," Giuseppe says.

"Yes. I already miss here, but I have two more nights and I plan to enjoy every moment."

With the drama of Angelo right now, I say this to convince myself more than the Captain.

22

Chapter 22

I leisurely walk back to my cute little apartment, plug my phone into the small speaker and the phone lights up with a million messages. All from Angelo. Ugh. I forgot I had turned the sound off. My body cringes. I turn on some music and read them, knowing damn well I shouldn't.

I get through only half of the messages, close the app and blast Coldplay's "Hymn for the Weekend"... again. This song has become the one that evens out my mind, makes my inner self relax and feel balanced. I am desperate to feel right again.

After a hot shower, I pick out this evening's outfit. With no idea what exactly I'll be doing, I do know it will be out in Italy and not here feeling bad about Angelo or myself.

My phone dings. Apprehensive, I look who it is.

Sebastiano: Ciao Mila. You are busy tonight? I would like to see you before you go.

Ciao Sebastiano! I am free tonight and would love to see you.

I'm so happy it's him!

Sebastiano: Perfetto. What time should I collect you?

How is 7 p.m.? 19:00

Sebastiano: Yes! 19:00 I will be in Sorrento to get you.

Great! See you then.

My phone dings again, I open the message and am blindsided.

Angelo: You are a bad person. No one wants you here. You should go home and never come back.

Oh. I thought it was going to be Sebastiano. The sadness I immediately feel, I try to suppress… then another message pops up.

Angelo: I wish you nothing but bad times. I hope you feel as I do one day and then you will see.

I touch the screen and close the app. My happiness of seeing Sebastiano tonight is overshadowed now by the sadness I cannot seem to control. Trying to keep up the *fuck it* attitude I've had all morning is becoming difficult. Of course, I don't feel great about slapping Angelo, but should I be condemned for it? No, I still don't think so. Last night was not all my fault.

My phone again. I hesitate; is it Sebastiano or Angelo?

Angelo: You are the worst person I have ever met.

I'm trying to be strong… to know that what I did… how I reacted… is justified.

The time is 17:00. My phone is loaded with unhappy tidings from Angelo and I'm broken. I pick up my phone and message Sebastiano.

Ciao. I'm sorry, I will need to make the time a little later. Is 20:30 okay?

He writes back instantly.

Sebastiano: Si. Yes, 8:30 is fine. I will message you when I am near.

Okay, perfect. Thank you.

Sebastiano: Of course.

I toss my phone on the couch and walk into the bathroom to look in the mirror. My face is blotchy. I can't see Sebastiano while I'm crying

240

this way.

I fill my cupped hands with cold water and splash it on my face, over and over. My fingers are crossed that it will bring down the swelling and redness in time to go out. I haven't responded to any more of Angelo's messages but they keep coming. I can't bring myself to block him; I still feel his pain. Maybe he's right. Maybe I overreacted. He's still hurting from his sister... perhaps he deserves to act any way he wants and I should have been a better understanding friend... just walked away.

More messages from Angelo.

I'm a mess an hour later and write again to Sebastiano.

Hello handsome. I'm sorry to do this, but I will need to cancel for tonight. I'm so very sorry.

Sebastiano: Okay Mila. But what is going on? Is everything alright?

You don't really want to know. It's a bit of drama and I think I won't be the best company tonight.

Sebastiano: Tell me. I want you to be okay and I want to see you.

As I give in and tell Sebastiano what happened last night, I can't imagine that any man would want to involve themselves in this mess.

Sebastiano: Get dressed. I will be there to pick you up at 7. You need to get away and your mind off everything. I will not take no as an answer.

I'm shocked.

Okay. I'll be ready at 7. Thank you.

Sebastiano: You are on holiday and I will make sure you feel good tonight. See you soon bella.

I close my eyes for a second and feel the now familiar warm wind against my face and whispering through my long hair, as I walk the usual path towards the square. Yes, this is... exactly what I need.

Inhaling deep, slow and until I can't anymore, I fill my senses with the wonderful smells and warmth of Sorrento town at night once again.

This is why you're here, I remind myself, as I make the turn down the last little street before popping out into the square. My phone dings and I'm nervous again to look. Even though Angelo has been silent for the last hour, I'm still jumpy.

Sebastiano: I'm here. Right in front of restaurant Sirena.

Sebastiano: I hope you're close. I can't park here long.

I walk out of the little street and onto the edge of the square, the same side as the restaurant he said he's in front of. I scan the cars but don't see his. I message back.

I'm here too.

Oh wait, I see him. I spot the cute little silver and blue car, walk quickly through the crowd, open the door and slide into the passenger's seat all in one fluid motion. Fast enough to startle him.

Sebastiano grins big. "You were very quick!"

"Yes… we have perfect timing," I say, smiling back at him. "I'm happy to see you."

"I feel the same," he says and puts the car into gear. "Now let's get outta here before they give me a ticket."

I love having someone drive me around in a different place at night. The unfamiliar scenery, so many different colored lights, going through tunnels that Hawai'i island doesn't have. To travel in darkness with only the dashboard's blue or red lights to see. It's more like being transported… to another time; and there, you can be whoever you want.

There are strings of lights above the street we're driving through, from one end to the next and Sebastiano explains there's a saint for each town, city or even village. It's time for this town's patron saint celebrations.

"Oh, I love it. So many festivities!"

"Si. It is very nice. And some can last for weeks."

I smile at the thought of living here and experiencing all of the traditions. How enrichening it would be to submerge myself in another's culture. Why didn't I think of these things before? You know, when I was twenty and had nothing but time to play with.

My whimsical thoughts are suddenly distracted as I feel Sebastiano's touch. His hand; warm on my bare knee as it glides slow, up my inner thigh, under the front of my skirt and stops just before his fingers reach my panties. He squeezes my inner thigh gently, then pulls his hand just as slow, down to where he began and back to gripping the steering wheel.

"Mmm… that was nice," I say, turning to see what look is on his dimly lit face. A slightly naughty one, and with that touch, the feeling in the car has changed; to angst and want.

He turns and smiles with one side of his mouth higher. "I like what you're wearing tonight."

When Sebastiano had messaged me today, I changed the outfit I had originally picked out for my last night here in Sorrento. Since I would be with him, I decided on a short, cream-colored skirt, a loose and low hanging white silk tank top, no bra, an olive colored, thin jacket that stops at my waist with intricate cut-outs on the sleeves and copper-colored heels that wrap around my ankles.

I want to return the *touching* favor. I reach over and slide my hand over the top of his lap; slowly, meaningfully and with just enough pressure for the thickness of his jeans.

"Thank you," I say in a sexy whisper. "I dressed tonight with you in mind."

I mold my hand over the strain against his pants. "Mmm… and it feels like you might be enjoying my company so far."

I slowly pull my hand back and sit nicely in my seat with an accomplished smile on my face. I've learned since I've been here, there's a wonderful, small feeling of power when they want you this much.

"Si, pretty Mila, but we are going to a restaurant for dinner first."

We both laugh at the thought of him walking into the restaurant this way, and then I notice he's turning down the road to Positano.

"Umm, I thought we would be going to where you live… to Salerno."

Sebastiano's head falls back with a quick and loud laugh, then collects himself again.

"We *are* going to where I live… Positano. I only told you I lived in Salerno for an excuse to drive you to Sorrento the day we met at the beach."

"Ahh you were being sneaky on day one!" I smile and secretly appreciate that he wanted to spend more time with me, badly enough to lie.

"I've thought about that day often since, and wanted to see you again," he says as he cuts his eyes to me then back at the road.

"Well, I'm really glad you did. And I'm grateful… very happy to be here with you now."

This crazy, curvy, downhill road to Positano isn't nearly as scary in a tiny Fiat as it was in the big city bus. I'm sure the company I'm keeping tonight has something to do with it too, but I'm still not going to distract Sebastiano anymore until we reach the bottom.

I look out of my side window. Intermittent headlights wind around the corners we just left and dotted lights from boats glow in the vast darkness of the sea down below. Time has seemed to stall each night I've been out in Italy and tonight it creates a much-needed reprieve from the day's drama.

We pull up to a beautiful old building. Sebastiano exits the car, walks around and opens my door. It's the little things… it really is. I honestly can't remember the last time, if ever, a man opened a door for me; and here, in Italy, it is consistently the way.

Lights shining from the ground onto the outside of the restaurant show green vines, thick at the base and thinning as they climb high up the walls; pretty purple flowers adorning every few inches. Exquisite.

I relax, feeling Sebastiano's hand gently rest against my lower back as we ascend the stone steps to the restaurant door. This is already a good evening.

23

Chapter 23

Dinner was perfect. Sebastiano ordered a plethora of amazing food for us and a wonderful bottle of red wine – my first red since I've been here.

The meal... this night... is exactly what I've been wanting all week.

We reach his place, ten minutes from the restaurant and I can't help but gasp as we walk up the stone steps to his front door.

"How much do you make as a personal trainer?" I ask, with high eyebrows as I take in the vastness.

"Ahaha! You are funny, Mila." Sebastiano smiles. "This home of mine, it was my grandmother's until she passed away a few years ago."

"Oh, I'm very sorry. I'm sure you miss her."

"Yes, she was a wonderful grandmother, and she cared very much for this home. I'm happy I am able to carry on for her."

I spin in a slow circle and fill my eyes. The door is colored a light blue through a large, faded, pastel yellow archway adorned with bright green vines and raw marble statues on either side. There is a pond with lily pads, a flowing fountain to the right and bright green grass everywhere. Surrounding the house are wonderful trees growing against and over wooden tunnels. Lemon trees.

"Oh, I love your lemon trees!"

"Si. It is what this part of Italy is famous for. You have had limoncello yes?" he asks, then smiles. "Oh, but of course you have."

"Yes, I love it. After the first time I tasted it, I bought my own to take home."

"Si, you must always have more." He smiles.

His hand lands on my lower back again, as he leads me through the yellow archway and into his home.

The door opens directly into the main room; it's spacious and airy with vaulted ceilings and a wide staircase to the right. Decorated contemporary and with splashes of color. His art tastes are large paintings sporadically placed. Intricate vases and mood lighting in soffits around this main room make it very inviting.

"Would you like a glass of wine?" Sebastiano asks as he leads me to the middle of the room and in front of a large black couch.

"Yes please, I would love one."

"Please, make yourself comfortable."

I sit, take off my heels and tuck my feet underneath me. Leaning sideways on the couch, I watch him in the kitchen.

"Have I told you how happy I am you're here with me tonight?" he says, looking up from choosing a bottle of wine.

"You don't need to, I'm extremely happy to be here too. Thank you again for talking me into coming with you. I wasn't in a good place all day."

Sebastiano walks to the couch and I take the glass of red wine he has in his outstretched hand. He sits next to me with his own glass and we toast with our wine; to meeting and being in the same space together this evening.

For the next two hours we talk all about our lives. He asks me every possible question about my children and in turn, I find out he's not only a physical therapist and trainer; he's also a musician. He loves classical music and creates his own mix of it and the eclectic music he writes. Color me impressed and I wonder why he is not taken by some smart and lucky woman.

"I've been sitting here wondering…" I begin.

"Yes?" He turns away for a second, placing his glass on the coffee table.

"Why are you single?"

Sebastiano turns back with a devilish smile on his face. His warm hand lands on my naked knee once again, slowly sliding up my thigh as he leans in closer and closer, his body following his naughty hand.

"I had a girlfriend, American, a few years ago. I just haven't found anyone I wanted to be with again yet."

His hand slides up. Between my legs, his fingertips lightly touch the front of my panties.

Wet and eager, my breathing has turned deep and slow.

"Hmm… I can understand that," I say in a whisper.

Sebastiano's lips touch mine.

He pulls my body towards his and lays me down; the soft cushions cradle my back and head. My hands wander intentionally up his arms so I can feel the muscles tighten as he holds me under my body. He pulls my lower back upwards into an arch and presses my breasts against him… against his beautiful body. He leans down, our tongues dance slowly together, deep and passionate as he skillfully spreads my legs open with his body. I moan into his mouth when I feel him hard against my clit.

"Do you like that?" Sebastiano breathes. He slowly moves his hips.

"Yes… I do."

My head falls back and he gently bites my neck, my shoulder; kissing down to the top of my breasts. And stops.

Oh… I don't want him to stop. I reach down and slowly unbutton the first tiny button on my tank top, the second and then the third. I fold back the now loose sides, exposing my breasts for him.

"I could tell you weren't wearing a bra, but, Mila... I didn't think your breasts would be this beautiful."

He reaches out, cups my left breast, leans down and places my hard nipple gently into his mouth. Wet and warm is his tongue and breath. The sensation tingles from the top, down my body, to between my legs.

Sebastiano stops and looks at me.

"How old are you again?"

"What?!" I laugh and smack his arm.

"Ahaha! You don't look like you are in your forties."

"Thank you." I smile.

"Thirty-nine maybe..." he laughs.

"What?!" I smack his arm again and can't help but laugh too.

"No, no, no... ha ha! I am only joking. You are amazing, Mila."

His mouth quickly on mine, I suck his tongue deep, wanting him even more. He leaves my mouth, sliding his tongue slowly down my neck and over my breasts. I feel my skirt sliding up to my waist.

"Mmmm..." I moan with my eyes closed and my head back.

His body shifts and leaves the top of me. I feel his hot breath between my legs and his wet tongue slowly slides up the inside of my thighs. Finally, his mouth lingers on the outside of my panties; gently teasing me.

"Oh my god," I whisper.

One of his hands reaches up, squeezes my left breast while the other moves my panties to the side, exposing my naked wetness. The tip of his tongue on my clit, I inhale sharp and my knees fall outward; opening up for his skillful mouth. Lightly flicking my clit with his tongue, my insides already start building, then his tongue is inside of me.

I'm lost in the ecstasy of it all. His body shifts again and I gasp so loud and long as I feel him push inside, deep and wide. That is *not* his tongue.

My body moves with his, meeting his deep strokes as I fuck him too. My head is held back by my long hair wrapped in his hand and I know he's watching the rapture on my face as I take him over and over.

We finish together.

Sebastiano kisses my lips and excuses himself to the bathroom. I roll over onto my stomach, close my eyes and squeeze my legs together; prolonging the euphoria.

"You're smiling," Sebastiano says, standing close again.

"Yesss. I am," I say with an even bigger smile.

"Are you satisfied?"

"I am."

"So, then you are done? That was only 15 minutes."

"Oh," I say, opening my eyes. "I can go as long as you will give me. I can be satisfied again and again."

Sebastiano smiles sweet. "Then I want to try something."

Curious as to what he means, I watch him walk to the other side of the room to a small shelf of random personal things: a little book, a few figurines, a couple of candles and an empty wine bottle, half the size of a usual one. The last thing is what he grabs and walks with into the kitchen. I see him run the bottle under water then I close my eyes again; I'm terribly comfortable, finally, fully relaxed after an extremely emotional day.

Angelo pops back into my head. Ugh. I push him into the back of my mind and relax again.

"What do you think?"

I open my eyes to see Sebastiano sitting on the coffee table beside the couch, holding the bottle out for me to inspect.

"I'd like to put this inside of you." His eyebrows rise up. "Can I?"

"Mmmm..." I pause and picture what he must have in mind and my body gets excited. I've accepted the fact now, that naughtiness makes me wet. "Yes, you can."

"In your pussy... or...?"

I look up at his handsome, wanting face. "What would you like to do?" I say with a coy smile.

"What would you like me to do...?"

"Anything you want to. I have never tried that, but right now I'm not against it. I *am* on this trip to experience new things."

"Perfetto. Then we will try it all. Tell me whenever you are uncomfortable and I will stop."

"Okay."

Sebastiano's face lights up and becomes naughty all at the same time. He reaches over, rubs my ass and squeezes it just right.

I know what he wants to watch first, so I open my mouth. I tilt my head back just enough and he begins sliding the neck of the bottle through my lips and over my tongue. As he slowly pushes and pulls it in and out, I let him fuck my mouth with the bottle as long as he wants. I imagine that he's thinking of something else in my mouth... I suck it as sensual as I can.

"Mmm oh my god, Mila, you are so sexy. I can't wait anymore."

He slides the bottle neck out of my mouth. I drop my head down and smile as my skin tingles with his touch; over my ass and between my legs. Quickly, I pull my knees underneath my body and push my butt up higher to expose everything he wants to play with. I feel the tip of the bottle between my lower wet lips.

"You are still so wet," he says.

I feel the bottle slowly slide inside of me while he gently rubs my clit. "Ahhhh... yes..." I moan. He slides it deeper. I moan again. "I love... how naughty... you are."

I'm holding the top of my body up with my elbows on the couch under my breasts, my head drops lower and hangs just above the cushion as I push my ass up even further. I feel his fingers against my mouth and I keep my eyes closed. One by one I suck them until he's satisfied they're wet enough, and soon... I feel soft, wet pressure on my ass. My eyes close tighter, feeling filled by the bottle in my pussy and his hand grasping, spreading me fully open; he licks me with his whole tongue. Three long licks then the tip of his tongue slides in just a little... back out, then his fingers; one... two... then three. My ass is stretched.

"Oh my god..." I whisper.

I feel the gentle absence of the bottle, then his fingers leave me. I am empty and I exhale.

Warm from being inside me, the smooth glass slides up and down where his fingers were. I try to relax my body, but keep my back arched down and my ass up high for him. Pressure... then my body accepts it. Slow and steady, he slides the neck of the bottle all the way in and holds it there. My god.

A pause and I hear a wrapper tear. With one hand, he rolls on the condom and enters my very wet pussy, pushing in slow and deep; over and over. Completely filled and perfectly naughty, I build fast.

"Oh fuck..." I moan. "Yes..."

Deep and filling, Sebastiano keeps sliding in and out of me. With each of his thrusts, he pushes the bottle in and out of my ass half way.

Then, as he gently pulls, the bottle slides out at the same time he does. Sebastiano replaces the bottle with himself. I'm stretched wider as my ass accepts him. I grip the material of the couch and moan as I feel his body press against me. Buried deep inside, his hands filled with my hips, he pulls my body even tighter into him. A low and deep moan from Sebastiano, then slowly, he begins to fuck me.

Half out... then deep; he buries himself inside me again and again.

Two handfuls of material as I grip the cushions; I'm in ecstasy, bent over with Sebastiano inside of me. In and out. In and out. I scream in pleasure... and orgasm. My body quivers, my ass pulses around his cock as I slowly come down from my release. Sebastiano moves in and out faster. He shoves deep inside me one more time and holds my ass pressed tight against his body; he moans and his hands squeeze my hips.

He releases my body and slowly slides out. We collapse on the couch. "Mila," Sebastiano says, kissing my shoulder. "That was amazing. Thank you." He takes another breath. "I've been wanting to do that for so long."

My brain is in a dream state. His naked body on mine, the warmth and closeness, all of my nerve endings still tingling and I'm loving his touch. After such a personal session, I need this attention; affection. I know now this is not something I could have done with just anyone.

"I'm happy you liked it... I did too," I say slowly, feeling each word as it enters the atmosphere. Everything tingles; from the top of my head, to between my legs and down to my toes.

Sebastiano looks into my face and seems to know he did a good job; I'm spent and fading from all the exercise. He lifts me up into his arms, traverses the stairs and lays me in his bed. His body is warm and comforting as he slides under the covers against me and wraps his arms around me.

I stir awake, lying on my side... the wanting ache between my legs is predominant. I guess I passed out for a little while, but Sebastiano is slowly waking me. I feel the soft tip slide up and down between my lower lips and he starts to fill me from behind. I'm still very wet and swollen from earlier; I want to feel him now, more than ever.

"Sebastiano..." I moan. "I love the way you wake me." I push back against him.

His arms wrap around my naked breasts, mouth by my ear, his body pressed up against my back. "I couldn't help myself," he whispers. "I seem to stay hard around you, sexy Mila. I keep wanting you."

"It's perfect," I breathe. "Please, don't stop."

24

Chapter 24

The sunbeams that flood into my borrowed bedroom let me know it's definitely earlier than I'd like it to be. Sebastiano brought me back by four this morning and the sun is telling me it's about 7 a.m. Oh... but Sebastiano. I stretch and revel in the flashbacks of everything he and I did. I also appreciate the conversations; *that* made everything else ten times better. Such a lovely night and definitely one of the best here.

I smile and roll over onto my side, look towards the bright, marvelous view of soft blue sky and the tops of old Italian architecture; I realize this is the last time I'll see this.

Sometime yesterday, between the tears and anger, I made the decision to leave Sorrento a day early; you know... since I slapped my early Monday morning ride into Naples out of existence. I had messaged Lorenzo and he let me out of our agreed amount of nights in this apartment. It was Airbnb that I found Lorenzo and had rented a different apartment from him first. Shortly after I had, Angelo realized I was renting from his friend and Lorenzo told me to cancel the first one. He instead, made a verbal agreement with me for this apartment right in the middle of town. It really is a much better location for me, but it's also one of the reasons Angelo thought I should take whatever treatment he wanted to hand out. It doesn't matter now; Lorenzo will be here at 11:00 a.m. to settle up.

One last minute taking mental pictures of this view, one last minute of relaxing in Italy in a bed all by myself and one last minute of peace and inner thoughts...

"Okay, that's good."

If I stay in bed any longer, I'm going to get depressed. I bounce up and head to the shower... I have lots to do in the next few hours.

With my hair wrapped in a towel and my playlist blasting, I run around the apartment packing and cleaning. The music fades out a bit as a message alert comes through my phone.

It's Lorenzo. He's here. Perfect timing actually; I just finished putting the apartment back in order.

I pull the towel off of my head and smooth out my hair just as I hear the doorknob turn.

"Ciao," Lorenzo says, cautiously opening the front door.

I suppose I could be running around the apartment naked. I laugh at the thought, but now wonder, is he even interested in me like that?

"Ciao! Hi Lorenzo!" I say and meet him with the customary greeting. "Come in, come in. Thank you for coming over."

"Of course. I hope everything was okay?"

"Oh yes, everything was excellent! I love your apartment; it was perfect for me." I walk over to my purse on the couch. "I wish I wasn't leaving."

Lorenzo follows and sits down at the table by the couch.

"And how did you enjoy Sorrento?"

"I loved it so very much," I say with a big smile.

I hand Lorenzo the money for my stay, sit across from him at the

for more than just a talk." I lean forward and rest my elbows on my knees. "What did you have in mind?"

"I like your mouth, bella Mila. I was thinking something quick." His smile turns up on one side and I swear his eyes twinkle a little.

"Wow. That sounds like it's all for you," I laugh and sit up straight. "Sorry Giovanni, but I have to leave here in 20 minutes. I'm taking the ferry to Naples in a couple of hours."

"It won't take long... you're very good actually," he laughs.

"Ahaha! Well, thank you. I do try my best."

I've learned quite a lot of lessons on this trip. One of them: being more assured in knowing what I want, not just what *they* may want. Seems easy enough, but not for someone who has been taking care of everyone else's needs for the last 15 years. Some things have to be *unlearned*.

"As much as I enjoy being naughty... I did already put on my makeup and I'm not going to do it again," I say with a wink.

"Haha, si. Yes okay, I understand. It was worth the try. You are a good girl, Mila," Giovanni says as he stands and retrieves his sunglasses. "A real pleasure meeting you... and other things." His smile is devilish at the end.

"Grazie. And you are amazing, Giovanni," I beam. "You were a big part in making my trip here so wonderful." I reach out and squeeze gently under his bicep. "I truly enjoyed meeting you and I'm really glad you stopped by today." An evil smile crosses my face. "Even if I didn't wind up sucking your dick."

We both laugh together one more time; easy and real. Honesty and straightforwardness being our mutual appreciation. I'm surely going to miss him.

Downstairs; slowly, I pull the large distressed wooden door closed one last time… sigh, grab hold of my roller carry-on and turn. I'm face to face with Tommaso from the restaurant.

"Ciao bella Mila."

"Ciao Tommaso!" I smile, so happy to see him before I go.

His eyes dart down to my suitcase then up to the purse and bag on my shoulder; his smile fades.

"Oh bella, don't tell me you are leaving already?"

My smile grows bigger; I'm touched he looks so forlorn to see me going.

"Yes, I'm sorry. I really don't want to… but I do miss my children, and so now it's time."

"Ah, yes. They miss you terribly I'm sure. Well, it was a pleasure to meet you… Miss Hawai'i." His smile returns and he gives me a kiss on one cheek then the other; his hands squeeze my shoulders in a kind of hug.

I drop my purse and bag on the cobblestones and wrap my arms around him. "I need a proper hug," I say into his shoulder. "Thank you for your friendship. It's been so nice seeing your smiling face almost every day I stepped out of that door."

Tommaso returns the hug just as hard, then holds me at arm's length. "Now you be safe and come back to visit again. You are always welcome here."

"Yes sir." I smile. "I have a feeling I will have to return."

I pull up the handle on my suitcase, shoulder my bags and walk one last time down the narrow street. The thumping sound of suitcase wheels on cobblestone is a beacon to all of the now familiar faces standing outside the other restaurants, each one giving a wave or nod. I never thought this would be such a solemn walk.

Finally, I stand at the lookout where it all began and take in the scenery one last time. A deep breath to remember the smell of the sea in the Sorrento breeze and one more mental photograph of the Sorrento coast. Well, it has been an experience; an invaluable, albeit crazy at times, amazing experience.

I gather my thoughts and focus on the task at hand. I can take the walk down the side of the cliff again... or, Giovanni did mention an elevator that has eluded me this entire time. To my right, I see the gelato wagon with many happy little faces surrounding it, smeared with pastel goodness. I turn to my left and look through the trees. Something shines in the sunlight.

"No way," I whisper and tug my suitcase in that direction.

Yep. There it is... the elevator down to the sea. Ugh. I really, truly need to be more observant of my surroundings. It's a wonder I didn't get irreversibly lost on this trip.

One euro and I have a ticket. The elevator opens to a small space for the four people waiting. We all squeeze in, stare at the numbers above the door as they change, then squeeze out; into the mouse maze tunnel to make our way, again, into the sunlight.

Back outside, I see the back of the same cute, young Italian man standing in front of my first ever restaurant here.

"Ciao," I say, surprising him.

"Oh, ciao bella!" he says, turning and startled. His eyes dart to my suitcase. "You are going home now? You are leaving Italy?"

"Yes. My holiday is over, sadly, it's time for me to go back."

"I'm sure you will return. But next time, be sure to make some time for me." He winks and smiles.

I'm definitely going to miss all of this.

25

Chapter 25

I find my way to the correct line to buy a ferry ticket to Naples. Buying a ferry ticket is more challenging than I expected. After standing in the wrong line for fifteen minutes, I overhear an English couple making the same mistake and I follow them to the correct line.

It's extremely hot now standing here and I'm wondering why I have so many heavy things in my bags; finally, it's my turn to step up to the little window.

"One way to Naples please," I say saving both the tired man behind the Plexiglas and myself the time of me trying to speak in Italian.

He says nothing; just passes my ticket and change past the window. I stick the ticket in an easy but safe place in my purse. Now – I'm starving. I skipped breakfast this morning and the wonderful smells from the surrounding restaurants have been teasing me while I waited in line.

Thump, thump, thump... back up the cobblestone walkway to the restaurant above the ticket booths. There is an impressive, multi-colored cluster of suitcases at the base of the stairs leading to the tables. Not caring anymore if someone mistakes mine for theirs, I leave my carry-on in the front of the pile and trudge up the stairs to an open, shaded seat.

"Holy hell," I mumble under my breath; hot, tired and relieved to slouch down into my white, metal chair.

The wind picks up and brings some relief, as does the server with ice water. She informs me it's a very busy time, so it would be beneficial to make an order now. I tell her what I would like, then watch her rush to the next table. My attention drifts past them as I focus on the distant view of Sorrento town, proudly settled atop the cliff. Such a glorious eyeful; pastel buildings on the edge, the hypnotic sea gently splashing against the massive black rocks and the blue umbrellas lining the piers, shading various colors of sunbathers, just beginning their vacation.

I've seen this sight for the past nine days, but now it doesn't seem long enough.

The chicken sandwich I ordered comes and goes quick, as it's inhaled. Just enough nourishment to get me to Naples and to dinner.

As I leave the restaurant, I dig my suitcase out from the middle of the cluster and roll it slowly to where the ferries dock and board... at least, I think this is the spot. Thirty minutes later, the ferry is backing into the pier and about 60 people start to jockey for position. I stay seated on my end of a bench, while I wait for most of the line to board, before I finally stand to wait my turn. A distinguished gentleman motions for me to go ahead of him. I smile and nod at the nice gesture, step up and hand the ferry man my ticket, only for him to hand it back and say something I don't understand.

"Let me," the distinguished man intervenes.

The two men have a not too happy, albeit short conversation when he tells me to hand my ticket to the ferry man again. This time it's accepted and I'm directed to step aboard.

"You needed to have a ticket for your suitcase," Mr. Distinguished whispers behind my ear as we walk through the large door, where we are met by yet another ferry man.

The two have a quick exchange of words and I'm told to leave my suitcase on the other side of the ferry with the others.

"We should sit together," Mr. Distinguished says quietly.

I was planning on taking a short nap until we reached Naples, but I'm feeling inclined to keep following his instructions. I think he may have just saved my day.

So happy to finally be on my way to Naples, I relax in the seat next to my new acquaintance. We exchange pleasantries and I find out Mr. Distinguished is really Matteo from Vomero, Napoli and he was in Sorrento for work. I also find out I almost didn't make it on this ferry, as I needed to purchase an extra ticket for my suitcase. Matteo told the ferry men I was with him and his annual ticket included a suitcase. He only had a briefcase, so mine was covered. He *did* save my day.

"Ah, and this is why we need to seem like we're together. Oh, my goodness, thank you," I say profusely, realizing I probably wouldn't have made it to Naples tonight if he hadn't stepped in.

"It is my pleasure," Matteo says. "I had noticed you sitting, waiting. I was wondering how I could talk with you." He laughs.

We have 45 minutes to chat on our voyage to Naples. I tell him of my divorce, briefly why I divorced, about my children and how much I love Italy. Matteo shares that he has a fiancée and of his hesitation to get married.

I probably should have let him talk first since I didn't have anything nice to say about marriage.

Soon, we see the Naples shoreline. So many buildings and a very different look from Sorrento's side of the bay. I'm instantly anxious. I've never been to a big city in all of my years and it looks extreme. I can do this, I think. I only need to find my way to the B&B I reserved off of the internet, find a place close by to eat, have a drink and then… sleep. Four-thirty tomorrow morning to get to the airport will come awfully quick.

Matteo and I walk off of the ferry together; I need to find a taxi.

"Are you heading into the city?" I ask.

"No. My house is just outside of the city. Why do you ask?" Matteo smiles.

"Ahaha! No, no," I laugh, knowing quick what he's thinking. "I thought we could share a taxi if we were both going in the same direction."

"Oh, okay okay," he laughs back. "The taxis are parked over there." Matteo points in the direction we are already walking. "But... most do not speak English. How will you get to the place you rented?"

"I guess I will show the driver the address? I saved it in my photos on my phone."

"Ahh. Yes. That is good. That could work."

Matteo is still walking with me, but suddenly stops. I stop too. Concerned with the look on his face, my breath is held in anticipation. Oh god, this could be either good or bad.

"I was thinking... I find you very attractive." He looks down at the ground, then back up to me. "So, I will help you talk to the taxi, to make sure they take you to the right destination..." Matteo clears his throat.

Oh god... what does he want? My head is swimming with the possibilities of the impending deal it sounds like he's about to make.

"But I would really like to kiss you."

In seconds, my mind races with all the pros and cons of his request. The initial feeling: *'of course he does';* with a huge phantom eye roll. I'm sad to find out he's not helping me just to be nice, but on the other hand... can I blame him? Is it really that big of a deal? It's just a kiss. A kiss for all of the help he's already given me and for the help he's still willing to give. I'm sure I'm blowing this out of proportion.

"Okay, yes," I hear myself say and watch a smile grow across his face.

"Really?" he asks, then catches himself. "Okay, wonderful."

Matteo, being five inches taller than me, in a suit and tie, places his briefcase next to his feet, gently holds the tops of my arms and pulls me softly, closer to him. Bending his head, his lips touch mine. Soft and slow, then suddenly, he takes his liberties. Sliding his tongue onto mine, he fills my mouth and kisses me hard and deep. Somewhat passionate, but mostly, it feels like he's getting his money's worth so to speak.

The only thing I can think about is his fiancée.

26

Chapter 26

"He will take you to the B&B," Matteo says after helping me into the first taxi in line and relaying to the driver, in Italian, where I need to go.

"Thank you, Matteo." I smile, grateful for the help but relieved to be parting ways.

"No, thank you, bella. Ciao."

With a wave, I'm on my way to the B&B, dinner and a drink. I'm exhausted.

"You will miss your boyfriend?"

I look up into the rearview mirror, and see the taxi driver smiling at me.

"What? Oh… no, I met him on the ferry," I respond without thinking.

His smile disappears. "But I saw him kiss you. Kiss you very much."

Shame washes over me as I join the taxi man in judging my actions. Why did I agree to that kiss? Shit. I really thought it would only be a quick kiss, not one seeming to be the last of his life. I basically wound up paying for the help. And of course, this taxi driver knows English.

I'm uncomfortable with explaining myself, so I change the subject with the taxi driver and ask if he understood the address to the B&B.

He says "yes" but then asks me to repeat it. We both laugh and I instead, show him the picture of the address.

"Ahh si! I can take you there. Very small road but I will get you close."

Close works for me.

With the deflection of uncomfortable conversation accomplished, I relax into the back seat of the minivan. I can't help but contemplate the kiss again. Why do I feel so much shame giving a man a kiss for helping me but not shame for the very naughty acts I've done these past nine days? Should I condemn myself or him?

Matteo is the one with a fiancée, but am I looking at this the right way? Maybe she's not the right woman for him... maybe he's not the right man for her. Maybe I'm in another country and things are done differently here. I *am* supposed to learn, to open my mind to everything.

Maybe, just maybe it's my American Pentecostal upbringing that's clouding my thoughts. Or maybe, even the 42 years of society brainwash, run by men, telling women how they should behave. So much so, that we basically mentally flog ourselves... and not in a good way.

Kissing him for gratitude wasn't the problem. The problem, the shame, is because I trusted a stranger. I wasn't expecting him to dive down my throat like a kid being told he has thirty seconds to grab all of the candy he can. I don't appreciate that he took advantage of my *yes*. I found out he really wasn't the distinguished gentleman I assumed he was and that disappoints me. But that again, was my fault.

Fuck it. It's done. I just hope I've learned my lesson; a lesson I seem to endlessly repeat.

I push the unfortunate event out of my mind and look out of the large van windows at the tall, old city. It's completely the opposite of Sorrento and I'm feeling more excited the deeper into the city we drive. This is where I was supposed to have come in the first place. I'm not upset about my decision to go to Sorrento, instead, I'm just happy I'm now in Naples... it feels like the perfect progression.

A mass of cars; modest and small, delivery trucks and scooters, all funneling in and out of the tunnel into the heart of the city. I notice a tiny, random amusement park while awaiting our turn through the tunnel and think of my kids; how much they would lose their minds to try every single one of those old rides. I want to bring them here, show them everything and watch the excited wonder on their happy little faces.

Well now I'm sad again.

One more night; I don't want to be sad on my last day in Italy. I think I've been sad quite enough lately. So, instead, I direct my attention to the lovely chaos that is this big Italian city. I researched Naples before my trip. Everything from pizza, to how Italian women dress, to crime and the Mafia. I came across a journalist that wrote something along the lines of: *Naples is like a beautiful woman in an ugly dress.* That stuck with me and I'm very excited to see this beautiful woman in her ugly dress for myself.

The taxi driver turns into a square, off of the main street and parks.

"I am sorry. I know the place is near, but I am not sure where."

"Okay, it's okay. I will message the B&B lady."

I send a text message to the owners and they respond immediately. I show the driver their message and he drives us down a narrow alley, where there is a woman waiting in the middle of the cobblestones.

"Okay, this is the place. I leave you here," taxi man says.

A bit concerned he's just kicking me out because a random person is in the way, I look out of the window, up and to my left. There it is; a small metal sign with the name of the B&B I booked.

"Oh! Yes... si! This is the place." I smile big into the rearview mirror at the driver.

"Si." He returns my smile.

"Wonderful. Thank you so much." I pay him and include an extra tip for being so helpful and taking the stress out of my evening.

I find out the woman in the middle of the alley is the owner of the B&B. She speaks very, very little English and I know zero Italian. Somehow, we both understand enough body language and she knows just enough English for us to communicate our way through the glass front door, up the stairs and for her to take the 50 euros in exchange for the keys. She shows me to my room; a double bed, desk and chair, tiny bathroom, tall closet space on either side of the bed and a window with a ledge on the inside. Definitely a one-night stay type of accommodation... but that's all I need.

"Scusi," I say, as she turns to leave. "Umm... dinner? Food or drink? A restaurant?" I point towards the window.

The owner looks at the window, then back at me. "No. Sleep."

What? Maybe she didn't understand. I say it again.

"No. You." She points to me. "Sleep." Then points to the bed.

Did she just say for me to sleep? It's 6:00 p.m... 18:00. Even early for European dinner. I think she just doesn't understand. How else can I say it?

"Um... eat?" I say, this time moving my hand to my mouth like I'm putting food in with a fork.

"No," she says again. "Come."

The owner steps out to the small hallway. Standing between my door and the door to the room beside mine, she somehow explains enough for me to understand; there is a young mother with a little boy already asleep in the next room.

Holy shit... she really *was* telling me to go to sleep! The woman makes a *that's final* face at me, turns and leaves.

What... the... fuck?

I'm starving and more in need of a drink now. I drop all of my bags on the end of the bed and look at the closets. There's no way I'm going to open those; I feel like a body just might fall out of one side. I make the executive decision to leave this place. I drag the one chair over to the windowsill and take the paper, pen and Wi-Fi code off of the desk.

"What the living hell?!"

The Wi-Fi code is fifty thousand letters and numbers. Maybe a bit of an exaggeration, but it might as well be. I try the code five times and finally give up. Screw it. I'll pay for the minutes of data. I don't care anymore.

I find three hotels that are close by, call each one and finally, the third has a room to rent. It's twice as expensive as this place… but again, I don't care. Now, I need a taxi.

The taxi company answers in Italian and I spit out the address where I'm currently sitting. They say something else but of course, I don't understand. I ask if they speak English. Nothing… they hang up.

"Ahahaha! Of course, I can't get a cab."

I try calling for a taxi a third time, but finally give up. There has to be another way. My mind quickly scans all of my possible options. I could try my luck walking back to the square my taxi driver stopped in before we found this B&B. Suddenly, I remember social media. I was trying to avoid all of the men I had previously made connections with here in Naples since I only want to eat and sleep, but I am in dire need of help.

I send out four messages on Messenger. Four different men. The first to answer back is Vlado, the friend of the younger of the two Italian brothers I met in Hawai'i. He had introduced us so I would have a connection I could trust while visiting. It's poetic I think, that he's the first to respond.

Vlado: Ciao Mila! How are you?

Hi Vlado!! I'm so happy to hear from you! I am in need of your help! Lol

Vlado: Of course. How can I be of service?

271

Well, I am at a very bad B&B. I need a ride to a hotel I booked instead.

Vlado: Oh I would love to help you but I have a broken hand. I cannot drive.

Ahahaha! Of course! It's okay. Maybe you could call a taxi for me instead? I will send you the address of where I am now.

Vlado: Why can you not call the taxi?

They only hang up on me. I cannot speak Italian and they do not speak English. It makes sense, I just really need to get a ride.

Vlado: Okay. Wait. I will message you back in 5 minutes. Okay?

Yes! Thank you

I close the app to wait for Vlado, smile and lean back into the chair. The realization of the connections I have made over the last year hits me. The very amazing people I have met... the amazing men... if it weren't for them, I don't know what I would do.

Even Angelo. I can't be mad at him, not for long anyway. If he had just said he couldn't do anything we had talked about, or even if I could have drawn the line; been the one to put the limitations on our time together and any communication. This was not the time or place for my bleeding heart and I don't think I was a helpful distraction for him; definitely not with all of my own uncertainties I'm here to figure out. What he's going through is extreme. He *did* introduce me to his friends and they *did* take care of me. I could sit here and go back and forth on the subject, but at least the hateful messages have stopped coming my way.

My phone dings, pulling me from my thoughts and making me focus back on the task at hand.

Vlado: Send me the address of your location. I am coming to pick you up.

Omg really?! Thank you!

I send the address and he returns instructions of when and where to meet him.

As per his instructions, I have to leave here and find my way to the only place he can park his car... and now, with the time it's taken, the sun has faded; it will be dark soon.

27

Chapter 27

With my bags and B&B keys in hand, I quietly walk down the short hallway. I nervously set the keys on the corner of the small table I was instructed to, carry my bags down the narrow staircase and hesitantly push open the glass front door. It's been twenty minutes since the last message from Vlado and he said he would meet me in thirty.

I look down the alleyway in both directions before allowing the door to close behind me. There's no turning back now. I think I'm supposed to go left. I look to the right, up the little road and decide yes on left.

The wheels of my suitcase on the very old cobblestones sound louder than ever. The words from Angelo resound in my head; how the city of Naples is dangerous for a single woman such as myself, how I need to be wary of basically everyone. And now, here I am... at night, not knowing if I'm walking in the right direction; my suitcase basically calling out to all bad guys; *"easy prey is alone."*

I shake my head and scold myself for being scared for no real reason yet. Yes, I'm in a big city. Yes, I'm a small woman walking in the dark... alone. And yes, I have a very loud, obnoxious suitcase, but I'm here to be adventurous and strong, right? There's no growth or learning what you can accomplish, without taking some chances.

The corner at the end of the narrow road comes faster than I thought and it opens up to a large rotunda. Cars are parked and running all along the edges. Oh, and there are the taxis! I laugh and want to smack my forehead at how close they were to my B&B. Then out of the corner of my eye, I see a man I somehow feel is who I'm looking for. Vlado and I have never met in person, of course; I've only seen a few pictures of him on Facebook. It's dark out now, but I just know that's him. Very tall, perfectly proportioned, in a mid-length leather jacket and standing behind a black luxury car with the trunk popped open. I pick up my suitcase and quietly walk up behind him.

"Vlado!" I say suddenly.

Visibly startled, he turns and focuses on the height challenged woman standing in front of him.

"Mila!"

The massive smile crossing his handsome face betrays his intimidating stature. I love it. Like long lost friends, I drop my suitcase and we embrace in a big, long hug. I exhale all of my anxiety into his jacketed chest and slowly inhale deep; he smells of leather, alluring cologne and a hint of cigarettes. Feeling perfectly safe now, with all of my stress melted away in his strong arms, I'm happy I booked that scary B&B.

Vlado pops my suitcase and extra bag into the trunk, walks to the driver's side of the car and I open the front passenger door, while recapping to him exactly why I needed his help.

"Ciao."

I'm startled and confused; there's a face looking at me from the front seat.

"Ummm, ciao?" is all I can stammer.

"Yes, my friend is here. Already in the front," Vlado says over the car.

"I see that." I laugh, close the front door, open the back one instead and slide in.

Warm, dark and cozy. The music plays loud from the car radio while I listen to the two men talk to each other in Italian. Out of the windows, I watch the wonderful, colorful lights blur past us from the streets and I'm ecstatic to be in Naples.

The talking and music fade as I focus more on what I'm seeing. There are so many buildings, cars, construction sites and people walking on the random sidewalks as we drive past. The grey and black city; streaked with red, yellow, green and white lights.

"Mila."

I look forward and see Vlado's eyes in the rearview mirror. He uses the fingers that are sticking out of his casted hand to turn down the music. Oh. I didn't realize he was now speaking English.

"Ha ha, sorry. I didn't know you were talking to me."

He smiles. "Yes. Where do I take you? What hotel?"

I pull the address up on my phone and pass it forward to his friend.

"Ah yes, I know where this is. It's not far from here," Vlado says.

"Perfect. Thank you again for doing this for me. But I thought you couldn't drive because of your hand."

"Yes, of course. My car is a standard so I asked my father to use his car. This one is automatic. This one I can drive. But please talk slower," he says with a smile. "I know English, but not so fast."

"Oh, I'm sorry. Okay, I'll slow down." I pause and smile back. "You do good with English. I didn't know… I couldn't tell it was difficult for you."

Vlado laughs at me and we drive with the music turned back up, both of them singing along to a classic American rock song.

I can't tell we've arrived at the hotel until the car is parked and turned off. The men get out and I scramble to keep up, grabbing my purse on the way out. The buildings, to me, all look unassuming. Beautiful with their old structure, but each door or opening looks the same. No big signs announcing: *you have arrived*, no flags or arrows trying to outshine the other businesses.

I follow my two men into the bright foyer, through a decorative green gate and to the right, where we enter a bright, but small reception area. One younger man, tall, thin and cute greets us as Vlado takes the lead. He and the agent talk in Italian for just a minute then Vlado looks down at me.

"He says he has no rooms for tonight."

"What? I called and they said they did. I'm sorry... I don't know." I look to my phone. I really thought this was the right place.

The front desk man interjects, again in Italian to Vlado and they both laugh. Vlado responds, laughs again and motions for us to leave.

"He said they have no rooms but he will be off work in 15 minutes and that you can stay at his place." Vlado breaks into a hearty laugh and holds the green gate open for me.

"Oh my god, you're lying... he didn't!" I say, laughing and embarrassed.

"Yes, he did. He liked you. But Mila, what now?"

I've been looking at my phone since we walked from the cute agent and through the gate; oh god we *are* at the wrong hotel.

Oh shit.

"Umm, Vlado?" I say, nervous and like a little kid. I hide my face behind my phone, only my eyes exposed; big and guilty.

"Yes Mila?" His eyes cut down at me.

"I just looked and... well... I just realized we *are* at the wrong hotel. I'm so sorry! I called three places." I turn my phone around. "Here is the right one." I show Vlado the website of the third hotel. "I swear."

He gives me a disapproving look then breaks into a smile.

"Okay, it's fine. It is close too, but you are sure it is the right one this time?!"

"Ahaha. Yes, I'm sure."

He gives me another *look* as we all exit and pile back into the car.

I love how all the younger men I meet are relaxed and positive. After living with an older man who was always angry and yelling for everything and nothing, this… they, give me hope.

The second… and correct hotel, has a very large, non-smiling doorman. We walk up a short staircase in the large foyer and enter a larger, bright white room with a long, tall reception desk. An older gentleman is working behind the desk and he also doesn't seem to be a smiley guy. Vlado leads the conversation once again in Italian, and to me, it sounds like an argument until Vlado laughs and relaxes sideways against the desk. The agent ticks away on the computer, still with the serious look on his face.

"What did you say?" I look up at Vlado.

"Well, he said you don't have a reservation."

Another *look* down at me. Cringing, I smile up at him. Yeah, shit. I remember now, the lady on the phone never took any information from me, except for my name. Damn.

"So, do they have rooms?" I ask, barely audible.

"He said yes. I told him he should give you a suite," Vlado says with a laugh. "He is looking for one now."

"Oh my god really?" I smile and shake my head.

The gentleman behind the counter asks for my passport and credit card. He switches his demeanor to very nice, and now, with a smile, hands me the keys… to a suite.

"Grazie… thank you!" I say not really knowing how to act. I've never stayed in a suite before.

"You are very welcome."

I gather my things, Vlado rolls my suitcase for a few steps and his friend starts walking towards the way we had come in.

"Where will you go after this? Are you going out?" I ask, taking my suitcase.

"Yes. We are meeting other friends for drinks."

"Could I come?" I ask a bit desperately; I really want to go out now.

"Of course you can come."

"Perfect! Great!"

"We will wait for you outside by the car."

"Why don't you just come to the room with me? I need to change my clothes. I won't be long... and I'm in a suite!" I look up at him and smile. "It won't be weird."

"Oh yes! That is right, you have a suite. We will come with you. I'm always looking for new places to stay and I'm curious how this is."

Vlado tells his friend what the plan is and the three of us squish into the *private* elevator. I'm so excited!

With my never-ending, wonderful sense of direction, Vlado again, steps in and finds the correct door to the suite. He swings it open and moves the key over the wall right next to the door. The lights slowly illuminate, showing off a massive, bright, white room. There are long windows to the right, behind sheer white curtains that open out above the street and gently blow periodically in the breeze. A staircase is straight ahead at the far end of the room, and to the left, closest to us, is the bathroom. That's my area right now.

"Okay, I'll see you boys in a few minutes. I promise I won't be long."

"No problem, we will make ourselves at home," Vlado says, walking to the white wooden desk against the wall, across from the far window.

The bathroom; elegant, with rust and cream-colored marble throughout. There are two sinks spread far apart in the long marble counter, with the entire wall above, covered in a huge mirror. There is the toilet and of course, a bidet, which I have noticed is a staple here in Italy. The shower is amazing; huge and with two *rain* shower heads, one on each end.

As much as I'm enjoying this bathroom, I quickly change my clothes from jeans and t-shirt to a tight, cream colored dress and heels. Screw it – my last night in Italy, I'm going out all dressed up.

I walk out of the bathroom into the big white room. I see Vlado and his friend by the window smoking a cigarette and looking down on the people walking on the road. They turn and notice me.

"Oh. Mila… you look… very good." Vlado smiles.

"Yes. Very, very good," his friend says with an approving nod.

He speaks!

"You *do* know English," I say, joining them at the window. I squeeze between them and look down to the street.

"Si. I know only a little."

"So, what is your name?" I ask, looking at him and realize it's a joint they're passing back and forth, not a cigarette.

"I am Dante," he says and holds the joint out. "Would you like?"

"Um, no thank you. I'm okay."

"Are you ready?" Vlado asks.

"Yes! Very ready! I need a drink and I'm dying for some food."

"Okay, let's go."

Out of the door, the men decide not to take the elevator and find a wide, stone staircase instead. Dante skips down the steps ahead of us, but I'm in heels. I hesitate, not wanting to fall in front of them, I need to take my time.

I notice Vlado is still standing beside me. I look up at him and smile. Without a word, he bends his elbow to offer his help. I love that he knows what I need and didn't just leave me to fend for myself. I slide my hand through his arm and hold on as we descend the stairs together, and happily, without incident.

"Thank you," I say as we reach the bottom and walk out to the car.

"That was perfect."

Vlado opens the door for me. "Yes, of course. I saw it was going to take you a long time to walk down the stairs in those shoes and I'm thirsty." He cracks himself up and laughs loud.

"Ahahaha! Wow… you're terrible!" I love how terrible he is.

Music blasting, enveloped in the darkness and speeding through the narrow streets; my men are singing and talking while I sit back, directly in the middle of the back seat, and take it all in. Forty-five minutes, one toll booth and two tunnels later, we have gone up a hill and are now parking on the side of a very worn, curvy road. As I scoot to the left door and out of the car, Vlado barks instructions to Dante and immediately, Dante has his arm out for me to hold on to. Okay, I'm loving this treatment tonight. I should make life difficult for men more often. This is very nice, but really, I almost don't know how to act.

I look down and see why Vlado has Dante assisting me; with the road being mostly broken up, huge holes and chunks of street scattered about. I guess it wasn't the best choice to wear skinny high heels tonight.

Vlado catches up with us just as we enter the establishment. Dante takes his arm back and I fall in line, letting the men take the lead so I can look at my surroundings. Not only did I wear the wrong shoes for tonight, I definitely wore the wrong outfit too. The bar/restaurant is outdoors, the only seating is at picnic tables. It's great and I love it; I'm just a little overdressed. Oh well, at least I'm here… and with good company. I follow Vlado and Dante to a table with three other people – and one of the three is a woman! I'm elated to see another one of me. I love my men, but I'm excited to finally talk to a female.

On the empty side of the picnic table, I sit with Vlado on the end. Flanked by him and Dante, I watch the others continue with their conversation after a brief pause of looking at the new person.

"This is Mila," Vlado says, then explains more in Italian.

"Buonasera," they all say and wave.

"Hi!" I wave back.

They turn back to each other and continue their conversation. Reminded again how I really suck at meeting new people, I search my brain for something to say. I feel I'm getting better at the unfamiliar, but I'm still not quite there yet.

"What do you want to drink?"

I look up at Vlado. I'm still exhausted from my day of getting to Naples and decide to take a cue from my time with Christian in Sorrento.

"Vodka Red Bull please."

"And what to eat?"

"Anything, really. I trust whatever you want to get."

"Okay. I will be right back. Wait here for me," he says with a smile.

I watch where he goes to make the order.

"Where are you from?"

I turn back around and see everyone's faces waiting for my answer.

"I'm from Hawai'i," I say with a smile.

"Oh, that is nice," says the man across the table.

Everyone goes back to having a funny conversation in Italian, as each person interjects a comment and the rest laugh. Vlado returns with two drinks and a hot, grilled, ham and cheese sandwich. Oh, god yes!

The wind is blowing slightly and it is a cool night. I'm grateful I brought my long jacket; even though it's thin, it still helps, but a hot sandwich is heaven. I quickly bite into it and down my drink. Vlado and I joke around about going to the wrong hotel, finally meeting in person and discuss our mutual friend; Younger Brother.

Two more drinks and I'm feeling wonderful. Vlado is at the bar getting us a fourth drink and I'm listening to everyone talk at our table.

I can tell now when they are teasing each other and since I'm starting to get a bit tipsy, I laugh when the woman of the group pokes fun at Dante.

"You understand what we're saying?" she suddenly turns and asks me... *in English.*

I'm as shocked as she is. I thought she didn't know any English.

"Uh, yes and no," I say. "I can just tell you're teasing him about his haircut."

"How?"

"Well... body language. He touched his hair after you spoke... and it definitely helped me understand, with the look on his face."

Everyone laughs.

"Yes. That's right!" she says.

The night is perfect. I forget that I'm in a dress and heels, the woman and I have constant conversations and it feels as if I've known everyone here for much longer than just a few hours. Vlado and I kiss for a picture he sends to Younger Brother and after that, we are very touchy with each other. I don't know what this is supposed to be, so I'll just relax and go with whatever I feel. I'm tired of overthinking life.

28

Chapter 28

"Hurry, Mila, hurry!"

We stayed at the bar laughing and drinking with his friends for hours. After we left there, Vlado drove us around to various other bars, stopping and talking with other friends of his. I can't even recall how many people... men... I met tonight. Now, with only one hour left to get me to the airport in time to check in, we're back at the suite to get my things.

"Wait," I call down to him as I climb the staircase at the far wall. "I have to see the bedroom. I can't have a suite and not see the bedroom."

Still pretty drunk, I can't even remember how many drinks I had after the first three. I fell asleep in the back seat of the car on the way back to the hotel and have no idea how long or short that ride was.

I reach the top of the staircase and two king size beds are looking at me. Wow. This really is a beautiful suite; I wish I could have enjoyed it more. Well, I should enjoy it as much as I can now. I jump up and flop on the first bed, roll around and off on the other side. One step and I jump again, bouncing onto the other big, perfectly made bed; my hair in my face, my legs and arms spread as far apart as possible as I relax, lying in the middle, on my stomach. Oh god, it's so soft and cool, I just want to fall asleep here... right now. My eyes close.

"Mila," a soft, soothing voice whispers in my ear.

My eyes slowly crack open to see Vlado sitting on the edge of the bed, facing me. His warm hand on my lower back.

"Hi Vlado." I smile. "I had a really wonderful time tonight. I'm so glad you came to get me," I say, rolling halfway onto my side.

"I had fun too. But now you need to pack and take a quick shower to wake up."

His hand slides down and caresses my butt. "How old are you again?" he asks louder and with a true question mark in his voice.

I giggle. "Forty-two. Why?"

"Where did you get an ass like this?!" he exclaims, grabbing hold of one side.

"Ahahaha! Stooop," I say, laughing. I smack his shoulder. "Okay, okay, I'm getting up."

The gigantic shower is fabulous and does the job of waking me up. I have 36 hours of travel ahead of me and I'll be happy I started off clean.

Dressed and now realizing we're cutting it pretty close with time, I shove everything into my suitcase and bag. I throw my purse over my shoulder, Vlado takes my suitcase and both of us scan the room for any stragglers. Satisfied I haven't forgotten anything, we go out and the door to my one and only beautiful suite clicks closed. The sound echoes through the hallway and through my heart. This is the sound of the end of my life-changing adventure.

At the airport, Vlado parks illegally and, at this point, I expect nothing different from him. We find the correct ticket counter and it's scary to me that no one else is in line, but the woman agent is wonderful, relaxed and helps me check in my suitcase for free, all the way to Hawai'i.

I actually have exactly one hour now until my plane boards. We made fantastic time.

"Okay Mila, take care of yourself and be safe," Vlado says, leaning down with a hug and two cheek kisses.

"Thank you, Vlado, so much. And I will. You take care and be safe too," I say with a bittersweet smile.

He leans down and kisses my lips; soft and sweet.

Vlado turns and walks toward the doors to outside. "Ciao!" he calls out, turning around with one last, huge sarcastic smile.

Why is he so silly?! I wave and revel in the permanent smile he's put on my face.

Upstairs, at the departure lounge, is a small restaurant serving breakfast. Oh definitely, yes. I'm starving again after all of the alcohol I apparently consumed. I order a breakfast croissant, a latte and a water. I sit at the far end of the oval counter and watch all the people in a sort of airport dance, maneuvering around one another, until my food is called out.

With a happy stomach, but in a surreal state, I find an open seat next to the corresponding gate on my ticket and wait to board. I message my daughter and let her know I'm on my way home. Fifteen minutes later, I'm in one of three lines, checking four times that I have my ticket and passport in my hand, as I inch closer to the agent. A silent sigh of relief as I pass through, make my way onto the gigantic plane, walk all the way to the back, up an extremely narrow, curved staircase and to the second floor. Best seats in economy on a plane *ever*! I settle in and exhale. With no one in the seat beside me, I lift the adjoining armrest, relax my body and insert my earbuds into my ears to cancel out the noise of my fellow passengers. My mind begins to recap the last ten days.

Holy hell. I did a lot. I've learned a lot. I've definitely accomplished a lot. I smile with every flashback playing through my mind. Sorrento. Positano. Naples. Pompeii... the train, the bus, the beach, the castle, the ferry and all of the amazing people I had the pleasure of meeting. I did it. Good and bad, doesn't matter. *I did it.*

With my newfound feeling of liberation, I turn on my playlist and go straight to "Hymn for the Weekend." The plane starts up its engines.

My phone dings. Then keeps dinging...

Angelo: Ciao Mila. I hope you are well and have a safe trip back home.

Vlado: Let me know when you are safely home. It was good to finally meet you.

Giovanni: Ciao tesoro. I enjoyed being naughty with you. Have a safe trip home.

A smile as big as the adventure I had stretches across my face.

Julian: Hello beautiful. I hope you had a wonderful trip. I also hope to see you again very soon. Thank you for the perfect time in Pompeii. Be safe.

My phone dings several more times. Messages from Bruno, Michele, Sebastiano, Christian, Marco... and Francesco.

Francesco: Amore. You did not meet me. Why? I was ready for you. I wish we could have seen each other. But I wish you a good flight home. Please tell me when you arrive there safe.

I close my eyes, turn up the song that for me, is now synonymous with Italy. I relax more into my seat, a satisfied smile still lighting up my face.

The plane speeds down the runway, butterflies in my stomach as we lift off...

I will be back.